40 Ways to Lose a Guy

TALES OF A MIDLIFE WITCH

BOOK TWO

DONNA MCDONALD

Cover by *MYST Partners*

Edited by *Teresa Beck and MYST Partners*

Dedication

This series is for the real life Peter Landerman, who is most definitely not a priest, but is definitely one of the nicest readers I've ever met.

Acknowledgments

Thanks to T. Beck for the edit. I appreciate your way with words. I'm so lucky to have you.

Thanks to my mother for showing me how tough some women can be.

Thanks to my sister, my niece, my daughter-in-law, my daughters, and my granddaughters for all the inspiration to write strong women heroines.

Book Description

My bad luck with men is a joke in my family.

The two other women in my family think I attract only bad guys. Rasmus morphing into some ancient winged creature and flying away convinced my mother she was right. Working with Colonel Benson and the sexy elf Conn recruited to guard my daughter is worsening her opinion. Can you believe my daughter at twenty thinks I'm the naive one? Well, the joke's on both of them.

Turning forty didn't make me extra picky, but they need to stop judging me for saying no. Colonel Benson is happily married, and I turned down the sexy elf Conn dangled in front of me on principle. I don't have time to deal with ancient winged creatures, eccentric fairy folk, and back-stabbing demons. The last thing I need is another man determined to ruin my life. Jack Derringer did a bang-up job of that already.

Speaking of my ex, and I really wish I didn't need to, but it seems Jack is involved in something extremely shady. It turns out that the reason Jack sent me to prison was to line his wallet. Should I be flattered that my absence was worth so much to someone? Finding out Jack betrayed me for money is why I informed my daughter that I couldn't promise to not kill her father when I saw him.

No one's paying me these days, but I still need to sort this out, find a way to permanently lose the guy I divorced, and maybe find the one that flew away from me before he gets captured again.

40 Ways to Lose a Guy is an exciting new paranormal women's fiction tale from USA Today Bestselling Author Donna McDonald.

Chapter One

We chose a booth at the back of the bar and I sat where I could watch for our visitor. I had chosen seats as far away from the music and pool tables as I could get.

If Father Peter Landerman was wearing his hearing aids this evening, we'd be fine. If he wasn't wearing his hearing aids, I would ask the waitperson to move us next door to the restaurant where we could be sure to hear each other. If he was wearing his collar, which I fully expected him to be doing, I'd have to seat the priest where he wouldn't draw attention.

Why would I go to such extremes merely to talk to an old family friend? Because I planned to shamelessly pour Peter's favorite booze down him until he told me what I wanted to know.

I turned to Conn, my demon familiar and the caretaker of my not-so-great wealth to ask about our finances. Fresh out of magickal prison, I had no idea if I had any money or not. Every time I asked Conn about it, he told me not to worry and started throwing around financial terms like safe money market accounts and high-risk high-rewards investments.

There was usually a bit of bragging in his comments as well, which I also tuned out. Anything more complicated than negotiating payment for work confused me.

I admit I took a more practical approach to my earnings. Either I had money to spend on something or I didn't. Tonight, I wanted to be sure I could spend it as freely as necessary

"Are we solvent enough to pay for top-shelf liquor tonight?"

Conn grinned at me and chuckled at my question. "Yes. I cashed out one of our money market certificates. Renting the house for a year took most of what I converted, but I know you need the stability."

It was good not to have to explain to Conn the reaction I'd had leaving the cottage for good. I hated the place the whole time I was there, but it was all I'd known for seven long years. The house I'd shared with Jack was his house and not mine. It wasn't stability I needed so much as it was to establish some other place as my sanctuary.

This was why I'd jumped at the first house whose energy felt right. Conn hadn't offered a single argument against it. I think it mattered more to both of us that we were together again. Finding a new normal would be easier with a place to call home for a while.

I smiled at him. "I'll look for a normal paying job after this is all over. My 'after prison' plan was to move home to Ireland but that's not going to be possible for a while yet."

"You just want to be far away from Jack."

I considered it and then nodded. "True, but now I'm not sure one ocean between the two of us will be enough. How would ya feel about not staying here in America? Ya have a stake in where we live as well. Are ya done with America yet?"

"I go where you go, Aran. That's the deal between us. I would only miss one person here in Salem, and it's not Lilith. Seeing her has reminded me that she never truly returned my interest, not even when I loved her madly. Besides, there are too many females in this world to ever believe only one will do."

"I won't move back unless it works for both of us. We're a team. We always were and always will be."

"Which is why I choose to imitate you in my human form. No other keeper has ever given me so much freedom."

I snorted. "If I hadn't treated ya well before I got out of prison, I certainly would now. That was a hard lesson learned about the ability to move around this world freely."

The wait person interrupted our serious discussion when she brought our drinks. It was a dark beer for Conn, which was his usual choice. I didn't drink much, so I didn't have a usual. I ordered a fruity rum drink that wasn't very strong.

Conn chuckled low. "Sitting here, waiting on a priest to join us feels like we're setting up a joke."

I laughed as I shook my head. "This is no joke, Conn. Father Landerman's knowledge of angels is renowned. He even knows about beings not recognized by his own beliefs, including djinn."

Conn took a sip of his frosty beer and smirked at me. "A witch, a demon, and a priest walk into a bar. The witch asks, 'Have you ever heard of a friendly Nephilim, or at least one not looking to destroy the world? The priest, fearing the being his god once destroyed, runs out of the bar screaming in terror. The demon laughs at the irony of a being made by the gods who are scarier than him."

He stopped talking to smirk at me because he knew I'd have to know. When I broke, I broke hard. "Okay. I'll bite, Conn. What happened to the witch?"

Conn's grin stretched wide. "Fearing neither gods nor the beings created by them, the witch was shocked that her question caused all hell to break loose." He snapped his fingers. "Wait... you're right. This isn't a joke. We're talking about your normal life."

"Shush," I said, elbowing him as I chuckled. "Peter doesn't know ya're a demon and he can't tell. He also doesn't know I'm a witch or that I wield the power of a child of The Dagda. So *ix-nay* on the *emon-day*."

Conn nearly spit out his beer laughing. *"Pig Latin?"* he asked.

I grinned at him. "It's the closest to real Latin a pagan like me can get."

Grinning back, Conn took another sip. "That's blatantly not true. Some of your favorite spells are in Latin. The druids turned their Roman conqueror's language against them. That was a superb historical irony."

I waggled a finger at him. "No druid talk either, Conn— nothing pagan at all. We won't mention any other religions to Peter unless he brings them up. Father Landerman is a respected family friend. He and Ma talk about angels together. I'm hoping he'll talk to me about them. Who knows? Maybe he knows about the guardians."

Conn laughed as he studied me. "I can't imagine anyone talking to you for five minutes without realizing you're a far more powerful person than they have ever imagined existed. Your witch powers don't often show, but The Dagda's power in you always makes itself known."

I sipped my rum drink. "Is that a compliment? Or are ya saying I suck at fooling people?"

"Both," Conn said. "I guess I'm here keeping you company because the priest believes I'm your brother."

"Not this time. Father Landerman thinks ya're my cousin because he knows Ma only had one child. No imaginary love children are allowed in this conversation, either. Ya're here because I need a second pair of ears to hear what he has to say."

Despite being in human form, Conn gave me a toothy demon smile. "How can you broach a real topic with the man if you're constantly filtering reality for him?"

"That's what the top-shelf booze is for, of course. I intend to ply him with liquor to loosen his tongue, as well as his religious affiliations."

Conn's deep, masculine laughter drew the attention of the woman serving at the table closest to us. She stared as he tossed his head to move his thick hair out of his eyes. He smiled back at her when she smiled at him but then looked quickly away. He looked too much like me to be my date and he knew it. That meant there was only one reason Conn was playing things so cool.

I smirked at his actions. "We can't talk about the Wu Shaman tonight, either. Her magick is too tribal."

Conn smiled but kept his gaze on his beer. "I'm obsessed with her—I admit it. It's very limiting to my social life."

I smiled as I sipped my drink. "Limiting for ya? What about me? I haven't gotten a haircut in two months. Do ya know why? Because I refuse to listen to Mulan ranting for hours about ya in multiple languages. I'd rather waste my long-distance minutes listening to Ma lecturing me about my poor grooming habits, and ya know how much I hate that."

Conn rattled off something in a Chinese dialect. I didn't understand a word, but I didn't have to. I wasn't the person meant to understand.

"Good goddess, ya learned her language to impress her." I

shook my head in shock. "I sure hope she appreciates yer efforts."

His smile was wide. "Not yet, but she will. And that reminds me of something."

Conn pulled an envelope out of his pocket with my name on it.

I took it, opened the flap, and saw a stack of money inside. "What's this?"

Conn's smile was wicked. "It's thirty percent of the ninety-percent profit, which ended up being one thousand three hundred fourteen dollars and change, which she generously rounded up. I know this because the Wu Shaman told me several times. She also said to tell you she invested the ten percent victim's share into an account which at the end of one year if left unclaimed will be divided among the three of us. She agrees with me that the Rasmus we knew is never coming back —hence the investing."

"That woman is crazy, Conn. She hocked the scimitar the guardian used on Rasmus. *That's* what she's calling profit."

His pleased and proud chuckle had me grinning.

"Yes, I believe she sold it online to a collector for a very healthy sum. Leaving the blood on it would have brought a higher value, but she didn't want the responsibility of some random person coming into contact with guardian blood and turning into an evil, man-made guardian monster. She cleaned the blood off, burned the cleaning rags to prevent it from spreading, and removed the guardian's energy before she shipped the sword to its new owner."

Conn's wicked-happy grin told me he was proud to tell that story in precisely that manner. The Wu Shaman was one of a kind—part medicine woman and part opportunistic thief.

I stared at the envelope of money for a while before shoving

6

it out of sight in my new purse. We'd had to replace all our belongings after the fire in our previous rental house. It had taken a second visit to the coin dealer just to buy new clothes. Hopefully, we wouldn't end up losing everything again. A year's worth of rent was a hefty investment.

"Tread lightly with the Wu Shaman, Conn. I've seen her power and I may not be able to stop her from casting ya somewhere. If ya break her heart, she might capture ya, stuff ya, and sell ya to a collector to buy her family's herb farm back."

Conn snickered at my warning. "The same thought already occurred to me. That's why I bought her family farm back before Mulan got any ideas about making a profit off me."

My mouth fell open before I laughed. "Tell me ya didn't. Does she know?"

Conn rubbed his nose. "Her father does, but he promised not to tell her. She's been sending money home for that purpose for years. He told her he got a good bargain and thanked her profusely for helping him restore their family's honor. Her sister is still complaining about her, though. I thought about cutting out her sister's tongue but feared that might make Mulan mad."

"Do ya think?" I exclaimed, knowing he was not joking— not in the least.

Conn looked serious for a moment. "Mulan doesn't need me, but she wants me."

"She needs ya more than she realizes. Mulan needs someone strong enough to deal with her crazy. And I need ya to woo her because I refuse to be the only one dealing with her. Ma is determined to make Mulan and me the best of friends."

Conn's laughter filled the bar. One of his most winning male traits was the deep masculine laughter that so easily rolled out of his throat whenever he was amused. He caught the female server's eye earlier, but now every woman in the bar turned to look longingly at him.

I appreciated it too, but all too often, I was the cause of his humor. He laughed at me more than he should. There were plenty of times Conn's teasing made me want to cut his tongue out.

And that's how Father Landerman snuck up on us.

"Is this a private party or can an old man join in on the fun?"

"Father Landerman!"

"Now, Aran, you know my name is Peter. That Father stuff is for parishioners," he scolded.

"Okay. *Peter*," I said with a smile, scooting from my seat. "It's so good to see ya."

I hugged the elderly man and helped him arrange his robes to sit in the booth. I waved the waitperson over. "Bring us two more dark beers and two top-shelf whiskeys—one single and one double, please."

"I feel spoiled," Peter said with a smile.

"Thanks for the refill," Conn also said with a smile.

"Ya gentlemen are both welcome." I saved introductions until the server ran off to get the drinks. "Peter, I don't think ya've met my cousin. Conn is from Da's side of the family. He's here staying with me for a while."

The priest nodded to Conn but didn't offer his hand. Very few people did. Women had no fear of touching my familiar, but men instinctively kept their distance. Conn said an ancient male instinct warned them away from him because an imperial demon was an apex predator.

Passing for family was never hard for Conn and me, but sometimes we had to get creative in labeling our connection. Brother. Cousin. We changed it to suit ourselves.

We'd gotten strange looks from the other bar customers when the robed priest sat down with us, but it wasn't because Conn was a demon. No, I was the one who got the stares, especially when I hugged him and helped him sit.

Maybe a confirmed pagan like me didn't put off the right vibe to be entertaining a man cut from Catholic cloth. But Peter was a family friend, and I didn't care what others thought.

Peter knew Ma and I didn't share his faith... or any faith he could readily explain. I never asked Ma how many details she'd shared with Peter. He didn't seem to be ashamed about knowing me, so I refused to be worried about being seen with him.

"Your mother said you were interested in talking to me about angels. Bridget and I have had many wonderful talks about them. I wish she'd stayed in the States with you. I miss her."

I smiled and nodded. "I miss Ma being here too. Next time she comes for a visit, I'll make sure she looks ya up."

"Thank you, Aran. You're a good daughter. What was it you wanted to know about angels?"

I smiled again. "What can ya tell me about the Nephilim, Peter? I read they were the hybrid children of angels and humans. I also read they were more evil than good. Does the very mention of them make ya want to run screaming from the building?"

Peter laughed at my dramatic teasing. "You joke, but they affect certain people that way. God considered them to be abominations and outside intended creation. Along with the bulk of humanity, most of the Nephilim were destroyed during the Great Flood."

"Ya said *most* of them, Peter. What happened to the

Nephilim who survived?"

"Many ancient texts claim those that didn't die hid from God's sight. In the years after the Great Flood, I believe that the ones who remained alive got called 'giants' and even 'heroes' sometimes. I think many of the famous myths about alleged demigods were based on them. Some scholars think the tales of Hercules were about a Nephilim because he was a hero who went insane and killed his family. Insanity from having too much power is their fatal flaw."

"Are they evil to your religion then? Tales I read of them didn't paint a pleasing picture."

Our wait person chose that moment to slide our drinks onto the table. I indicated for her to put them all in one place and I moved them around while I waited for Peter to answer.

"I disagree with the view that Nephilim were abominations. The reason I disagree so strongly is that scripture says God instantly regretted the flood and the earth's destruction after he lost his temper with humans and Nephilim. What is evil anyway? Often, one person's evil is another's salvation. That's why there are so many scriptures warning us not to judge each other. I believe the actual issue with the Nephilim was that they refused to take sides. They didn't dare because their side would always win. The immense powers they inherited from their heavenly parent were far more than their earthly side could handle. Insanity was inevitable."

I nodded and sipped my drink, thinking of Rasmus changing into a being that flew like a rocket through the skies. "What would ya say if I said I was fairly sure I'd met a Nephilim?"

Peter's eyebrow arched upwards. "Hold that thought until I can hear it better," he ordered.

Then he drank the single shot of whiskey straight down

without stopping. There was no coughing or sputtering. Instead, Peter simply took a small sip of the dark beer I'd ordered for him and sighed in pleasure.

Still without speaking, Peter picked up the double and took a healthy sip. I feared with that sort of drinking he would become incoherent before I got the first real question out of my mouth.

"Let's get some food too," I said with a smile.

I waved our server down and ordered a variety of appetizers. Keeping this casual was hard when I was impatient for answers.

After the wait person scurried off to place our food order, Peter found his voice again. "So, you think you met a Nephilim and lived to talk about it?"

I smiled at him and shrugged. "I did the being a favor. Or at least, I believe that's how he saw things."

I pulled a tiny feather out of my pocket, the one left by Rasmus after his transformation, and held it out between two fingers. "He left me this as a souvenir of our encounter, which is the only reason I don't think I imagined him. I will admit that I haven't told Ma yet. She's got a soft spot for angels. I didn't want to alarm her if my encounter turned out not to be with one."

I laid the feather in the palm of my other hand. The feather instantly changed from dark gray to brilliant white.

"May I?" he asked, reaching out to touch it.

His ancient fingers lifted the feather after I nodded. It immediately turned gray again. He sucked in a breath. "It wasn't a Nephilim you met, Aran, but that was a very good guess about the being you saw. The being you ran into has similar powers."

"What was it then?"

"You met a custos, a praeses, a defensor—they're known by many names. In English, we call them *guardians*."

Conn stiffened beside me but stayed silent.

I tilted my head. "What is a guardian, Peter? I heard that term before but couldn't find anything written about them."

Peter drank the rest of his double shot before he answered me. "There's nothing to find because no one knows what they actually are. The Church quietly recognizes them as part of heaven's army, but we don't know enough about their powers to talk about them with confidence. They show up in dire times and do things to correct the balance of power in the world. Or that's what we think they're here doing."

"How long have they been here?" I asked.

Peter spread his hands. "That's also something we don't know, but they appear at troubled times in history. Even when they take human form, I've heard they don't give many explanations. We concluded they have little or no power while walking the earth in human form. Or this is what we believe based on the few stories we have. It's hard to find someone who has talked to them who also remembers what was said. Making people forget them is only one of their many talents."

I refused to believe Rasmus could ever make me forget him. "Are ya saying that a guardian is a shapeshifter of some sort?"

Peter nodded in his solemn priest way. "Yes, but not like one of those fictional beings people make up to tell a good story. Think of him more as a Skinwalker like in First Nation legends. A guardian will take on whatever form they need to in order do whatever it is they intend to do—animal, human, maybe even a god. I've studied them all my life, but I've never seen one in person. People who see them only tell me about it during confession, especially if they believe the guardian was an angel."

Maybe Peter would think my question rude, but I had to ask it. "If ya have never seen one, how did ya know what being this feather belonged to?"

Peter snickered. "You're a sharp woman, Aran. The reason I know is because I saw a feather like that once before. The person who showed it to me said he'd gotten it from a *confirmed* guardian. That person knew more about them than I did, but he refused to give me details. He said it wasn't allowed but refused to tell me by whom. He was a completely reliable source, and I have no reason to doubt his story."

We stared at each other for a few moments. As usual, I was the first to break. "Are ya going to tell me who the person was? Or keep me dangling?"

Peter crossed himself making the symbols of his faith, then linked his ancient fingers together in front of him on the table. I expected the rosary to appear in his hands soon, but it hadn't made an appearance yet.

"I don't really want to tell you, Aran, but I will if you insist."

I held his gaze. "He left me this feather on purpose. I believe I need to know."

"Fine. It was your father who had the other feather," Peter said finally

"Da?"

Peter nodded and pointed at the feather. "Either that feather in your hand is the same one he had, or you both were visited by a guardian. And I have to tell ya that the latter worries me sick. Seeing a guardian is not a good sign based on what happened to your father. He was in perfect health and should have lived as long as I have. After his encounter with the guardian, his death came sudden and far too soon."

Conn straightened beside me. "It was my understanding

that my uncle died of age-related illnesses. Sometimes the solitary burdens we keep secret age us beyond our years. Don't you agree, Father?"

Peter nodded. "Yes, I do. That was well said, young man."

Those profound words were the only ones Conn spoke in the priest's presence. Church officiants weren't his favorite people. I always figured the animosity between demonkind and humankind had its roots in a lack of empathy. But I'd given up trying to change that many years ago. Inspiring compassion in all beings for each other was a big job and for a better person than me.

On the way home that evening, I couldn't shake off learning that Da had met a guardian too.

It also intrigued me that the Rasmus I met and had been attracted to might be only one form of the being he became after Lilith broke his demon compulsions.

What other being could he masquerade as?

I wondered if he had taken the form of some random stranger and kissed some other woman who turned out to be a witch. The thought upset me, but I couldn't help thinking about it. I felt deceived somehow for believing in his human form.

I twirled the feather in my fingers and wondered which side of the good versus evil fight I had landed on with my supernatural talents. Both as a witch and a child of The Dagda, I felt I was doing true good in the world. That said, I'd dispatched magickals in the past with no more regard than Jack had shown when he'd imprisoned me. Was I right to think I knew who was good and who was bad?

Ya could have said I was having a true mid-life crisis and not been wrong.

Chapter Two

W hen the level of coffee in my cup hadn't lowered in fifteen minutes, Conn took my cup to the sink, poured it out, and refilled it with fresh hot brew. I thanked him when he set the cup back in front of me.

Moments later, he answered the doorbell when it rang and brought back a bag of food with him. "I refuse to let you starve us while you brood about what you don't know."

"Sorry if I've been sullen, Conn. I've been thinking about a lot of things. Ma is adamant that the man who gave the ring to Da was an angel. She said the only thing he left Da was the ring itself. She found no feathers among Da's belongings after he passed, nor did she remember ever seeing him with one."

"Maybe the being your father met *was* an angel. That feather your priest mentioned doesn't mean a guardian didn't come later without Bridget knowing. Your father was good at keeping secrets—he and Bridget both were."

My frown deepened at the thought. Was I keeping things from Fiona? As her parent, I meted out information as I felt she was old enough to understand it. Would I stop talking honestly to her if she married someone I didn't trust? The answer was a resounding yes, but that was the *only reason* I'd block my child from learning the truth.

"What if the being who delivered the ring wasn't an angel, though, but something else, Conn? What if it was Rasmus or one of his kind? Guardians have a purpose that they seem determined to keep secret or they wouldn't be hanging out on a mountaintop hiding from people."

"Okay. What if that's all true, Aran? It changes nothing."

I thought a sentient ring that hid from everyone but me changed a lot. I held out my hand. "Conn, there's something about Da's ring I haven't told ya. It's far more than what it appears to be."

"I want to hear about it, but can we eat first? Your blue funk has been worse than being on a diet."

He sounded so pathetic that I smiled and nodded. We ate silently, which depressed me further. I couldn't help remembering how much more lively meal conversation had been when Rasmus was still with us. But then thinking about him spiraled into wondering how he came to be a demon hunter and how he had forgotten what he originally was.

What had Jack and others done to a guardian to make him forget his true self? If he was as powerful as Peter said he was, why had he and his comrades ever allowed Jack and his fellow bad guys to do that to him?

I gave up after two bites and set my sandwich down. I had no appetite for food. I was only hungry for knowledge about guardians and answers to my questions. This was the one aspect of my nature that family and friends often hated about me. I couldn't let things go until I'd gotten to some reasonable point of understanding.

Conn's sigh across the table was loud. "We're going to have to look into his human past, aren't we?"

I lifted a shoulder and let it drop. "If I track down Jack and he lies to me, I'm going to remove the father of my child from this world. My anger lingers no matter how I try to forgive and forget what he's done. What am I going to do to get past this? Fiona thinking I'm a criminal is bad enough."

"I knew her total absence was bothering you."

I spread my hands in the air. "My daughter hasn't answered a text or asked how I am in weeks. I send a message to her every day. Why would I bother to invite her to lunch or ask her to stop by? I told her the house we were in burned down and she didn't even ask why. Trying to talk to her is like communicating with a wall."

Conn held up a finger. "But she hasn't blocked you from sending texts to her so there's still hope."

I grunted. "Not answering back is the same as blocking a person. The effect is the same."

"Yes, I suppose that's true." Conn finished his breakfast sandwich and grabbed a muffin. "So, what do you want to do today?"

"I don't know."

"Yes, you do. You just don't want to admit it."

I glared at him. "What is my purpose in this quest, Conn?"

He froze mid-chew and tilted his head.

I waved my hand so he would go on eating. "I'm just feeling philosophical this morning. Maybe it would help me to talk this out."

After Conn nodded, I waited until he returned to chewing.

"No one's paying me to look into this. No one's threatening my family. Lilith and the baby are doing fine. Rasmus hasn't come back to visit since I found the feathers. If I walked away from this mystery right now, I would lose nothing I haven't already lost."

Conn paused to answer. "Okay. Then why can't you move on from what happened?"

I blew out a frustrated breath before letting the truth spill out. "Because I spend every day wondering what I'm supposed to be doing with myself. That isn't something I've ever felt before. Before I went to prison, I was getting ready to open the magick shop. Now all I can think about is how nice it would be to go home to Ireland. But what would be different for me there? All my dreams and plans were ruined seven years ago. I don't know what to do with myself, and there are all these mysteries swirling around me."

Conn finished his muffin and then stared at me. "Jack and Fiona were your entire life seven years ago, Aran. They both kept you too busy to think about what you wanted for yourself. Fiona was a child, but Jack did it on purpose."

"Maybe he did, but so what? My problem is that I see a stranger in the mirror every morning. She's forty, has kinky gray hair, and looks like my older sister might have if I'd had one. I feel nothing like that woman on the inside, Conn. Time stood still for me when I was at the cottage, but it moved on for everyone else. Now I'm estranged from myself, which sounds odd, but that's how I feel."

"Aran, your biggest problem is that you're celibate. It's been years since you let your second chakra bring you joy. How many more times do we have to have this discussion? I don't want to fuss at you about your non-existent sex life. That's not my job."

Though he wasn't Hindu, Conn often used Vedic terms to describe the invisible energy centers that powered human forms. Chakras could get blocked with actions ya didn't take and get clogged from yer confusion about life's problems. Blocked chakras could make a person miserable until they got whatever was messing them up worked out.

Conn wasn't wrong about the primary issue with mine, but I couldn't go for the quick fix. Rasmus and I had slowly grown into our little attraction. The possibility of us had felt natural, hopeful, and sweet in a way I hadn't felt since I was a teenager.

Until I put my memories of *that* version of human Rasmus to rest, no matter whose bed I jumped into the only face I'd see above me would be his. Knowing that for certain, I couldn't disrespect that brief but wonderful connection we'd had. I simply couldn't.

"Sleeping with a stranger wouldn't help me. I don't know myself as well as I once did, but I know that for certain."

Conn's sigh of disappointment was loud and echoed in the kitchen. "Maybe if we found out what happened to the guardian to trap him in his human form, you could leave your pity party and meet someone new. If you believe what your priest friend said, the demon hunter you think you rescued never existed. Or at least he didn't exist any more than some other person he could have chosen to become. You saw what he truly was when Lilith removed the compulsions, Aran. Rasmus even left you a reminder so you wouldn't forget."

"I admit I didn't like the human Rasmus when we first met," I said with a head shake. "He was so negative and grumpy. But I liked he was honest about his feelings. I liked he did the hard things, even when he complained. He was a person like you and me, and I think a good part of him was human. I guess I can't help wanting to believe that his human form was part of him."

When I saw Conn's disappointed expression, my sigh was

as loud as his had been. "I know ya think I'm obsessing, and maybe I am. Rasmus also must have suspected that he wasn't the being he saw in the mirror. I guess he and I have an identity crisis in common."

Finally, Conn nodded in agreement. "Yes, I suppose you indeed have that in common with him."

"And ya and I would both be fools to get involved in his past. Asking questions will only lead us into more trouble with demons and demon hunters."

"Also, right," Conn said.

"And tackling the military would be especially foolish. I might have to flee the country if they took a strong enough dislike to me. Ya can't brainwash an entire nation to save me from a bad decision. We could pay every demon caste we know to put compulsions on everyone, but it would bankrupt us."

Conn jumped in to make it worse. "Not to mention what might happen if we run into more of those angry man-made guardians like the one that escaped us. The one we captured is back out there, Aran, and he's not our fan."

"I know. And if ya're right about Rasmus, what gain would come of us even looking for someone who no longer exists? There's no gain at all in it. All I see for us is trouble if I research his past just to learn something that won't help me put this away."

Conn smirked. "You're one hundred percent right. I don't see any gain happening unless we relieve a few more man-made guardians of their ancient, expensive swords."

I chuckled at his grin. "Ya're spending too much time with the money-hungry Wu Shaman. Mulan might help again for the pleasure of making another of her deals. She will not settle for her one-third next time, though. She's convinced I'm a slacker in the magick department and she's the one who does all the work."

Conn laughed. "Does her opinion matter to you?"

"Only a little," I admitted, chuckling again. "That sword she stole was so big it dragged on the floor when she carried it. Her Wu Shaman staff looked strange enough in her hands all dressed up like she was, but her half-carrying half-dragging that giant sword was hilarious. She is helpful, but her entertainment value is also high."

Conn grinned at my joking. I think it relieved him.

"We're still going to look into this, aren't we?"

I shrugged at his conclusion. "Ya probably think I'm being my typical contrary self, but I can't let go of my obsession with finding out the truth. At least this isn't about Jack. I know he's involved in this mess, but outing his evil deeds is no longer my primary motivation for solving these mysteries. Now, I want to know what the man I knew as Rasmus suffered and why."

"Call Mulan then. She's bored with doing hair. I bet she would jump at the chance to use her magick skills. If you need treasure for your bargain with her, we have those Greek plates we recovered from the troll. I kept them in storage since we never found their owner."

The idea of bribing Mulan with the plates made me smile. "I guess she could shake her shaman staff and put everyone to sleep while we riffle through filing cabinets looking for records on someone named Rasmus."

Conn waved his hand. "We need to take some action so I'm going to go get one of the plates. You can show it to Mulan when you see her. Be sure and tell her you have five more for her when the job is finished. Maybe she'll think of them as a salary."

He seemed so happy for a good excuse to torment Mulan that I couldn't burst his bubble.

"Fine. Get me the plate while I make an appointment. My hair needs a trim and good conditioning. I'll make this errand a two-fer."

Conn popped away from me to collect the plate from storage before I realized that I never told him about the ring. It was like everything in my life conspired to keep me from telling anyone its secrets.

Conn acted like Da's ring was the one in Plato's story. But I wasn't a devious king trying to steal a kingdom, and I seriously doubted invisibility was one of its talents. If it had been, the ring would have made itself disappear, instead of simply morphing into something no one paid any attention to.

I pulled the ring off my hand and looked on the inner band for an inscription. When I found nothing, I studied the edges looking for more symbols. There was none of those either. The ring looked rugged and masculine, but not magickal at all. As I stared at it in my fingers, it morphed into what it truly was. King Solomon's Seal rose out of the stone while the rest of it turned to shiny gold.

"Ya're just messing with me, aren't ya?" I asked it in challenge.

When I got no answer, I shook my head and slid the ring back onto my finger. It instantly morphed back into the plain man's ring I'd been wearing since I got it.

"Ya are as full of secrets as Rasmus and his brethren," I said to it as I rose to fetch my phone.

Chapter Three

I followed Mulan to a wash station. She was quiet, so I let
her wet my hair and work up a froth of suds in silence. It
was one of life's genuine pleasures to let someone else wash yer
hair.

Appreciation and gratitude wafted over me in waves, and I
closed my eyes to enjoy it.

"Do I charge too much for haircuts?" Mulan asked.

My eyes opened abruptly. "No, I think yer rates are
reasonable. Plus, yer work is wonderful enough to command a
higher fee. Are ya asking me because I haven't been in for a
while?"

"No. I know you mourn. Healing heart like yours takes
long time."

I stared at her in disbelief. "Why do ya say that? I'm not in
mourning."

She stopped scrubbing to stare at me. "Why do you lie to
me, witch? Wu Shamans see all lies. Thanks to you making me
use magick, I see more now than ever."

I glanced off as she chanted and coated my wiry hair with a

thick conditioner. "Okay, well, I may not have realized I was in mourning, but I wasn't lying. And I didn't mean to cause ya trouble."

Mulan made a sound somewhere between a grunt and a cough. "Did you cry yet?"

"No. Why would I cry?"

Mulan rolled her eyes and made a disgusted sound as she wrapped my head in a towel. "Denial. Just like my whiny sister. You will buy leave-in conditioner today. It makes hair curl but not frizzy."

I didn't want a product I had to leave in my hair, but I nodded to keep her happy. "Wait..." I said before she rushed away from me. "Do you want another Wu Shaman job?"

She turned back to me. "What now? Are there more demons to save from their bad decisions?"

"No," I said, swallowing hard. "I'm going to see if I can find out what happened to Rasmus when he was in human form. I talked to a priest friend and he confirmed guardians exist. No one knows much about them except that they were created by the gods. Did you look into them?"

Mulan crossed her arms. "My people have a name for them." She said something in Chinese. "It translates to *violent protector* in English. I do not know if it's the same elsewhere."

"Father Landerman said the guardians were known by many names all over the world. His faith knows of them, but he had no real details. They're not angels, humans, or Nephilim like I thought. He said they could shift into any form they wished."

"Guardian who was spying on demons could not shift. If he could have, he would have shifted and escaped Connlander of the Fir Bolg. Strength always loses to stealth. This is shaman training. He was fake guardian, but still very strong."

24

"Yes, I agree he was a fake guardian—a man-made version. My friend also said one of the real guardians visited my father before he died."

Mulan's eyes studied me closely. "And now one has visited you. You believe this is no accident. I agree with your theory."

"The night Lilith freed the being from all demon holds, I received a visit from the being Rasmus turned into. He left me a trail of feathers and then landed at the end of them to make sure I knew they were his. It was a very bizarre thing."

"What did he say to you?"

I shook my head. "Nothing. He just nodded to me and flew off. Father Landerman told me that people who saw them reported that the guardians seemed unable to speak. Apparently, they can only speak when they take a human form and maybe they're helpless in that state. Based on what I observed with Rasmus, though, I don't think they remember everything during their shift between forms. He seemed unsure of himself and a bit confused about being drawn to communicate with me."

"If true, perhaps being human is how bad guys caught your real guardian."

"That's my guess as well."

Mulan snorted softly. "More than good guess, I would say."

That was very close to her complimenting me, but I didn't dare point it out.

"I'm going to see if I can find the military medical records Rasmus thinks were withheld from him. He told me he woke up in a hospital with no memories of his life before that day. His only choice was to believe what they told him. He also said my ex-husband and other demon hunters were there. Lilith said my ex became his *keeper*—whatever that means."

Nodding, Mulan stared at me. "It is big mystery."

I nodded and caught my towel as it came undone. Bending forward, I wound it back tighter. "I have to find out what happened. If I don't, I may never sleep again."

"Okay. Before we make our bargain this time, I have question. Did Connlander of the Fir Bolg buy back my father's farm?"

When I didn't immediately deny it, Mulan snorted before walking away. I spoke to her back as I raced to keep up. "Wait... why would it matter to ya if he did?"

"I am beholden to no one. I refuse to owe him."

I reached out and grabbed a shoulder to stop her. "Conn didn't do it to make ya owe him. He did it so ya wouldn't kill him, stuff him, and sell him for a profit online. He's as scared of ya as he is attracted."

When she turned to look at me, Mulan's eyes widened. And then she laughed.

Her pleased smile was a beautiful sight, and I wondered if she'd ever smiled like that for Conn. If so, no wonder he was obsessed with her. The Wu Shaman had charisma in spades, even when she wasn't wearing a sexy red dress and makeup.

"Ya have a delightful laugh, Mulan."

"Get in chair," she ordered, smirking as she yanked the towel away from my head. "Is there victim this time?"

Goddess, she was still fixated on making the deal. I'd all but forgotten. "Yes, there's a victim. It's the same one as before. Rasmus—the human version—is still the victim."

That's what I told her, but it probably wasn't true. The Rasmus I knew was just the human form of the guardian who was something distinctly different than human. I admit I wanted to confirm the version I knew was never returning. My plan of how to do that was by figuring out what the people who captured Rasmus had done to him.

Maybe I was crazy, but that was the path I was following.

Mulan was thoughtful as she combed through my wet locks. "Fine. We reserve ten percent for him *again*. Same deal about end-of-year split if he never returns. Maybe by then you cry out grief and move on to actual human man instead of strange being with secrets."

"Yer deal sounds fine," I said, not bothering to argue that I wasn't grieving.

But if I *was*, it would have been over someone both human and real. There was no need to grieve, though, because Rasmus wasn't dead. He simply was assembled differently. His human body had ripped apart to reshape itself into a being with wings. As a woman who borrowed demon powers when she pleased, I had no right to judge.

I studied Mulan in the stylist mirror I faced. "I don't think there will be sufficient profit in doing this research to suit ya. If we find nothing, I can offer ya a set of six ancient Greek plates for yer trouble. The Metropolitan Museum in New York would probably buy them from ya. There's one in my purse if ya want to see a sample."

She stopped combing my strands and went to my purse to pull out the plate. Before she looked at it, she peered deeper inside the purse. With the plate out, all that was left was my wallet. I had carried the purse today only to hold the plate.

"Where are your woman things?" she asked.

Well, that was a very personal question. I wanted to tell her it was none of her business, but she might refuse to help me if I did. I lifted my chin and glared to let her know I did not consider this line of questioning okay. "I only carry tampons and pads when I need them. Who wants to look at those all the time?"

Mulan gave me a bewildered look. "I don't care about your monthly cycle. I want to know where is your comb, your brush, your makeup. You know.... your *real* woman things."

My anger deflated. "Oh, I never carry that stuff unless I'm going on a date or going to a party. That's the only time I care about a purse. Most of the time I tuck my protection in my wallet like men do, which allows me to only carry one thing."

Mulan's huff vibrated through the air. "Sexual protection you carry on your person, but no makeup or hairbrush? This is why you don't have dates."

I blinked at her reflection. "No, I don't date because I've found no men I want to date. Well, I found someone but he morphed into a being with wings and flew away. Maybe I'll join a dating site when my life settles into something more normal."

Sighing in defeat, she turned her attention to the plate. "Is this best one of set?"

"I don't remember them well, but Conn says they're all the same. We recovered them from a troll twenty years ago. The troll said he traded a Greek merchant for them, but they were stashed with a lot of other stolen goods that had owners. We never found out the truth about the plates, so we put them in storage. Conn says we're way beyond the finders-keepers limit."

Mulan nodded as she gazed at it. "High demon is right. There is no value for items collecting dust. You must convert them to money and then invest money for gain."

She slipped the plate back into my purse and returned to me.

I swallowed nervously as the scissors flew around my head as she lectured. Mulan wielded scissors like they were weapons. I waited for her to finish cutting my hair before I spoke again.

"Are the plates okay? Do we have a deal?"

"You make poor bargain this time. I will sell ancient Greek plates for only fifty percent profit so my ancestors will not haunt me for taking unfair advantage. Profit from search for your winged boyfriend we will split one-third each of ninety percent."

I made a face as I watched her squirt a big glob of gel into her hands. I hated hair products but I loved the results. "Rasmus was never my boyfriend—not really."

She sneered at me. "Yes, and with your empty purse, we know why he made no sexy moves on you."

My lack of makeup was not the reason... and I counted his kiss as a move. If he hadn't changed back into his real form, would he have made a more serious move?

I had no idea what he remembered. Rasmus had been told he once had a wife who'd divorced him. Was that untrue? I secretly hoped it was.

I glared at my nosy hair stylist, but it had no effect. Her face wore a nearly blank expression as she gelled my hair and used a loud diffuser to set the curls.

I wisely kept my mouth shut. My hair had never looked better.

Mulan set the diffuser down and looked at me. "Use leave-in conditioner to take care of frizz every morning. Use gel you bought last time on wet hair before drying. Can you do those two things?"

"I will *try*," I said because I was unwilling to commit and fail.

Mulan muttered to herself in Chinese as she went to pluck a tube of the conditioner off her shelf. I admired my hair in the mirror before I slid from the chair.

The Wu Shaman had many talents. What she did to my hair was nothing short of miraculous.

I paid for the haircut and conditioner making sure to add a generous tip. Her work was worth it, but I also feared what would happen if I didn't.

I put my wallet back into my purse with the plate and waited until the Wu Shaman looked at me. "If the search seems too dangerous, ya can leave off helping me with no hard feelings between us. I don't want ya to get hurt, Mulan. But I could use yer help."

"Then I will help," Mulan said, shrugging her shoulders. "Maybe I will take time off from doing hair. Work for you could be my second job."

"No, we need to be clear on this. I'm not making ya a job offer. I'm looking for answers to my current questions. That's all. Yer unique skills will only be necessary if I need to make a whole army sleep on command. Do ya understand what I'm saying?"

"I'm not worried about finding profit, witch. It will find us. Trouble finds you every day," Mulan said. Then she waved her fingers in the air. "You create work for us with your chaos magick."

I glared at her. "My magick is not chaotic. No, I don't think that's true at all."

"Whatever," she said, finger-waving my concerns away. "Text me plan. I warn manager I may leave in a hurry. She will handle my clients."

"I guess I appreciate that ya're willing to accommodate my schedule."

Mulan shooed me with a hand. A bracelet of tiny turtle shells jingled on her equally tiny wrist. How did she find such small ones? I shook my head to stop from wondering about it. "I'll tell Conn ya're helping us."

"Good. I will settle my debt with him in my own time. You will keep his secret until then."

It was clear to us both that she wasn't asking me to keep silent about her knowing that he'd helped her family. No, her statement was an explicit threat. Since I liked my tongue and wanted to keep it in working order, I thought it was wisest to go along.

"I'll not say a word to Conn—I promise."

When the sneaky Wu Shaman smiled at me again, I fled her shop without a backward glance. I'd go to the coffee shop down the street and call for a ride home.

Waiting in Mulan's shop felt too dangerous today.

Chapter Four

My technological skills were lacking. This was no secret to anyone who knew me. Conn did most of our online searching and took care of our finances. Mulan's technology skills proved to be even more exceptional.

While Conn charmed the night duty nurse at the veteran's hospital, Mulan searched the nurse's computer for records on anyone named Rasmus. We found only one person listed with that name, which didn't surprise me a bit. His was a name ya didn't hear often.

"Paper records are in basement. Nothing electronic for him. Too much time has passed and they are not up to date here. This computer is ancient."

"Let's go to the basement then," I said.

We strode confidently through the hospital corridors because we'd nabbed two white doctor coats from a break room to disguise us. Underneath our white doctor coats, Mulan and I were dressed in dark jeans, dark shirts, and dark jackets. Conn wore something similar. On the way here, our driver who kept speaking in TV references, told the three of us we looked like a couple of *Charlie's Angels* who'd dragged Charlie along as our third.

I looked up the TV show on the phone so I could praise his humor and set a bit of a spell on him to make him forget he'd seen us. Making people forget about me was another new habit I'd picked up after being imprisoned. Not trusting people as easily as I once did was yet another legacy from Jack.

The door to the records room was locked when we got there, and the lock was electronic. The hospital had upgraded some of its equipment and technology after all.

I was looking for cameras to spell so we could break in without risk of discovery when I heard a badge hit the electronic access and click it open. My sticky-fingered Wu Shaman had lifted the nurse's badge when I hadn't been looking.

If her thievery kept up in my presence, Mulan was going to single-handedly prove Fiona's view of me as a criminal was right.

Once inside the room, Mulan went unerringly to the correct filing cabinet. She pulled out the file on Rasmus and handed it over to me without even looking at it. Maybe she did that because the lighting in the room was too low to read, but I wondered if she even cared about Rasmus or his story.

"Tuck folder under arm and look professional," Mulan ordered.

I did as told, and we walked back out quickly.

We returned to the floor with the nurse's station and I heard Conn's voice down the hall somewhere. Mulan tossed the badge back on the desk.

And just like that, we walked out of the hospital with what we came for. It all seemed rather anti-climactic.

Did the hospital not know what Rasmus was and what he

could turn into? I had expected to have to navigate through tons of records to dig out the information. It never occurred to me I would leave with a file summarizing his hospital time.

"We will study it later," Mulan said. "I will make brownies to fuel our research."

I grinned at her and nodded. Then I grinned at Conn as we walked by him. His smile was wide as he checked his expensive watch and started saying his goodbyes.

Who could argue with any plan that involved brownies warm from the oven?

Definitely not me. I loved brownies.

THE MAJOR PROBLEM with being a thief is that each time ya stole something ya never knew if it was going to be worth the trouble ya went through to get it. This was one of those times when it had not been worth it.

"Stealing that file was a colossal waste of time. The only good thing about this evening was Mulan's brownies."

"Because I am great baker," Mulan said, favoring me with a small smile.

I ate another brownie and decided she was right.

Conn chuckled at her bragging while he addressed my complaint. "You're just mad, Aran, because the complete story wasn't in there. I think we found out a lot this evening."

I frowned at his cheerfulness. "What did we learn, Conn? That veteran hospitals are understaffed and don't have enough money to upgrade their computers? Yes, we learned that. We danced in there and got his records without running into a single guard."

"His records were marked sealed by the military, *and* we

have the name of the person who sealed them. That's as good as activating a demon signature on a compulsion. We can track down the person who sealed the records by his name."

Mulan helped herself to another brownie. "I have military boyfriend. He will tell me secrets if I ask."

"Since when do you have a boyfriend?" Conn demanded, his frown wrinkling his normally smooth forehead.

"I have many boyfriends," Mulan said with a shrug. "Training men to please you in bed takes long time. Why would I train new ones over and over? I am too busy for that."

I stood there grinning at both of them like any third-wheel friend would when witnessing a romantic breakdown. Unconcerned, Mulan blissfully ate her brownie and ignored Conn glaring at her.

Finally, she turned to look at me and ignored his continued glaring. "My boyfriend is top general. I can charm him into telling me."

"Like Conn charmed the nurse tonight?" I asked.

"Yes, or maybe more. Do not worry. We are business partners. I will do my part."

The combination of her no-nonsense answer with the innuendo of potentially sleeping with her 'top general' was making Conn vibrate with irritation. Not laughing was the hardest thing I'd ever done.

"I really can't ask ya to make that sort of sacrifice, Mulan. It wouldn't be fair."

She looked me up and down. "Do you want to charm him? Your gray hair looks okay now, but that boyfriend does not like plump women. Maybe you wear tight underwear as disguise. That might work."

My mouth twisted into a smirk. "Thanks, Mulan. I'm so happy ya think I'm too round to attract men."

She offered me another shrug. "At least your hair looks good."

I stared at her. Was the woman truly that clueless? "Yes, because my hair looking good is the most critical thing in my life right now. How could I make it through a single day without that being true? I should come into yer shop every week and let ya do my hair."

Somewhere in the background, I heard Conn practically choking as he tried hard not to laugh at my sarcasm.

"Now you are learning," Mulan said proudly, jabbing her finger in the air at me. "Carry makeup and then you have many well-trained boyfriends like me."

I walked away before I got any more tempted to set her on fire than I already was.

I'd been calling fire since I was six. For insulting my weight, which I worked hard to keep in check, Mulan deserved the 'fires of hell' version of my flames. The only reason I didn't roast her was that I was a better witch than that.

"I had no idea getting my hair done every week would solve all my problems."

The oblivious look on Mulan's face couldn't be faked. I'd been mocking her with my answers, but she'd meant every word. I guess my alleged business partner thought all women our height ought to look like skinny pencils the way she did.

Conn was laughing hard and all but rolling on the floor when I left the kitchen. The joke was on him, though, because Conn wasn't yet in the running to become one of Mulan's well-trained-in-the-bedroom boyfriends.

***

MULAN CALLED the next day to say she had our answer. It wasn't even lunchtime when she called, so I doubted she'd had to do any extensive charming to get her military boyfriend to talk.

"Program is now disbanded. They trained ten special soldiers for secret missions. Man who signed hospital form has retired. Men in program were reassigned."

My sigh was loud. "So, we hit another dead end."

"No. We must interrogate retired man and make him talk. Do you not watch TV? I thought you were experienced."

"I think we watch different TV shows," I told her. "But I suppose talking to him might help. Let's not call it an interrogation. People react badly to that word."

"Fine. I will only think it," she said.

I couldn't help laughing. Mulan was a master at bending ethics in ways that let her keep her illusion of being a holy person intact. Were all Wu Shamans like her?

I quickly discarded the idea. She was so unpredictable that I was fairly sure there was only one Mulan.

"Do we know where this retired military man lives?"

"Conn is looking for him. I am confident he will succeed."

"Okay. I'll prepare my list of questions."

"Yes. Good idea. Do chaos magick to charge up your persuasion."

By the time I hung up the phone, both my eyes were twitching.

Chapter Five

While Conn tracked down the military man who signed Rasmus out of the hospital, I poured over a giant pile of books I'd checked out of the library. I'd been reading them for a week now and knew little more than I did before I'd started.

This morning, since there was no one else to talk to, I called my mother in a time zone five-plus hours away. It was evening in Ireland and she was getting ready to go out to dinner with her friends.

"He was right, Ma. Father Landerman wasn't joking about how little was available about the guardians."

"Peter would know better than anyone," Ma said.

"I appreciated that he told me his theories and shared what he knew. It only cost me a beer and two whiskeys. My wallet got off easy."

"Yes, ya definitely got off cheap," Ma said, chuckling over me bribing a priest to talk.

"The Dagda once told me not to worry about the trappings of anyone's religious beliefs, because underneath they were all the same. But now I wonder if that was true. All these books are about sins and punishment. The idea of punishment angels doesn't fit well next to the idea of them as luminous beings singing in a heavenly choir praising their deity. How am I supposed to sort them out?"

"I don't know, but I still find them fascinating. I think it's their flying with wings that fascinates me so much."

"Modern stories cite angels being invisible beings who require ya to use telepathy to communicate with them or to write to them in a sacred journal that somehow notifies them. I understand the need for tools, but ya would think communicating would be easier with something that's supposed to be perfectly made."

"Ya are looping on hearsay, daughter. Ya need to find something more productive to do."

I ignored her criticism and talked on. "Nearly all angels are thought to be attached to a religion of some sort, but the man-made guardian we encountered had very different leanings. I know because the man specifically said he did not recognize my sovereignty as the daughter of The Dagda. Of course, his idea of sovereignty probably rested on whichever guy among them developed the biggest muscles. I swear reading all this stuff is enough to make ya feel insane for asking questions about angels in the first place."

"Aran, ya're babbling. Take a breath before ya pass out. Ya know how ya get."

I laughed at the chastisement. "I'm forty, Ma. How is it ya can make me feel seventeen again with just a few words?"

"It's a mother's gift," she said.

Maybe it was a mother's gift, but I lacked it. My child seemed completely unaffected by anything I said to her. Not that we'd been talking lately. I hadn't spoken to Fiona since Ma left. I sent daily text messages Fiona never answered and I was about done dealing with that modern humiliation. She was going to owe me an apology when she stopped being stubborn.

I hung up with Ma and set about making myself some strong tea to help me go back to my boring reading. My plans changed when Conn showed up and announced he'd found the man who sealed the hospital files.

"Thank ya for seeing us, Colonel."

"I'm not sure why I agreed. You're not the police or part of any branch of the military."

I heard Conn grunt beside me but ignored him. "We're a private investigative group, but my brother can be quite convincing. Our questions won't take much of yer time. Yer name came up in our search for a missing friend."

Colonel Benjamin Benson led us through a nice, but modest home until we exited into his backyard. It was a gardener's dream and a landscaped heaven on Earth, including the natural pool built into the yard's surroundings.

"This is beautiful, Colonel. I fancy myself quite the gardener and recognize the hard work here. Did ya do all this yerself?"

"Most of it," he said, waving us into chairs at a table. "So, what can I do for you?"

"As I'm sure Conn mentioned, my name is Aran O'Malley. I'll get right to the point of why we're here. Ya signed a hospital release order for a man named Rasmus. Only his first name was listed on the form. The rest of his name was obscured and marked 'sealed' as were all his other records. I don't think 'sealed' means he was an elite member of yer US Navy. I think his actual records were hidden on purpose. I also think I know why, but I need to verify it with ya."

"Is this Rasmus person a family member? Why are you so concerned?"

I held his mistrustful gaze. His questions were ironic since I could already tell he knew exactly who and what Rasmus was. His attempt to lie to me was weak.

"I'm tired of looking for answers and finding brick walls, Colonel. I know Rasmus was never in yer military. He's a supernatural being. I've spent the better part of the last two months trying to figure out why Rasmus turned himself inside out before transforming into a being with feathered wings that flew away from me."

"I don't know what you're talking about."

I snapped my fingers and created a ball of fire in my hand. The colonel hissed and leaned away when I held it out to him. "While I'm not a being like Rasmus, I'm powerful in my own unique way. Now, I need to know the truth about Rasmus, and I swear whatever ya tell me will go no further. However, if ya don't volunteer to tell me, I can arrange for ya to become more helpful. I'm sure ya have seen how cooperative someone with a demon compulsion can be."

Benson crossed his arms and glared. "I thought when I retired all this shit would be over."

I let the fire I created in my hand go out and spread both hands in the air in front of him. "I'm sorry for yer sake, but it's not over yet. I'm sure ya deserve to retire in peace and live out yer life as normal as ya can. Every being on Earth has that innate right."

"How did you find out about him?"

I looked at the man's gorgeous pool and envied him his

backyard sanctuary. I hoped our visit would not ruin the enjoyment of it for him.

"I rescued Rasmus from some trouble he was in. He told me what he could of his story but couldn't remember the critical details. His transformation—or rather, *transmogrification*—was the culmination of us calling in some favors from supernatural friends as we all tried to fix him."

"How many people know about these sorts of things?" he asked.

"I have no idea. All I can tell ya is that no one was more surprised than we were when Rasmus changed from a normal-looking human into a winged being that almost nothing is known about. Until that point, Conn and I both thought he was simply a demon hunter involved in some underhanded scheme."

"Your life sounds complicated."

I nodded in answer before I spoke. "Yes. My problems are many. Rasmus is only one of them."

Colonel Benson avoided my eyes as he leaned forward and rubbed his forehead. "I knew it was only a matter of time until he broke free of our hold on him. He came to talk to us and we captured him. That being is powerful, even in his human form. Once he was rendered unconscious, scientists took all kinds of samples from him. Then they hit him with every drug they had that could erase a person's memories. We've used that cocktail of forgetfulness plenty of times in the past and it's never failed. When Rasmus left the hospital, we thought it had worked to neutralize him. He was assigned to someone whose job was to keep tabs on him."

"Did they use Rasmus to make some kind of serum? We ran into a fake version of a guardian during our search. The human didn't have feathers or look like a birdman, but he was incredibly strong—much stronger than a typical human."

Benson shrugged. "I heard the being's blood was potent. Whoever got it immediately became ten times stronger. Everything in their body adapted quickly, except for their minds. They became less stable mentally. Turns out our bodies make their own drugs to keep our minds level. We don't know how long our test subjects have before they grow too unstable to constrain."

"How long has this testing been going on?"

He hesitated, stared at me, and then gave in. "It's been about seven years. Follow-up injections have to be given every month or the effects fade. Once they gave the being all those memory drugs his blood lost most of its potency."

Conn's grunt was followed by a head shake and a growl. Our minds had traveled the same path in drawing conclusions. Jack knew I'd stop what they were doing and not let them use demon tricks to hide their activities. It was easy to see his thinking about removing me from the picture. He'd warned his partners about my powers and then sold my incarceration as a way to manage me. There could be no other explanation.

I pulled myself out of my epiphany and stared at the colonel. "Rasmus never stopped being conflicted. His lack of memories ate at him until he was willing to risk whatever it cost to recover them. My understanding is that he lost the majority of what he'd experienced as a human during the last seven years."

"Including you?" he asked.

"No, I just met him. And he didn't lose me, which is why I'm digging into this. He's just not here in human form to tease me about looking into his story."

"He's not human, Ms. O'Malley. That creature will

probably return to kill us. He took human form to talk to us and try to stop us from wiping out the demons. Those above me viewed his defense of demons as a potential threat to the security of our country."

I chuckled at the irony. The demons Rasmus was trying to save ended up being paid to help enslave him. I shook my head at the contradiction. Leave it to modern humans to break ancient contracts while thinking they could squirm out of the consequences.

"Rasmus was being practical in trying to stop ya from killing demons, Colonel. Demons can't be killed—not truly. They regenerate over and over, even when they take a thousand years to come completely back from the dead. It would be wise of ya to work with them."

The colonel snorted. "You can't work with demons. They're abominations."

I rolled my eyes. That was exactly what was said about the Nephilim. And the guardians. And any being that didn't fit whatever the norm was for people during some particular period of history.

I stared hard as I answered. "We're all made of the same stuff and were created by the same powers, even if we now call those powers by different names. The demons come back eventually in their original form that never changes. They're what ya and I would call immortal. Humans regenerate too over time, but we die and return in different bodies that lead different lives. I'm only now learning about guardians, but I'm sure they're not outside the natural rules of this planet."

"The guardians are dangerous—more dangerous than anything we could ever imagine. They're more dangerous than demons. We had to constrain Rasmus for everyone's safety. No guardian we create will ever come close to doing what he can do."

Talking to Colonel Benson was like talking to my contrary mother. Both of them believed what they believed... and believed that I was wrong.

"Okay. Maybe ya were right to fear the real guardian, but I didn't get the impression that killing humans was his purpose the last time I saw Rasmus in person. And he's not the only one of his kind. Why haven't the rest come to rescue him or kill ya all in his stead? Yer narrow focus isn't helping ya, Colonel. Ya have much bigger problems than Rasmus and his intentions."

"Like what?" Colonel Benson asked.

I snorted at his belligerent tone. Now this felt like arguing with Jack. The military man simply wasn't able to hear me. Was I wasting my time with Colonel Benson? Maybe I was.

"Yer people need to worry more about yer altered humans that are calling themselves guardians. We know they're man-made... and so do the real guardians. Conn and I captured one and someone burned down our house to get to him. No human ashes were found, so I know he survived. But that man and those like him are going to be problems if they don't stay in their right minds. Humans are not ready to wield guardian powers. Ya told me yerself that it drives them insane."

"Ms. O'Malley, your wisest course of action is to never ask another question about guardians—the real or man-made ones. And after you leave, I'm going to pretend I never met you. I wish I knew nothing about Rasmus and his kind, and all I want to do is forget what I learned about them. I highly suggest you do the same."

I smiled sadly. "Well, ya see, Colonel Benson, I have no choice except to be involved. One of the fake guardians is terrorizing a pregnant demoness. He's been hanging around to steal her newborn child after its birth so yer scientists could experiment on it. My job is to maintain balance and I won't let stealing a demon child go unanswered. Watching over demons is part of my higher purpose in life."

"You can't single-handedly stop human evolution from happening, Ms. O'Malley. That's what is happening with the guardians we made. They're evolving humans and they will help us fight the demons."

I smiled at him. "There are all kinds of forces in this world, Colonel Benson. My family upholds a bargain with the beings from the Underdark that is as old as humankind itself. I'm a hereditary witch from the line of The Dagda, who put that bargain in place. Ya probably don't know who my ancestor was, but in Celtic lands, The Dagda's name invokes the same fear and respect that I hear in yer voice when ya speak of Rasmus."

Colonel Benson shook his head. "One person can't change the minds of those who wield their wealth like the blade of a weapon. The military makes deals with the wealthy for the good of our country. Necessary sacrifices are decided by those far above my pay grade."

"Yes, well, my powers and I are not part of yer military. That fake guardian I met was flawed enough to think his new powers made him untouchable, but what it did was show that he was an unreasonable bully. He's not using his powers for any good purpose."

"Your word choices could use some work."

I narrowed my eyes. "Yer man-made guardian thought he could walk away with someone's child because no one was powerful enough to stop him. Now he knows that's not true because we showed him that he could be stopped."

"The program is just beginning."

I refused to drop my gaze from his. "The real guardian—Rasmus, the human form of the being yer people tortured—was conflicted about his powers despite yer wickedness. He chose to fly away rather than retaliate. One of the guardians I met is an abomination, Colonel, but it isn't the one nature made. It's the one yer scientists created with stolen blood."

"What are you planning to do about it?"

I kept staring at him as I stood. "I'm intending to end yer program. I will do whatever I have to do to stop yer man-made guardians from upsetting the balance of power among the world's beings. Ya can either help me or hide out here in yer backyard paradise and try to forget ya know what is happening. Whichever ya choose to do, I appreciate ya talking to me this much. I'm a little less in the dark now."

"Where do you think Rasmus went when he flew away?" Colonel Benson asked.

I shrugged. "I don't know where he went, but my instincts say he's coming back. It wouldn't be good for yer people to try and capture him again. He knows yer intentions this time and I don't see him letting ya use him again."

Chapter Six

"What are you doing?"

I lifted my round crystal sphere and slipped a feather beneath it. "I'm going to use one of his feathers to scry for the winged creature Rasmus became."

I finished setting up my scrying tools before I turned and looked at the Wu Shaman. Mulan was dressed in jeans, boots, and a sweater today. I never thought to ask her age, but she looked young enough to be heading to class at some university.

Well, she didn't look as young as Fiona did. Faint worry lines crossed her forehead. Maybe she looked more like a graduate student. The idea of Mulan being in school at all made me grin. I felt sure her confidence had terrorized her professors when she'd been a pupil.

"Scrying? Does that work?" Mulan asked.

"This is what a witch does to find someone."

"I would use internet instead of fire pit and glass ball. It is less complicated," she said in a tone dripping with sarcasm.

I glared up at her from where I knelt on the ground. "How would ya search the internet for a man with wings and find any truth? We don't have a picture outside of the memory in our heads. Conn and I searched for the term 'guardians' and found nothing helpful. We tried all kinds of terms: angels, Nephilim, Seraphim, djinn, and pretty much every paranormal being imaginable. With an actual feather he shed from his body, my magick can make enough of an energy connection for me to find him. How is that beyond what ya're able to do with yer shaman stick?"

She shook her stick in front of me. "This is not stick. It is staff. It is shaman tool."

I snorted and waved her off.

Giving up her discouragement campaign, Mulan stomped away to stand next to Conn, who was noticeably shorter today. He'd shrunk his human form another two inches. The five-feet-nothing Wu Shaman didn't seem to particularly notice, but I did. The difference between their heights was a scant few inches now. I was nearly able to look Conn in the eye.

Was he trying to lessen the intimidation he radiated? Or was he adjusting his height to find the optimal one to kiss her without bending his body in half?

I couldn't imagine a man ever making such an accommodation for a five-foot-nothing woman like me, but I also would never expect him to. I liked tall men. Or rather, I liked men who walked tall and with confidence. It was simply my good luck that most turned out to be tall with wide shoulders and long, muscular legs that filled out their jeans nicely. Maybe it was a visual thing. Given Ma's booty man, desiring men was something shared by all the women in my family.

I had no idea why Fiona wasn't dating right now. She'd dated in high school, so I knew she liked guys. I wouldn't have cared one whit if she wanted to date women, but Fiona might not know that. We'd covered the basics over the years, but not shared experiences. If she'd had other leanings, though, I think she would have looked for and found the perfect time to drop her sexual preferences into conversation on the off chance she could embarrass me with the details. Since that hadn't happened yet, I felt pretty confident that my daughter still preferred men.

My runaway thoughts, especially about my non-communicative daughter, were a clear sign that my head was not in a proper space to be scrying for a being with powers I knew nearly nothing about. Colonel Benson had seemed to know more but asking him wouldn't have gotten him to confess. Maybe after I located Rasmus, I'd track him down and ask him to talk to me.

I took my metal bowl that doubled as a miniature fire pit out of my newly restocked witch's kit. I dropped a few wood shavings into it and added some compressed sawdust pellets for heat. When I had a good flame going, I added herbs, and essential oils, and performed a spell for my safety. Astral travel was hard on the body and I would need to sleep afterward.

When I'd finished my preparations, I placed my hands on the crystal sphere and spoke my intentions to find Rasmus out loud. The moment my fingertips touched the cold crystal, my spirit self was transported to a mountainside cave. It was so real that I shivered in the cold air and blowing snow. Eventually, I heard the crackle of a fire cutting through the silence of the weather and I followed the sounds inside the cave to find it.

Around a fire sat three winged men. They weren't talking or moving. They all sat like statues contemplating the flames. Since my physical body wasn't present, I never expected to see all three turn to look directly at me, including the one whose feather I used to find him.

Rasmus looked exactly like I remembered, only more luminous. But he looked enough like his human form that I could never mistake him for another of his kind.

"*Witch,*" one of them said.

The word echoed around inside me until it exploded in my ears and brain. The being that used to be Rasmus shoved the shoulder of the one who had spoken to me.

And then my spirit got violently yanked back into my body.

When I finally found consciousness, I realized I was on the ground by the fire pit and looking up into Mulan's worried face. I turned my head and saw a worried Conn bent over me. He seemed to be speaking, but I heard nothing he said. I could feel myself bleeding from my ears.

Had I hit the ground hard when I returned?

I reached up and patted Conn's face to let him know I'd survived whatever had happened. I'd found Rasmus, but something must have gone wrong with my scrying.

Before I could pull the answer to my pain from my mind, the world went black.

THREE DAYS LATER...

THE SECOND TIME I woke up after scrying for my missing guardian, I discovered the top of my head was completely bandaged. Even my ears were covered. My hands felt the bandages and the thick pads beneath them, and I wondered what they were for. Had I fallen? How could I have, though, when I'd been sitting on the ground while I was scrying?

It hurt to turn my head enough to look around, but I managed. As soon as my eyes focused, I discovered I was in the bedroom of the house Conn and I rented. Next to the bed, Lilith in human form sat in a rocking chair that had not been part of the room's original décor. Conn must have bought it. In her arms, an infant also in human form lay sleeping peacefully. The demoness looked up when I made a sound and studied me quietly.

"Can you hear me?" she asked.

Not only could I hear her, but it was like Lilith was screaming at me. I winced at the pain. "Yes, and ya don't have to yell."

"I wasn't," she whispered. "Your eardrums ruptured and are still bleeding from it. Conn said you were scrying. What happened?"

My mind reached for the answer again and this time pulled forward some hazy memories. My hands went to my head as I recalled the pain when the guardian spoke. "I believe I've figured out why the guardians don't speak to us in their natural forms. How long was I out of it?"

"You nearly died, Aran. Conn came and got me. Before the Great Rebellion, I was a healer. It took me a whole day to stop the bleeding and two more to repair your eardrums. It's like the inside of your head exploded. The closest I've seen to this kind of damage is a sound weapon the human military invented."

I closed my eyes to think about what had gone wrong. The one-word greeting uttered by one of the winged creatures had been spoken beautifully. But his voice had been as destructive as any weapon I'd ever faced.

"Thank ya for saving my ears, Lilith. I owe ya one."

"You owe me nothing, witch. Connlander of the Fir Bolg *ordered* me to heal you."

I snorted. "Well, that was nice of him. Is that why ya did it?"

"No," Lilith said, smiling at her baby. "But Conn thinks it is why."

"Well, I won't tell him any differently," I said, closing my eyes again.

Lilith reached into the nightstand with her free hand and pulled out something. She stood and walked until she leaned over me. "Hold out your hand. This was clutched in your fingers when I pried them open."

She put something light into my hand that tickled my palm. I pinched it with the fingers of the other hand and lifted it until I saw a snow-white feather glistening in the light. I immediately knew who had sent it.

"Conn said it must be a message because everything you used for scrying crumpled to dust, including your crystal ball. All that survived were you and that feather you brought back with you."

I lowered the feather, put it back in my palm, and closed my fingers around it.

"I admit I'm curious. Is it a message?" Lilith asked.

I tried to shake my head, but the movement hurt too much. "No, I believe it's an apology, but I can't be sure. It isn't from the guardian I was scrying for. It's from the one who spoke to me and hurt my ears."

"Were they all guardians?" Lilith asked.

"Yes, and real ones." Hurting still, I closed my eyes. "They have beautiful, but also terrible voices full of power. I'm lucky ya could bring me around."

"Sleep," Lilith said, patting me. "I'm going home now."

"Thank you again for helping me."

"You are welcome, daughter of The Dagda. May the gods be good to both of us."

AND SEVEN MORE DAYS AFTER that...

I SAT on the tiny patio at the back of the house Conn and I had rented and gazed up at the stars. The sense of having dodged death hadn't yet left me. My whole body still felt fragile and off-balance.

Conn had made me call his mantle today to make sure I still could do it. It hadn't been easy, but somehow, I managed. Moving energy or even attempting it hurt my body in ways I could not describe.

Despite my protests that it was unnecessary, Mulan visited every day. She'd come after work and stay to fix a meal before she left. I'd gotten used to seeing her and Conn sitting together. They shared stories while they shared a meal. They bent their heads close and laughed.

I was watching them fall in love, and yes, I was jealous. But the only man occupying my thoughts, especially the romantic ones, wasn't a man at all.

It would be petty of me to resent their happiness, especially for Conn who deserved to find another person to love after centuries of not replacing his deceased wife. Seeking to diffuse my resentment was why I'd banished myself to the outdoors this evening. The bandages were off at last, but every sound still got magnified inside my head and made my brain hurt.

My mind wasn't healed yet, and I didn't even know from

what kind of injury. Was I the first person to hear a guardian speak who had survived the experience?

How had something I'd experienced in my astral form damaged my physical form so much? If this was magick, I'd never encountered or read about anything like it. If it was some natural ability, why didn't we hear about more incidents of it happening?

And why didn't Father Landerman's church know that little factoid about guardians?

After carefully searching all those books for the least of details about dangerous heavenly beings, I still had no idea how any of what I saw was possible. I was no closer to understanding the three beings I saw even though I felt sure now were genuine guardians.

No matter how stupid worrying about Rasmus was, I watched the sky every night and wondered if I'd ever see him again. I also wondered if the real guardians were good guys, or if I'd done the worst thing possible by putting Rasmus back in touch with his past.

My leads on the real guardians were now officially exhausted, except for one I didn't want to pursue. I was back to thinking that my only recourse for more answers would be talking to Jack, no matter how much I dreaded it. Unfortunately, the heavy price my ears recently paid for getting answers about Rasmus made me a coward about finding out anything more.

I'd have to work on that fear. Maybe tomorrow I'd give it some thought.

Tonight, star gazing was all I could handle.

Chapter Seven

I held the phone away from my head so Ma wouldn't burst my eardrums with her frantic bellowing.

"No matter how ya feel about him, he's still yer daughter's father. Track Fiona down and see what she's not been telling ya. Jack's been missing for days, but that was the only detail I got out of her. He also hasn't texted, which is why I think she's genuinely concerned."

I closed my eyes. "I can't scry for him right now, Ma. There was an accident."

"Accident!? That's it. I'm getting a flight out of Ireland this evening. I should never have come home until things were back to normal over there."

"Ma, stop!" I ended up yelling to get her to listen. It was obvious where I got my stress babbling from and I would tell my mother that next time she fussed at me and mentioned it. When finally, all I heard was some heavy breathing, I cleared my throat and continued. "Ya don't have to run over here yet."

"Ya can scry for Jack using yer old wedding band. I know ya

kept it because it was genuine gold. I didn't raise a fool who would throw away something so valuable."

"I still have the ring Jack gave me, but as I was trying to tell ya, I lost my scrying tools when I was searching for my missing guardian. The crystal ball and my portable fire pit disintegrated and turned into ash. I haven't yet replaced them."

"Then get Conn to find him. I bet one of the demons knows where Jack is."

I nodded, even though she couldn't see me agreeing with her. "If ya promise to calm down, I'll go to the house this afternoon to check on Fiona. If Jack is truly missing, the people he's been working with might decide to visit the house."

"Ya're right. That's another reason I need to be there. I'm booking a flight the moment I get off the phone."

"We only have two bedrooms here, Ma, and ya can't keep paying for hotels. Ya would have to stay with Fiona at Jack's house, and then both of ya might get nabbed. I have enough to worry about. Please don't book a flight until I've looked into this."

"Call me back in a few hours or I'm getting on a plane, Aran."

"Alright, Ma. Alright," I said in as soothing a tone as I could manage.

"I have one child and one grandchild, and I refuse to lose either of them. Losing yer father was hard enough to survive."

"I know, Ma, and I love ya for worrying about us. But yer worrying won't help change the trouble Jack brought into our lives. Let me look into this first."

It took me another ten minutes to get off the phone... and ten more to change clothes.

I sent a text to Conn that I was going to see Fiona. He was out for the day looking into a demon matter. Conn had agreed to tutor Lilith on how to better rule her people. I knew he was also helping her improve her security. The man-made guardians—that was how we talked of the one we ran into at Lilith's—were still a threat to her child.

Goddess, could one of those man-made guardians be the father? Was that why they were invested?

I shook my head at the thought. Surely that couldn't be the case. Since she'd told Rasmus he was not the father, I doubted her tastes ran to beings more powerful than demons.

But it was someone Lilith didn't trust or she would have told him about the child before it was born. Every time I looked at the baby I either saw a vision of his future demon self or a human form that didn't look completely human.

It seemed rude to ask her to verify my vision, so I hadn't.

Even if the baby had been Conn's child, which it wasn't, that still wouldn't have been any of my business. I only cared about what the demon adults were up to, and only then if they stepped out of bounds.

I called Fiona multiple times as I prepared to go out, but never got an answer. I sent five texts accelerating the demands in them until I was using all caps, which she'd informed me was screaming in text language.

Nothing I did got a response and panic was setting in. Ma wasn't the only one worried now. If anyone did anything to my daughter, I would rain pain and death on them until they begged to be killed.

"Bloody useless thing!" I screamed at my silent phone as I shook it in the air.

Katie would have teased me about not using my power voice in the house and Conn would have laughed. But a missing ex-husband and a non-communicative daughter were not amusing to me.

When the leash finally snapped on my patience, I called for a ride.

After getting out of prison, I vowed never to step foot into Jack's house again. But here I was, rushing over there as fast as I could because that's what worrying mothers did.

I NO LONGER HAD MY keys so I couldn't get into the house the normal way. My old house keys, which Fiona and Jack both insisted I keep, had melted in the first rental house fire. Conn said he would meet me here, but he was caught up doing something with Lilith that he couldn't leave without finishing. I told him to stay where he was and that I'd call if I got into serious trouble.

When the wards didn't respond to my magickal requests for entrance, I hesitated only for a second or two before calling my second choice for help.

"Hair Divine. Mulan speaking. How may I help you?"

"This is Aran. I need yer help. Are ya busy right now?"

Her giggle was loud in my ear. *"You sound like TV movie spy. Have you been practicing?"*

"This is serious, Mulan. I need to break into a house. It's warded, and I don't know if it's safe for me to do this."

"Was house warded by better witch than you?"

"No... Ms. Smarty Mouth Shaman. I warded it myself, but my wards aren't responding to me. Jack must have paid someone else to layer their magick on top of mine. If I break that person's level of magick, they will be notified, which I'd rather not deal with. But I need to get inside and check to see if my daughter is okay. My mother talked to Fiona yesterday and is now frantic. My ex has been missing for several days. I thought maybe ya could break the other witch's ward and they'd think it was a fluke."

"Okay. I will come see if I can help."

"Thank ya. I'll send a car to pick ya up."

"I have car to drive. How do you think I get to work? The hair shop makes good money."

"Okay. Fine. Drive yerself here. I was trying to be helpful."

"Be helpful and wait quietly," she said before hanging up.

The house looked exactly like it did the day I left it. The lawn still needed mowing, trimming, and some new landscape plants. The only difference I could see was that the chairs on the porch were now a higher quality version with expensive, weatherproof pillows decorating them. I could see Fiona's preferences in the choices made.

Flowers in new tall pots flanked the door of the colonial exterior and were drooping from lack of water. Jack's absence was being felt by the yard and his porch plants. I knew he was too cheap to pay a gardener. By the time he got home, the flowers likely would be dead and there would be a bill from his homeowner's association for not mowing.

I paced on the sidewalk, trying not to look like I was intending to break into the house. This neighborhood mostly worked during the day, so only a few residents were home. Given it was lunchtime, there was little traffic whether pedestrian or car.

A blue VW convertible rolled up with Mulan at the wheel. She pulled to the curb, shifted into park, and grabbed something that looked like a wooden ball bat before she got out.

I held up both hands. "I didn't mean I needed yer help to knock the door down. That would be breaking and entering. I'm trying not to be any more of a criminal than I already am."

"For powerful witch, you have limited mind," Mulan announced while shaking her head. Right after that, she mumbled something to herself and held the ball bat out to let it transform into her staff, complete with jingling tiny turtle shells swinging from one end of it.

"Oh, it's yer staff. Sorry," I said, shrugging. "Ma made me tense. Guess I'm overreacting."

"I do not need your excuses," Mulan said, waving away my comments.

"Oh, come on. I said I was sorry."

"Forgiveness is not instant. We are not that kind of friends."

Both my hands went to my hips before I glared at her. "If we're not that kind of friends, then why are ya here? I despise my ex-husband, but not enough to blatantly steal from him. Ya shouldn't get yer appropriation hopes up about finding profit in my ex-husband's house."

"Profit is not why I came. I am here because I am weak of character and feel sorry for you."

The weak of character part, I could believe. If she felt sorry for me, ya sure couldn't tell it. I grunted at her comment and added a glare for good measure. "Instead of paying ya, I thought I could teach ya to break magickal wards. The trick is to find the right amount of magick to take them out."

"I am Wu Shaman. Breaking witch wards sounds illegal and I was never in prison."

And she just had to throw that in my face, didn't she? It reminded me that Fiona was still upset and thought I was a criminal too. Finding what would change my daughter's mind about me seemed an unsolvable problem.

I turned my attention back to the wards. "The witch Jack hired to do this laid her magick over mine. All I need ya to do is banish her layer and the rest will obey me. I'll do the actual breaking and entering if we need to do that later. I'm not leaving until I find out if my daughter is okay."

"See? This is why I came when you called. You are tiresome and exciting—both at once—but also very good mother."

I rolled my eyes at her half-ass praise. "Can ya see the wards or not?"

Mulan mumbled a couple of words and shook her staff. A ring of magick burst from her and covered the grounds. "Yes. I see them now. Which color is yours?"

"Color?" I only saw black and white ones. I turned to study the wards. "There is a thick ward on the bottom with a thinner one on top. My ward is the thicker one."

"Other witch is lime green. Your ward is dark like red wine. How do I remove hers?"

I hadn't quite worked that out yet, but I had an idea. "Is the lime green color a solid line or are there breaks in it?"

Mulan hummed thoughtfully as she studied it. "It is mostly solid, but barely visible in some places. Is that what you mean?"

"Yes. Those are its weak spots. Pick one to focus on and see yerself lifting it up and cutting it with energy scissors."

"Scissors?" Mulan went rigid. "Scissors are tools of my other trade. Scissors are not weapon. I will use the spirit of the magickal dagger Jing Ke used to kill King of Qin."

I crossed my arms and stared. "How does a spirit dagger work?"

"Like regular dagger, only it cuts magick."

Mulan completely deserved the eye roll and the scoffing noise I made. The witch ward might not recognize the spirit dagger at all. Or it might read it as an intruder which could trigger the wards. The fallout to both of us could be anything from an explosion to being knocked unconscious by a rogue protection spell.

I should have risked breaking it myself, but Mulan was already here, and I'd asked her to help. It was only fair now to let her try to break it, so I waved her forward.

Mulan said a bunch of words in her favorite magickal language. Soon, a portal formed in front of her. She reached inside the portal and pulled out a dagger made of sparkling blue. Carrying it in one hand and her staff in the other, Mulan walked to the border of the ward. She stretched her staff over it and then made a cutting upward motion with the blade she'd summoned.

The ward over mine disintegrated into nothing. My wards quickened at my presence. I spoke the entrance spell and the door of the house swung open without being touched. When she turned back to me, she smirked. Since she'd done as I'd asked, I would have said nothing, even if she bragged.

"Thank ya," I said, hurrying up the sidewalk.

ONCE INSIDE THE HOUSE, I realized Mulan was still on my heels, shaman staff in hand. I prowled the living room, and kitchen, and checked outside before heading to Fiona's bedroom. There we found her lying on the bed like some princess from a fairy tale.

Her phone was beside her and the battery was at zero. That was so unlike her. No wonder she hadn't responded to me. "Fiona," I said, shaking her shoulder to wake her.

"Your daughter looks like her handsome father," Mulan said.

"Yes, she does," I said. I checked Fiona's pulse, as well as for any other damages that might give me a reason to kill Jack without remorse.

Mulan banged her staff once on the floor, bent over Fiona, and held out her hand. "She is in magickal sleep, Aran. No bad witch involved this time. I see demon magick."

I straightened at the news. "Stay here with her. I'm going to search for her father."

And when I found Jack, I was going to rip him from limb to limb. I knew how to do that. Conn had taught me. Severing the body into various parts was an effective way to stop a demon who wouldn't heed my warnings.

Most of them only needed a few months to regenerate from being torn apart, but those months got the point across. Destructive behavior or mistreatment of humans would never be tolerated. Jack needed to learn that lesson too. Being human, though, a torn-apart Jack would never regenerate.

I had been hoping to reason with him, but that was before I came in and found our daughter had become one of his victims. More and more removing her father from both our lives seemed to be the only way to get some peace.

Chapter Eight

J ack's bedroom was as stark a place as a person could create. The colorful covers and pillows I bought for the bed were gone. Jack had replaced them with a chocolate brown spread that looked masculine, dull, and well-used. The only thing I found of my ex-husband in there was a nightstand drawer full of condoms.

Everything of mine was gone, but there was an assortment of women's things in the master bathroom. It was more than I'd ever owned. I knew Mulan would have approved because it included hairbrushes, makeup, and several bright shades of lipstick.

What this told me was that Jack had a steady thing going with one of his women and that she frequently spent the night. My guess was they belonged to the head councilwoman—the one who'd been so pleased by my insistence on divorcing Jack.

The most remarkable thing about finding such concrete proof of Jack's infidelity was how little I cared. I felt no urge to sweep all signs of some other female into the trash. It was both depressing and liberating at the same time. It made me a little angry to be reminded that he'd felt no loyalty to me, but my discoveries validated what I'd said to him after our divorce was final.

I'd told Jack this was his house and hadn't been mine in seven years. When I looked around the room where I'd spent nights sleeping next to him, there was nothing familiar to me at all. Instead, I felt like a nosy stranger, which was odd considering my name was still on the deed to the place.

I left the master bedroom and headed toward the smallest bedroom that we'd turned into a study for Jack after moving in. An expensive door had been installed for privacy and it was locked. If I'd been in a calmer state of mind, I would have spelled the door open. But I wasn't in a calm place so I diffused my frustration the old-fashioned way.

I jumped up, spun, and kicked the expensive door open before stomping inside. If Jack had been on the other side of the door, I would have done the same spin move on him to take off his head. But more bad luck... he wasn't in there, either.

No, there was only me with my resentment of Jack's betrayal and the confirmation that both Jack and Fiona had erased all signs of me from their lives.

Everything in the house said that clearly as it could be communicated to the world. There were no pictures in the hallway of us together. I'd found no pictures in any room of our family of three. Fiona brought no photos to her room in my cottage prison, nor had she asked to take any photos of the two of us with her when she left.

All I found were pictures of her and Jack together, and I found pictures of Fiona alone. Did the ones he'd taken of me with Fiona as a baby still exist? I could hate Jack for that alone. He'd made sure that nothing in the house reminded my daughter that I existed.

Like the other rooms I'd searched, the study Jack and I both poured sweat into renovating had changed too.

The new desk and chair in it were worth far more than I ever would have spent on such things. Unlike the front yard and dying flowers on the porch, the expensive desk gleamed with signs of loving care. And a shiny laptop reigned supreme in the middle of a leather mat.

This was the room of a successful man who earned a good enough living to buy luxuries.

Around the laptop, I saw notes of all sorts containing cryptic sentences like 'subject thirty-four climbs' and 'subject sixty-two doubled in size' stuck to the mat. The notes about abilities indicated Jack was monitoring the man-made guardians. It was proof of something, but without Jack to confirm my suspicions, the notes were just suspicious scribbles.

Mulan appeared at the now broken door of the study. "I heard loud noise. Are you okay?"

"No. I am not okay," I said gruffly, waving my hand at the desk. "These notes are proof Jack is part of the program to make the man-made guardian. Each note talks about a 'subject' and what kind of new power the person got from the guardian serum. There's one number in the sixties. We can assume that means they created at least sixty of them."

"Your ex is evil man. We also know he paid some demon to force magickal sleep on his only daughter," Mulan said.

"And who knows what else Jack's done?" I exclaimed as I rubbed my forehead. I stared at his computer and the twenty yellow notes surrounding it. "Mulan, I'm about to become a real criminal because I'm taking Jack's computer and notes with me when we leave. I'm taking my daughter too."

"Conn told me your ex-husband say over and over that this is still your house. Did he truly say this?"

"Yes, but those aren't my woman things scattered across the counter in the master bathroom. They belong to someone who *isn't* me." My angry gaze raised to Mulan's. "Yes, Jack did say that to me, but it wasn't true. This is not my house, Mulan. He and Fiona erased all traces of me from this place. They probably did that years ago. There isn't even a single baby picture of me holding her."

"Too bad then," Mulan said, shrugging her shoulders. "One cannot steal from one's self in one's own house. Is this not true?"

Her argument was debatable in these circumstances but might be useful if I could bring myself to agree with her.

Deciding I needed some petty revenge to balance out my resentment, I looked around and spied the Babylonian god statue I'd bought Jack for one of our early anniversaries. It was a genuine artifact and cost me dear from my Shadow Breaker earnings.

I retrieved it from the shelf and brought it back to Mulan.

"Jack lusted for this for years until I finally saved enough to buy it. If ya have it appraised by a museum, ya might find out that it's worth a good deal of money. This is yers if ya search Jack's computer for me. I want anything about guardians of any kind, demon hunters, and that woman he's let take over the master bathroom. She might be involved in everything as well, so I want ya to show me *all* the dirt ya dig up on him. I don't see how I could get any madder at him."

Mulan's face lit with joy as she held the statue. I couldn't tell if she'd heard the details of my offer or not. She looked far more interested in the statue than she had in the Greek plates. The woman nearly hummed in pleasure as she explained to me what she held.

"This statue is Marduk. He was great leader who grew so

powerful that people of Mesopotamia made him their creator god. Maybe this is how your ex-husband sees his role in making fake guardians."

"Jack is not a great leader, but yer comparison may be accurate. My ex is plagued with delusions of being more than he is."

"Well, he was wise about this statue. It contains great power still. Maybe it came from someplace where the real Marduk visited often. I feel Marduk in it."

I didn't care about the power locked inside the statue, though hearing about it was a surprise to me. All I'd known when I purchased it was that the statue was a genuine artifact. A reputable antiques dealer had given me a deal. If it was anything like Da's ring, I could see how it could have hidden its power. The ring I wore hid its true form from everyone except me. Did humanity make that sort of magick possible with their strong beliefs?

Mulan seemed in touch with ancient magick in ways I wasn't. No, I wasn't jealous of what she knew, but rather I found it fascinating that she was so knowledgeable. Though I teased her often, I highly respected her Wu Shaman powers. Maybe one day Mulan could teach me how she did some of her shaman tricks.

I would enjoy expanding my skills to incorporate other kinds of magick. Right now, though, all I cared about was stopping Jack. He'd made our child a part of his agenda, which was a line I wouldn't allow him to keep crossing. This was true even if I had to lock Fiona in the cage we put in Katie's basement until I got the whole mess sorted out.

My mind went to my sleeping daughter. Lilith had healed me. Maybe I could pay Lilith to wake Fiona up. Or maybe Conn could wake her.

Most important was waking her in a way that revealed the demon responsible. After I found out the source of the sleeping magick, I would pay that demon caste a visit they wouldn't forget during their slow and painful regenerations.

My child was off-limits to them. I hadn't had to tell any demon that since Fiona was a toddler, but now it seemed they needed a reminder that no amount of money was worth risking my wrath. Or maybe Conn needed to be the one to convince them of why they shouldn't mess with their demon king or his keeper. I could feel my gut churning with the need to act, but first I had to finish this.

"So... can ya break into Jack's computer?" I asked.

"I have some skills in that area," Mulan said vaguely, still smiling at the statue. "We will split profit per our original agreement. Payment for me and Conn. Rebate from dastardly husband for you. No victim to pay this time."

No, Rasmus was not involved in this part of my life. But I wish he could have seen how effectively Jack had erased me from this house. Would he still think Jack was devoted to me then?

"Good. It's all settled then. Do with the statue as ya want," I said.

I texted Conn then that I needed his help.

Mulan went to the kitchen and came back with two plastic bags to carry our stuff. The statue got stored in one and the computer went into another. While we waited for Conn to appear, I gathered up every scrap of paper I found on the desktop.

The desk drawers held the usual stuff plus several bottles of top-shelf booze. All of it smelled of Jack and corruption, but that only made me more determined. I wasn't sure if this was going to be a one-time visit or not, but I knew I had no desire to return to this place ever again.

Conn said he would be there in ten minutes. Fiona had an empty duffle bag in the closet, which I stuffed full of clothes for her. No matter how much she argued with me, she *was not* coming back here to stay until I found Jack and strangled the truth out of him. If she returned to her room, it would be only with Conn or me, and she would not linger.

I wouldn't allow her to be hurt again—not while there was breath in me.

I was dwelling too much. A change of subject was needed. "What do yer people say about time travel, Mulan?"

Mulan leaned on her staff and tilted her head as she watched me pack. "To go back in time is forbidden. Only one shaman return from doing so. She aged fast and turned to dust while people watched. No one ever try again."

I nodded and sighed. "I don't want to go back in time to change the world. I just want to undo the damage I did by kicking the door to Jack's study open. He's going to know I did it when he sees the condition it's in."

Mulan nodded, as if both my temper and my drop-kick were legendary. "I will repair door and teach you shaman magick. Today, we trade training, witch."

Curious, I followed Mulan down the hallway to the study. She inspected the broken door and frowned at me. I shrugged at her chastising look. "What can I say? I was mad at Jack over the missing baby pictures."

She snorted at my excuse. "If I had cape, I would drop it around your shoulders and then you could be *super* mad."

Was that the Wu Shaman's idea of a joke? Or another chastisement? I sighed and looked away from the damage I had done to the door.

"I joke, witch. Come and stand beside me," Mulan ordered.

I reluctantly stepped close to her side.

"Your mending words are 'be fixed'. Wu Shaman's word for this is *guding.*"

I repeated the command. *"Guding."*

"Close enough," she said and planted the staff between us. "Now, grip staff with me and repeat command."

I did as she ordered, but nothing happened.

"Talk nice to Shaman staff first. Make friends, *and then* repeat command. I have been teaching it English. It may be confused by your odd accent."

Ignoring her insult about my speech, I gripped the staff tighter. Closing my eyes, I took a deep breath and sent a picture of Jack unlocking his expensive, perfect door and never knowing what we'd done *inside* the room. Jack might suspect me, but he wouldn't be able to be sure.

I'd magickly erased my DNA from the room already. I'd erased Mulan's as well. I just hoped the ruse extended to those working with Jack. Based on the notes I read, every man-made guardian had a unique talent. It would be my terrible luck that he'd bring one home who could tell him the door had been broken and repaired.

"Guding!" I said firmly and sent a bit of my energy into the staff. Mulan must have felt it too because she gasped.

In front of us, the door mended itself as we watched. Splinters left their hiding places and slid together like perfect puzzle parts. It was amazing to watch and I wondered if "be fixed" could be substituted with the same results.

"Is the spell reversing time?"

Her shrug was instant. "Staff decides how to do something. I do not control that."

Because I'd seen Da's ring making decisions, it was easy to believe her staff could do so as well. When the repair was done, the door closed with a click and locked back. I breathed out a sigh of relief, glad it had worked.

"Finished," Mulan announced.

I immediately released the staff. "That was cool, but if the staff does the work I won't be able to repeat the process."

"You will because I will make you staff of your own one day. As Wu Shaman, I can choose five students in my lifetime and make five staffs for them. You will be student three."

"What happened to students one and two?"

"One died in training. Student two decided the work did not suit her. She left to open bake shop."

"I guess it's hard for a shaman to find good help."

"That is true for both shaman work and hair salon. Hiring new people is very tedious but must be done."

I nodded in sympathy. "I'm honored ya consider me worthy to be trained."

Mulan shrugged. "I don't know your skills, but shaman staff is impressed. It says you need training. I will do that to keep staff happy. No breaking staff when you are mad, though. Repair of staff is very, very hard work."

Giving her a middle finger salute seemed rude after all she'd done for me, so I ignored my first response. Instead, I gave a brief nod to show I had heard her.

Conn opened the front door and walked in just as we headed back to the bedroom.

"I checked the wards before I came inside. Where's Fiona?" he asked.

Mulan decided to talk for me. "Her evil father paid to put his daughter in demon sleep."

In the blink of an eye, a large red demon with black horns

stalked down Jack's hallway. By the time I got to Fiona's bedroom, Conn was studying her like a diner studies a meal before deciding what to eat first. It had taken me years to adjust to his feral nature and even longer to trust he had control of it. By now, I knew the only genuine worry was what Conn would do to the demon who had harmed the child he'd helped me raise.

He studied Fiona for several minutes before jerking away like someone had zapped him. His low growl made every hair on my body stand up. This was the demon king at his scariest.

I grabbed Mulan by the arm before she could make a dash for the door.

"It's okay," I hissed in a whisper. "He's not going to do anything rash."

When I was sure Mulan was staying put, I turned loose of her and walked nearer to Conn. "Do ya know who did this, Conn?"

"Yes," he growled. "And so do you."

"Is it Lilith?"

Conn's frustration lowered a couple of notches. "No. That would have been worse."

"Indeed," I said, nodding soberly. "I still owe Lilith for saving my eardrums."

"She has been more than paid for her service to us," Conn said.

He morphed back into human form but forgot his clothes. Mulan hissed behind us, muttered something in Chinese, and turned her back to Conn.

I didn't know what game Conn was playing with the shaman, or why a woman claiming to have many 'highly trained boyfriends' was so shy around him.

"Sorry," he said, before magickly covering himself in clothes.

I smirked at him. "Do ya think Mulan and I are that desperate for the sight of a naked man?"

"No. I was angry and forgot my clothes," Conn said, looking at Mulan instead of me.

I shook my head. "Can ya wake Fiona up?"

"She'll wake up on her own tomorrow or the next day. Her sleep spell has a timer. I could wake her before then, but she'll have a whopper of a headache that won't go away fast."

"She can sleep the spell off in my room and I'll take the couch. I'm not leaving my daughter. It's obvious that she's not safe here anymore."

I blew out a breath. In the space of a heartbeat, I suddenly knew who had done this to her. I'd feared for the demoness and her posse when she told Conn that Lilith was back among the living. "Was it the demon princess from the church in Albany who spelled Fiona?"

Conn nodded, growling again.

Normally, it creeped me out when he growled in his human form. Today I would have growled myself if I could have. "Maybe this was her way of getting even with us for our surprise visit."

Conn's frown gave away his dark thoughts. "No one would risk your wrath for anything less than a small fortune. She more likely did it because she got paid an obscene amount of money. Working with Lilith, I've learned much about the castes in the surrounding states because she's been collecting intel on them. Most are not doing well enough financially to support their people. The royals leading them are highly susceptible to bribes. It's a bad situation all around. The demon hunters bribing them has made things worse."

I rubbed my forehead and tried to calm down. "I've been in the mood for tearing demons apart since I found out they knocked Fiona out, but we have a bigger problem on our hands. I found notes on Jack's desk about test subjects and their results. They have to be about the man-made guardians. Mulan's going to go through Jack's computer to see if she can get us more details."

A voice beside me jumped into the discussion. "Yes. My job is to dig for dirt on evil ex-husband."

I turned to her and smiled. "And I hope yer Babylonian god statue aids yer efforts."

Mulan smiled back at me. "I would also like to go with you when you seek revenge on the demons who put your daughter to sleep. It would be an honor to watch you work."

I shrugged. "If ya want to see me pulling demons apart limb by limb, I won't stop ya."

Mulan bowed her head. "Many thanks, witch. I love to see you work your chaos magick."

Conn looked between us before settling his gaze on me. "I'm not sure you two should be hanging out together without me. Mulan gets bloodthirsty around you."

I grinned at him. "Haven't ya heard, Conn? I'm the Wu Shaman's new apprentice. I got my first lesson today. Mulan even let me hold her staff. If I do well, she's going to make me a staff of my own."

I couldn't remember ever seeing Conn hide his face in his hands and groan before. The sound made me laugh and I suddenly felt better than I had in days. Mulan turned her face so Conn wouldn't see her smiling. Conn's dread of us working together was hilarious. For the first time, I felt like the Wu Shaman and I were a united team.

Conn dragged his hands away. "Next thing you'll tell me is you're going to teach Mulan to be a witch."

I gave him the most innocent look I could manage. "Why do ya think I called her today? I taught her to break wards. Not my wards, of course, but the one some hag Jack hired to lay a ward on top of mine. The hag probably got notified when her ward broke, but she won't act because a Wu Shaman's signature will be scary to her."

Conn chuckled. "You mean you *hope* that happens. Jack could send a battalion of man-made guardians after us. We're going to need the element of surprise to take them on."

"Hoping is all I can do until I find Jack. Will ya put Fiona in Mulan's car and take her to our home?"

Conn smiled at me. "I could... and will if you want. What are your plans?"

"I'm going to run to a magick shop and replace the contents of my witch kit. Once I get to the rental house, I'm going to layer more wards to keep Fiona safe until she wakes up. Unless the man-made guardians have witch powers, they won't get by what I set without being electrified."

"Fine. Go replace your witch supplies, but don't be scrying until you get home."

I nodded. "Agreed. No scrying unless I'm home."

Those seven years at the cottage had changed me enough to see the wisdom of not rushing into a fight I wasn't sure I could win, especially not alone. I had too many unknowns happening to end up incapacitated again.

And frankly, I was afraid to scry for Rasmus again. I couldn't afford to spend more time being healed from my rash actions. Besides, my guardian feathers—both Rasmus's and the white one I brought back with me from the astral plane—were locked inside the artifact safe Conn put in storage after my accident.

I needed to look for Jack to move forward in my search, but despite Ma's guilt trip over my old wedding band, I was reluctant to use it to find him. It was only right to tell Fiona what had happened before I went after her father. She might want to pretend nothing was wrong, but I couldn't let her do that any longer.

Jack hiring a demon to spell her had ended my tolerance of his shenanigans. I hoped our child was getting a clue so my fight with her wouldn't escalate into some O'Malley versus Derringer full-out war.

Chapter Nine

The ride I called for took me downtown to the magick
store next to the cemetery. The driver wasn't keen about
leaving me there but was appeased by the tip I gave him. My
request for him to wait and then take me home probably didn't
hurt either.

Sarah Anne Templeton, the witch owner of the store, had
pulled all I'd asked her to for my witch kit. It turned out that
she'd added a few surprises for me as well.

"I can't believe demons spelled your girl, Aran. Are you
planning to send them to visit their ancestors for a while? Most
supernaturals respect a child of The Dagda, but demons *always*
do. You and Conn are the scariest power couple in magickal
existence."

"Nobody's being torn apart just yet," I said, sparing her a
smile. "Fiona's safe and Jack's nowhere to be found. Everyone
who knows anything is worth keeping alive until I sort out this
mess."

"That's smart of you," Sarah said. "By the way, I have a new
scrying tool I want you to look at today. It's not a crystal ball,

though I did put one of those in your box per your request. I figured it couldn't hurt to have both tools if you're doing a lot of scryings these days."

My lips curved. "Ma once bought me a new scrying tool. This was many years ago now. It was only after I tried using it that I realized she'd gotten me a portable phone. I'd never seen one as a child. Da didn't enjoy having technology around. He said the antenna of a portable phone created a negative force field around everything within a mile of it. He was exaggerating, but his illogical loathing took root in me like a weed."

Sarah laughed loudly. It never hurt to keep yer favorite shopkeepers entertained.

"Oh, I wish you could visit me more often, Aran. You tell the best stories, and your mother is a delight. If Bridget O'Malley was content to live in Salem, I'd hire her to help me in the store. We'd have a great time scaring the humans who come in here looking for witches."

"Ireland has something for Ma that America doesn't, Sarah. Conn says Bridget O'Malley has a booty-call man these days. I've also been thinking about going back to Ireland to live, but my life is too unsettled at the moment to be making big decisions."

"Well, you're divorced from Jack now. Things have to be better than they were."

"Things are definitely better," I said.

I drew the contents of my witch kit closer to inspect them. Sarah had packed it all in a large box. I sorted through it with the joy of a child on Christmas morning.

Sarah smiled at my enjoyment and brought me an amulet. "It's not the lightest thing to wear, but I can't keep them on the shelves. It has a place where you can tuck a piece of hair inside and instantly see the person. I bought them in both locket size and hand mirror size."

I eyed the round crystal ball in the box. Reaching down, I picked it up. This one was a light smoke color. I'd used every stone imaginable and they were all fine once they were calibrated to me. I returned it to the box. "Would ya think I was old-fashioned if I just stuck with the crystal ball?"

"Goddess, no," Sarah said. "Give me your hand."

I knew she read palms for personal entertainment and I was willing to indulge her. But that wasn't her intention today. She put the amulet in my hand and chanted over it. "Consider this a gift to a good customer. Blessed be, Aran O'Malley. Don't refuse my gift."

When she turned loose of my hand, I held up the amulet and watched it spin. It was heavy, but it was well crafted. "It's beautiful, Sarah, and I won't say different. I thank ya for yer kindness."

"You're welcome. Give Katie my love when you see her. That banshee hasn't visited me in ages. I hope she's not settling for a mundane life."

I slipped the scrying amulet over my head. "No, I don't see that happening. Katie's healing nicely. I don't know what she suffered or I'd try to help her more."

Sarah sighed and stopped smiling to stare at me. "It's not my place to tell you, but it doesn't seem right that you're the only one who doesn't know."

"Oh, there are a lot of things I don't know, Sarah. That's why I keep buying scrying tools from ya."

Grinning at me, Sarah shook her finger. "You're joking, but I know you, Aran. Neither will tell you because they think you're too young to bear the burden with them. Their pain is centuries old."

"Well, that sounds completely ominous. Now I have to know. What burden do Katie and Conn carry?"

"Conn's wife was Katie's best friend. The banshee lost her ability to sing the death song after singing at the funeral of the friend she loved most dearly. The loss was too personal for her and banshees are too proud to get help."

I closed my eyes and gave the news the moment of respectful silence it deserved. When I opened them again, Sarah was staring at me with wide eyes. "Don't worry about sharing it. I'm glad ya told me, Sarah. I'll keep it to myself."

"Well, I'm getting older, Aran. Your mother and I are just regular human witches. Our lifespans are more finite than a child with the lineage of the gods in her blood. It may make no difference in the long run, but I'm not a fan of keeping secrets about painful things. I prefer transparency, except when it comes to nosy non-magickals who ask too many questions."

I chuckled low. Non-magickals were her pet peeve, but also her bread and butter. "Do ya get a lot of those in here?"

"All the time," Sarah said. "The other day some muscle mania guy came in wanting me to teach him how to scry. I told him he needed to read a book on it because my shop wares were for entertainment only."

That sounded like one of the man-made guardians, but plenty of men hit the gym regularly these days. Maybe I was itching to use my jump-to-conclusions mat.

Sarah snapped her fingers. "He also asked about other witches and if I knew any. I told him I was one and that my witch magick focused on making healing potions and salves. I gave him a sample of my muscle rub and sent him out the door. The man's eyes creeped me out. Even when he was looking straight at me, I didn't get a sense that anyone was home inside him."

Should I warn her about the man-made guardians or just let it go? My time was nearly up and my ride would be double-parking out front any minute. I looked around the shop and decided Sarah's ignorance might be an advantage to her and her business.

In the end, I smiled, paid for my purchases with cash, and headed out to meet my ride.

AT THE HOUSE, Conn was cooking dinner, Mulan was bent over Jack's computer, and Fiona was tucked into my bed still sleeping. I put together my witch kit, kissed my daughter on the forehead, and then slipped outside to do some more star gazing.

When Conn was free later, I'd ask him to retrieve my bag of guardian feathers. I wasn't planning on scrying for one of them again, but it comforted me to have part of Rasmus with me. No, when I got around to scrying again, it would be to find Jack.

I dreaded doing it but would need to after I talked to Fiona. If I was on better terms with my daughter, I might have invited her to join me in my search, but Fiona's good energy was still more with her father than me.

And I still needed to call Ma back and let her know what had happened. I'd texted her that we'd found Fiona, but I knew she'd want to hear the details.

I sighed and leaned back in one of the outside chairs Conn found tucked away in the garage. He'd brought two of the four down from storage and put them outside. I needed to buy pillows for them, but even the wood was comfortable.

I stared at the sky and wished Rasmus would come

swooping down. I couldn't talk to him if he did but seeing him would have reassured me he was okay.

It startled me when the amulet I'd forgotten about vibrated against my chest. It lay outside but on top of where the amulet of The Dagda now resided inside me. I wrapped my hand around the amulet and chuckled at the number of sentient artifacts I had on my person.

Was I going to deal with Sarah's new scrying tool making magickal decisions for me too?

A wind picked up and blew my hair back. That was strange since the sky was clear and ya could count the stars tonight. Before I could dwell on the strangeness of the weather, three feathered beings with glowing eyes landed a few feet in front of me.

I slowly stood to greet them. I didn't call out to Conn and Mulan because I was afraid my speaking would make them leave. They wouldn't be here if it wasn't something important. And I needed to know their purpose no matter how scared I was to interact with them again.

But I said nothing as I stood and watched them looking at each other.

The three finally nodded, and then the one in the middle—the one that had been the Rasmus I knew—stepped forward. His feathered form tore raggedly down the middle of his body, which sent feathers flying into the air.

Unable to stop myself, I caught one in my hand before turning away from the gruesome physical changes Rasmus endured when changing forms. I closed my eyes to shut out what he was going through. The violence of his transformation puzzled me since Conn never seemed to suffer the slightest bit of pain when he shifted.

"Aran?"

I forced my eyes to open and turned my head to face him. Yet another slightly different version of Rasmus now stood in front of me. He looked far less confused and far more sure of what was going on. I was relieved by his understanding of himself, and also a bit sad. But what did my feelings matter?

Being a real guardian was his reality to accept.

Mine was to accept that Rasmus was not human.

"Hello, guardian. Or should I call ya Rasmus when ya're in yer human form?"

"We normally don't stay human for more than a few weeks at a time. What the military scientists did to me surprised us. My brethren left me in that state to study how humans managed to constrain my true nature. That they kept me that way for several years is an astounding feat and far too ambitious given the limited scientific advancements of your species."

I chuckled dryly at his summary. "And then I came along and disrupted all yer plans to play guinea pig because I helped ya set yer true self free. One of yer fellow guardians could have stopped me, Rasmus. I probably would have believed them because of the feathers and the whole flying away thing ya can do."

"They viewed your intervention as a very positive event. It made all of us hopeful that your species has wise people with power looking out for the rest. Before I forgot myself, I had taken human form to discern the reasons for their DNA experiments. Their success in burying my memories was both unexpected and concerning. We cannot let anything stop us from our true purpose. We have been wrestling with what to do about the situation since my failure to initially reason with them."

"Would ya care to share yer ideas with me? I've been wondering what to do about them myself."

"If I told you what my purpose was, you likely wouldn't understand. Your father didn't understand the guardian who visited him. Orlin did his best to explain, but your father's beliefs about the world got in the way of his acceptance."

"I'm not Da, and it might surprise ya what I can accept as reality." I held up my hand. "The ring my father guarded all his life hides itself from everyone but me. I don't know why. It's making its mind up about who to show itself to. I'm going along because it's not giving me a choice. The day ya remembered yerself, it showed itself to ya on its own."

"It was taught self-defense when it was being made. It didn't try to hurt me, but it got my attention."

"Was it yer kind who gave the original ring to King Solomon of Israel?"

"The ring was given to a wise human who built a fortress to hide powerful artifacts meant to defend and save your world. The rings do not call demons to serve them. The rings are a special contract with demonkind. Each time demons complete a request of the active ring a female among them gets pregnant with a child."

"So, Lilith's child was part of that agreement?"

"Yes. She fully redeemed herself and many others. Even now, she continues that work."

What business was it of theirs what Lilith chose? "Is yer contract with yer creators like the one The Dagda made with the demons?"

Rasmus shook his head. "Our contract with our creators predates the one between the *Tuatha de Danann* and the original *Fir Bolg* people by thousands of years. It also doesn't include punishment as a motivation, but yes, it is similar in intention."

Rasmus turned and nodded to his comrades. They nodded

back to him and flew off. He turned back to me and said something I could never have guessed in a million years he would say.

"No human words can describe our existence in terms of time. We knew Danu before she became your goddess. We knew the beings who created her. "

"Are ya seriously telling me that ya were around before Goddess Danu?"

Rasmus nodded. "Yes. We assisted the race of ancients who created human life and we are the ones who made sure humankind survived when the decision was made to destroy everyone on the planet. My kind was around before dinosaurs roamed the Earth. In my natural form, I don't feel the passage of time, Aran. I feel time only when I'm in a human body. To become human is a major change for us in many ways. We do not take this form unless we feel it is absolutely necessary."

I felt my eyebrow arching and couldn't stop it. "Ya don't look that old, Rasmus. What's yer secret to keeping all the lines and wrinkles at bay for eternity?"

His mouth lifted at the corners. The signs of his amusement were faint, but I saw his lips twitching.

"Our secret is cellular regeneration at a scale and pace the demons would envy. That's how the hunters got the demons to go along with their plans—they promised them the secret of guardian regeneration. Unfortunately, their promises were empty. What we do to change ourselves is not something that can be learned or transferred via tissue or blood or passed genetically through human replication."

I grunted. "Now ya sound like a scientist."

"We're learners, observers, and recorders. We are rarely participants because it causes complications for your kind."

Waving my hand, I smiled at him. "Tell me more about the

man-made guardians and how wrong our mad scientists are in making them."

Rasmus narrowed his eyes at my demand but did as I asked.

"Human DNA was purposely limited to prevent too much evolution from happening. We made that change the moment we realized the harm genetic advancement did to your fragile human minds. Human-guardian pairings do not work out well for the offspring. When our hybrid children descended into human madness and resorted to cannibalism, we had to kill them all. The rest of humankind was not safe sharing the world with those beings."

His statements were loaded with ownership of things most believed were only myths. I'd have to unpack his stories later. Right now, I have something current and critical on my mind.

I looked at Rasmus as I spoke. "My theory is that the demon hunters or guardian makers or mad scientists— whatever ya want to call the ones in charge—made some sort of serum from yer blood or DNA or whatever it is mad scientists can use for serum making. Are ya aware of how dangerous the man-made guardians are? Do ya remember we captured one of them? He got away from us."

"His escape doesn't matter. The effectiveness of the science behind their experiment is limited to one lifetime per person. Whatever an individual gained from a serum made from me will never be passed to the individual's offspring. The evolution of my kind took hundreds of thousands of years. There is no shortcut to becoming one of us. Our level of power will destroy a human's mind long before the person's body realizes he has a problem."

I shook my head at the news. "Are ya aliens from another planet like some people say?"

Rasmus chuckled at my question. His eyes wrinkled

attractively at the corners when his lips curved. He looked as human as I did when he smiled like that. And Goddess help me, I was still attracted to him. But that attraction was a distraction I had no time for.

"It was a serious question, Rasmus."

He smirked as he crossed his arms. "Aliens are a myth humans created. That term is merely the label you give to those beings who show power beyond your current understanding of possibilities. Most of you find it hard to believe that five hundred thousand years or even a million years ago, even more advanced versions of yourselves existed and thrived on this planet. As Conn rightly observed, the evolution of life repeats itself over and over. Humans are simply along for the ride this time. The creators control who gets to live on your planet. Many other species preceded you."

I crossed my arms to mirror him. "Is that so? Who are these creators ya say are driving this repeating bus humans are riding on? Can ya tell me that?"

"The Creators started it, but *you* are driving it for *you*," Rasmus said with great emphasis. "If that were not true, we guardians would not be needed, and I would not be here talking to you."

"I'm not sure I believe ya got yer memories back, Rasmus. Ya sound nothing at all like the man ya were when we met. Or was that man merely a ruse ya created to fool people like me? Ya don't have to lie about things. Tell me why ya're here."

Rasmus turned away, laughed dryly, and studied the ground for several long moments before finally answering. "I came back and became human again because I missed talking with you. You make me feel hopeful about life, and this is not a small thing for those like me."

My disbelief verbalized into a humorless laugh drier than

his. His praise was too sugary to be authentic. "Is yer human presence here allowed by yer kind? Yer guardian buddies didn't look thrilled about leaving ya here with me."

He turned back to me and smiled. "Nothing is forbidden, but we know from knowledge gleaned through many ages that every action we take has consequences. Some are easily anticipated. Others reveal themselves in time. What you call karma is what we call the price paid for becoming a different type of being."

I crossed my arms and nodded. The last thing a woman wanted to hear from a man was that her presence in his life was more a problem than a blessing. I didn't see myself as part of his karma, nor did I ever intend to be.

Rasmus didn't have to say he considered me to be a lesser being. His condescension was in every word he spoke through his filter of superiority. It seemed ironic now that I once thought The Dagda had been arrogant. Rasmus made me feel like I had the maturity of a five-year-old compared to him.

His attitude royally pissed off the forty-year-old woman inside me whom I'd suffered so much to become. I liked that woman's maturity and claimed it gladly.

The real guardians could kiss my inferior ass.

A feminine throat clearing had me swinging around before I could voice my thoughts. Conn and Mulan stood on the patio staring at me and Rasmus.

"Everything okay out here?" Conn asked.

Rasmus nodded as he shoved his hands into his pockets. "Everything is fine. I have all my memories back, or at least, I think I have all of them. I did not return to harm anyone, though. My brethren and I do not kill any being except as a last resort. May I stay and aid you in your quest?"

I could feel Conn and Mulan's gazes drilling holes in my back as I stared at Rasmus. "Do we honestly have a choice?"

Rasmus shrugged. "You have the same free will that all of your kind has. You can exercise it any way you wish. If you wish me to leave, I will change back to my natural form and be on my way."

I no longer trusted anyone or anything the way I once did, not even my own instincts. If human Rasmus stayed, at least I could learn all I could and make notes about guardians.

After his terrible experiences at the hands of Jack and the others, Rasmus truly might be motivated to help us, but he didn't seem in a hurry to take them down the way I was planning to do. Would he try to stop me from harming the man-made guardians? Or would he truly assist me in our fight?

If he returned to wait the events out with his two guardian buddies, I would never know.

"Ya can stay and help, but accommodations won't be comfortable. We'll have to put a bed in the garage for ya. This place only has two rooms, but I suppose the garage is still better than that cave ya were in when I saw ya."

Rasmus smiled. "No one has been successful in locating us before. Your appearance caught Orlin off-guard, which is why he spoke when he recognized you. Once we learned to speak telepathically, our voices evolved into frequency weapons. He meant you no harm."

I shrugged off the apology. Demons apologized all the time but rarely meant it. They apologized to play nice with me once they realized my powers were greater than theirs.

How transparent were guardians in their motives? That question hadn't yet been answered to my satisfaction. I felt like Rasmus watered down every explanation he gave me.

"The scrying accident is water under the bridge now. I've survived much worse than what yer friend did to me."

Mulan touched my arm. "I have two extra beds at home. We will fix up the garage and put both men out there. Then I will stay in high demon's room until we are done. We keep everyone close and build powerful strike team."

I nodded at her dramatic suggestion and hoped Conn didn't mind sleeping in the garage for a while. His idea of getting Mulan into his bed didn't include him not joining her there, but he'd have to deal with it for now. His frustration was going to be one big ongoing issue until they worked things out.

The other big issue was that my demon familiar was used to having a lot of privacy. I liked privacy too, so it was natural for me to worry about Conn's. These people were our guests, but Conn and Fiona were family. Their needs came first, except for tonight. Hopefully, our houseguests wouldn't be staying long enough to disrupt our home life enough to irritate us.

If Conn started brooding, he'd turn himself into a dog and sleep on every piece of furniture in the house. It would be a nightmare to keep the dog hair from taking over everything. It was his version of a silent protest and would last until I took steps to resolve his issues.

"Can we get the beds for the garage tonight?" I asked her.

"Yes. I will take men and make it happen. I am good partner."

"I promise I will be properly grateful as soon as I can. Right now, I'm going to sit with my comatose daughter and call my irrational mother. If I don't get in touch with Ma, I'm going to end up with yet another houseguest. I should probably text Katie and see if she has any openings at her place, just in case."

"Is Katie a witch friend?"

"No, but she owns an inn that caters to magickals. Conn and I put a charmed cage in her basement for prisoners. Rasmus spent some time there."

Mulan lowered her voice to a whisper as she looked at Rasmus and snickered. "Your true guardian is handsome for such tall man. Instead of using cage, you should invite him to bed to keep eyes on him."

I glanced over at Rasmus explaining himself to Conn who was nodding at every other word. I lowered my voice as well. "If I could go back in time, I would laugh, say ya were right, and acknowledge that I blew my chance to be with him. He is very good-looking and oozes masculinity, but I can't see him as a sexual partner now that I know what he is."

"Really? What is he?" Mulan asked.

I grunted. "He's an infuriating enigma with a superiority complex that I know I couldn't stand waking up to in the morning without hating myself."

Mulan made a tisking sound with her tongue as she patted my shoulder. "You are feeling your oldness. I hope you get over that soon. Sex keeps magickal powers strong and nerves calm. So what if he turns into a big bird and flies away? No man is perfect, Aran."

Somehow I walked away without rolling my eyes over her non-helpful advice. It was rare for me not to fling back insults as good or better than the ones Mulan seemed to enjoy dropping on me.

I told myself I was too mature to be doing that as I went to check on Fiona. Conn would have told me I was in denial again, and this time he would have been right.

Thoughts of sleeping with Rasmus, despite all I knew of about him, were more alive in my mind now than they'd been when he kissed me.

Chapter Ten

F iona came back to consciousness in the middle of the night. She woke thrashing and screaming as she came out of the spell. I jumped up from my uncomfortable place on the couch and dashed down the hall to find Conn already there and trying to calm her.

My two hours of sleep had not been enough to deal with this.

Conn looked at me. "Our girl hasn't quite come around yet. She's caught up in what happened to her and is reliving it, I believe."

Knowing my daughter had fought her assailants and lost only made me madder at Jack.

When this mess was sorted out, I was going to see that she was never that helpless again. She needed magick training, hand-to-hand, weapons, and everything else I could talk her into learning.

"Switch places with me, Conn." Once I was sitting by Fiona, I pressed on both shoulders and shook her gently. "Baby, wake up. Yer wicked ma is here and ya're safe now. No one is going to hurt ya again. I'd cut their heads off before I let anything happen to ya."

My daughter opened her eyes, blinked until I came into focus, and then sat up to grip me hard. She sobbed on my shoulder for two or three minutes while I made soothing noises and rubbed her back.

Conn, Goddess bless him, disappeared from the room and came back with a pack of tissues for her. She took them from him with a teary thank you. I didn't ask where he got them, but I figured they'd come from Mulan's purse. My lack of having any in my possession would earn me another lecture over not carrying what the Wu Shaman considered to be 'necessary women's things'.

I brushed Fiona's hair back from her face. "Ya got spelled to sleep for few days, but I think nothing worse happened to ya. Conn and I checked yer energy for other compulsions and found none. It was only a demon sleep spell."

My daughter choked on her tears as she got the explanation out. "Dad... made them... do it. Why... would... he... do that... *to me*?"

The question got wailed on its way out. My grown daughter was so hurt that her voice had reverted to a child's. If Jack was here, I would have punched him so hard his brains would have rattled in his head. He would pay for hurting the beautiful child he helped create. I wouldn't rest until I made sure he would never betray me or Fiona again.

I took a few deep breaths before I spoke to calm myself. "It's okay, Fiona—everything is okay now. Ya're safe here. Gigi called me upset, which is how I found ya. I'm glad ya were at least talking to one of us."

Fiona's eyes teared up as she hugged me again. She wailed some more on my shoulder. I took that as the apology she was too proud to utter. She might be Jack Derringer's child in outward appearance, but her emotions were as passionate as anyone's in my Irish family.

Mulan hovered in the doorway. I waved her inside the room. She held up a steaming cup of something smelling like flowers and herbs. "I made her special tea to help with recovery."

I guess Mulan carried some necessary Wu Shaman things in her purse next to her lipstick, hairbrush, and tissues. She frequently made me feel like I wasn't womaning right—not compared to her anyway. That wasn't what friends were supposed to do, which is why I didn't think of her as one.

Since currently she was caring for my daughter, I held my tongue and didn't speak my thoughts out loud.

Fiona sniffled and dabbed at her eyes as she studied Mulan. My daughter no doubt wondered if the drink was drugged with something that would knock her out again.

"Let me introduce ya two. Fiona, this is Mulan. Ya've met her before but under far different circumstances."

Fiona's head tilted. "You're the stylist from Gigi's salon. You did my hair."

"Doing hair is good job and pays well," Mulan said proudly.

I cleared my throat to interrupt them. "Mulan is also a Wu Shaman from China, and she specializes in healing. We've become temporary business partners until we find..." I stopped and rethought my words. "There's a lot more going on than I realized when the demon hunters let me out of prison."

Fiona scooted to an upright, seated position. She cleared her throat and scrubbed the remaining tears from her eyes before looking at Mulan. "It's nice to meet you... again."

Mulan smiled, nodded, and set the steaming cup on the

nightstand. She also put a small dish of cookies next to it. "There is more food in kitchen. I bought cookies because there was no time to bake brownies. Maybe tomorrow I will bake."

Fiona did her best to smile back. "Tea and cookies sound wonderful."

I smiled when Mulan bowed to Fiona before she eased out of the room. Conn hadn't made a reappearance, which was worrisome, but I had to deal with my daughter's needs first.

Climbing into the bed, I sat with my arm brushing along Fiona's. She sipped the drink and nibbled one of the cookies. I waited to speak until I couldn't handle the silence anymore. "Are ya okay?"

"No," Fiona whispered. "I may never be okay again. There was this guy, Mom. Dad introduced us a few months ago. We hung out together several times. The day this happened, Dad came home after being gone for days with no explanation. Daniel—the guy—arrived at the same time, but he'd changed so much physically that I barely recognized him. He was excited and was going to tell me all about it, but Dad stopped him and made him leave."

"Did yer Daniel fellow have muscles like a football player or a weightlifter?"

"He was bulked up like a bodybuilder who'd been taking steroids for years," Fiona said, her voice faint. "He used to be built like me—nicely muscled but slim and not bulked up. We ran track together. I thought we were becoming a couple."

"Did he ever hurt ya?" I asked and held my breath for her reply.

Fiona shook her head and frowned. "No. After Daniel left, I went to my room and closed the door. Dad followed me and said he wanted to talk. He held my hand and said he was sorry that he hadn't allowed Daniel to stay. He said he would explain everything to me after my nap and that things were going to be better than ever for us."

I ran a hand over her hair. Her gaze slowly raised to mine.

"Dad talked to me like I was ten instead of twenty. We even argued about my age and maturity. I told him I wasn't taking a nap like a toddler and that he had no right to interfere in my relationships. He said he was my father and that gave him the right to do whatever he decided was best for me. Fighting with Dad is the last thing I remember until I woke up just now."

Her story made me hate Jack more than ever, but I didn't want to rant about it in front of our child.

I patted her hand. "Yer father..." I began, then stopped to take a deep breath so I wouldn't scream. I searched for calm and finally found a little. "I have reasons to believe yer father—and maybe all demon hunters—are involved in some military experiment that turns normal human men into very strong and powerful beings. The original being they used for their experiment is the guy they sent to make the deal with me to get out of the cottage. He's also the same guy I coerced to help me solve the bogus demon portal task. But there is no open portal, Fiona. I've spoken to the largest caste in three states and another smaller one."

Fiona sniffled again and waved her hand. "So was everything Dad did part of some evil plot?"

This is the biggest problem with being divorced. I wanted to tell my child the truth I suspected, but only after she saw an inkling of her father's wickedness for herself. Until that time came—whether she was twenty, thirty, or even my age—I would have to pretend to be neutral. It's what Da and Ma had done to me with Jack. And they were right to hold back because I wouldn't have believed them before seven years ago.

"I can say for sure that yer father's actions were part of a plot, but whether that plot is evil or not hasn't been confirmed. Demons are involved. Despite his job, I know your father has been paying demons from several castes to assist him. I don't know what yer father's big plan involves, though. Do ya have any ideas?"

Her head moved side to side as she thought. "Strangers came to the house often. I... I looked away every time I felt uncomfortable. Dad locked them in the study with him for hours during each visit. I wasn't allowed in that room after you went to prison. Dad kept it locked."

I nodded. "Yes, that's what I discovered while I was searching it for clues about what he's doing."

"Are you going to hurt him?" Fiona asked.

"For being a terrible husband and a questionable father? That's all I've got evidence for at the moment. That may be worth making him bald or unable to talk for a while, but truly hurting him? No, that's not what I'm planning. I would only hurt him if he hurts ya again or tries to hurt Conn. Oh, and Gigi too... though, Goddess knows, she's been looking for an excuse to put a curse on yer father. It was all I could do to keep her from flying over here to help track him down. She's worried sick about us."

My child laughed even as she scrubbed more tears from her eyes. "It's not funny and I don't know why I'm laughing. I truly don't understand any of this."

I nodded and sighed. "I haven't understood yer father for years. Before he betrayed me, I still loved him. Now I'm hearing from Gigi and a host of others about all the things they were afraid to tell me about him for fear that yer father would find out and use them against me. So don't feel bad for not realizing his true nature was shady. I shared his bed without ever realizing that he loved my power more than he loved me. It still makes me mad that I got fooled so much, but I'm mad at myself as much as at yer da."

"How did this happen to our family?"

"I have no idea, luv. Life sucks sometimes and all ya can do is deal with that fact. I don't like this situation any more than ya do."

Fiona released a breath that shuddered its way out of her body.

"Is the tea helping?" I asked.

"Yes. How long was I asleep?"

"Two days, I think."

Fiona bit her lip. "How could I possibly be tired then?"

"A spell affects yer body in strange ways. If ya're genuinely tired, I would say that's a good sign. It says yer body is healing from yer ordeal."

"Where are we?"

"We're at the rental house Conn and I leased for a year."

"Is this the small place you mentioned in your texts? If so, it only has two bedrooms. I'm guessing this is your bed I'm in."

I smirked at Fiona for reading my texts without ever acknowledging I sent them. "My preferred real estate advisor wasn't speaking to me at the time I committed to this contract, so I went with the best house I could find after the first one burned down."

Fiona lifted her chin. "I was mad at you for what you said about me siding with Dad."

"Yes, and I probably would have felt the same in yer shoes. But blocking me out of yer phone wasn't mature... or safe. Please don't do it again. Get mad as ya need to get but stay in touch. The life of a magickal isn't the same as a normal person's, Fiona. Terrible things can happen to ya simply because I'm yer mother and Jack's yer father."

Her head bobbed up and down. "You're right. I wasn't thinking of that. Will you sleep with me tonight?"

"Yes. Or I could send Conn in one of his doggie forms to curl up beside ya. He's been as worried as me about not hearing from ya. I almost sent him to spy on ya."

"Sleep here with me," Fiona said, curling up on the pillow. "If you're beside me, I know things will be okay."

"Okay. Let me get my stuff. We'll see about turning this one bed into two smaller ones for a while."

"Mattresses on the floor are fine with me," Fiona said.

"Goddess, no... not unless I have to. I've slept in strange beds and on strange furniture too many times. This may be a rental, but I made it my own the day Conn and I moved in."

"Thanks for coming to find me, Mom."

"I love ya, Fiona. No matter what happens, that will always be true."

Chapter Eleven

The next morning I woke to an empty bed. Waking alone was nothing new for me, but I'd held my daughter close as I fell asleep and now missed her. Holding her while she slept was something I hadn't done in a very, very long time.

The immediate panic I'd felt over her absence lessened when I heard masculine voices and Fiona's responding giggle down the hall. I rolled over in bed and pushed myself upright.

Today, I felt ancient. Not as old as Mulan made me feel, but much older than forty. I had held my twenty-year-old all night while she blissfully slept unconcerned about her fate. My poor arms had fallen asleep.

I now could say with mature certainty that forty *was not* the new twenty. Sadly, it was the same old forty it always was.

And sometimes forty looked exactly like I did this morning... and it felt like I did, as well.

I'd had too many surprises in too short a time without the luxury of being able to process them. My tired body wasn't keeping up well and today it was more obvious than usual.

After stumbling to the bathroom and pulling a sweatshirt

on over my pajamas to hide my braless state, I walked down the hallway in bare feet.

Rasmus sat at the table drinking coffee and wearing one of Conn's expensive shirts. His presence gave me déjà vu. We'd done this scene before. He looked well-rested this morning, but then he'd looked that way every morning I'd seen him this early.

As usual, I looked like a zombie freshly risen from death. Today I also looked like one who had not changed clothes in decades. Having seen my fair share of necromanced humans, I knew wrinkles were the least offensive problem for clothing stained from body fluids most humans didn't know they even had inside them. Decomposition was not a pretty process.

Goddess, Rasmus was right.

I was a terrible person in the morning and prone to morbid thoughts before I was properly caffeinated.

I scrubbed my face before speaking. "Good morning," I mumbled, heading straight to the coffee pot for a fix.

"Mom's not good until she's had at least two cups of java," Fiona said, grinning at Rasmus.

"Yes, I know," Rasmus instantly replied.

"That's very interesting," Fiona said slyly, letting her smile bloom. "So how many mornings have you and Mom spent together?"

I saw Jack in her smile, but I pushed the similarity away. The sound I made was a cross between a growl and a sigh. "Don't bother answering her, Rasmus. My daughter woke up sassy after her demon spell."

"I don't mind answering," Rasmus said, but then stared at her over his coffee cup as he sipped and made her wait. "I've spent several mornings with your mother, but no nights. Does that answer your *real* question?"

Fiona giggled. "Yes, even though Mom would say *that* information was none of my business."

I walked to the table and flicked her ear as I passed her chair. My daughter yelped and smacked my arm. Luckily, I'd already set my cup down in one of the vacant spots.

"I say that because who I sleep with—or don't sleep with— is none of yer business, Nosy Rosy. Did I ask for details about what ya did with yer Daniel fellow? No. I did not. It's called respecting a person's privacy."

Mulan laughed as she scrambled a mountain of eggs. "If I become mother, I want to be tough like you," she exclaimed, pointing her spatula at me.

I blinked at the Wu Shaman's words. Were they truly a compliment? I wasn't caffeinated enough yet to be sure, but even a poor compliment deserved a response. "Ya're going to be a great mother, Mulan. Ya got the guilting thing perfected already."

Mulan carried a giant bowl of scrambled eggs to the table. Conn, who'd been silently making toast, returned with his contribution to the meal. We ate the morning feast without talking much.

Eventually, I rose and made a fresh pot of coffee to make sure the five of us got a second cup—something I saw as critical for myself. The third cup I now nursed was my bonus for being the one who paid for the brew.

I sat at the table and leaned over my coffee cup like I was protecting it from being stolen.

"What happens when Dad comes home and I'm not where he left me?" Fiona finally asked.

Three cups had barely taken the edge off. Between Fiona's sleep spell and Rasmus showing up, resting well wasn't easy.

Jack's reaction to me rescuing our daughter from his house was the least of my concerns.

I raised my head and studied her. "He'll be texting ya when he discovers it because he knows I'm the only person with enough nerve to retrieve ya. What ya say to him about it is yer problem to figure out."

"What do you want me to tell him?" Fiona asked.

I could hear the petulance in her tone about to break through, but it was time for her to accept responsibility and ownership of her own life. I wasn't telling her what to do.

"I want ya to stay mad, and stay on yer toes, and not let yer father put ya in another demon sleep while he figures out a better way to control ya."

Fiona frowned into her coffee. "Maybe…"

I slapped both my hands loudly on the table to be sure I had her attention before I stated the obvious.

"If ya want to keep being a victim, Fiona, that's yer call. Anything could have happened to ya while ya were unconscious. At yer age, Goddess knows, I can't follow ya around keeping ya out of trouble all day long."

"I understand that Dad *made* them do that to me. I heard him telling those demon guys to make me sleep."

I swung one arm in the air. "And that's my whole point. Yer father can't be trusted. I know this is hard for ya to accept. He's given ya a lot over the years, and he's been there when I wasn't. In case yer brain hasn't figured this out yet, I feared for yer well-being. I stayed in that prison to make sure yer father treated ya well. Jack knew what I'd do if he didn't."

She looked every bit as offended by that truth as I knew she'd be.

"There was no need to do that. Dad would never hurt me."

I snorted before glaring her way. "Do ya count yer demon

sleep as someone taking good care of ya then? I seem to remember ya sobbing about his mistreatment for quite a long time last night. Ya seem all better this morning, though. Maybe I read ya wrong. He has spent more time with ya than I have."

Fiona looked away from me and stared at the wall. I knew this was hard for her. If I was a different mother, perhaps I would have softened my approach. But I wasn't. That man-made guardian swiped a giant knife across Rasmus's throat and drew blood. If we hadn't stopped him, he would have decapitated the guardian in human form without a single regret.

My child had no defenses against someone like that. I wasn't even sure if I had any, but I didn't doubt I'd soon find out.

As a mother, I had a right to worry, but Fiona had a right to feel she was safe with the man who helped create her. Jack's list of crimes against us wasn't getting any shorter.

I blew out a breath. "Yer father sold someone the guarantee of my imprisonment. He purposely took seven important years from us and now ya're all grown up. Ya may think ya know how to judge danger, but ya're not any good at recognizing trouble when it's smiling and being nice to ya. Killing yer father will be my next call if he allows any of his demon lackeys to touch ya again."

Fiona rolled her eyes. "You're always so dramatic."

"Says the girl who wept on my shoulder last night." I ignored her hurt expression and leaned back in my seat. "The people yer father keeps company with are dangerous. Maybe yer father is dangerous too."

"Or maybe Dad's just... I don't know," Fiona said before shaking her head.

"I've seen some of what the man-made guardians can do,

which justifies me screaming at ya. So the way I see it, this is your reality check, Fiona. It is now yer number one job to keep yerself safe, which is the only way to prevent yer father's death at my hands. And I'm not joking about it."

I paused to glare at her closed expression. What would it take to get through to her?

I sighed and leaned over my coffee again. "My highest purpose is to make sure demons don't harm humans and humans don't harm demons. I've already had to prevent an innocent baby from being kidnapped because of things yer father did. I won't have my own child go missing as well, because I promise ya that will tip me into a rage no one wants to see me unleash. Are we clear?"

Fiona frowned harder but held up both hands. "Yes, Mom—we're clear. I'll be more careful. Not trusting Dad is going to be hard, but a part of me knows you're right. I'm still angry about what he did and I don't know why he did it."

I nodded at her response and returned to drinking my coffee. I needed this third cup.

Conn cleared his throat in the awkward silence that followed my argument with Fiona. He knew I rarely showed that sort of temper in front of anyone outside the family. "Now that Aran's getting older, we may have to hold off talking to her until after she's finished *three* cups of coffee."

Mulan laughed with no embarrassment. She made no secret of the fact that I amused her. Fiona and I arguing over breakfast was probably high entertainment for her.

Rasmus said nothing. He rose from the table, gathered our empty breakfast plates, and loaded the dishwasher. Some might say I was overly suspicious. Ma would say she raised a witch who listened to her instincts.

"So tell me, Rasmus. Do ya know where the scientist bastards are doing their work?" I asked.

"Yes," he said without looking at me.

"Will ya show us?"

Rasmus stopped loading and looked at me. "Yes. That's part of why I returned."

Fiona's ego was still smarting, which always showed up in her tongue. It was an unfortunate inheritance for both of us. I got it from Ma and Fiona got it from me—passed down from mother to daughter through who knew how many generations. I saw the rude question forming in Fiona's expression before she asked it.

"What were the rest of your reasons for returning to Mom?" she asked Rasmus with a smirk.

Rasmus switched his gaze to hers. "Well—to quote your mother—*that* would be none of your business," he said.

Then he spoiled his rebuttal with a wink that made her grin at both of us.

I sighed and turned to Mulan. "It's about to get real, Wu Shaman. Do we need to make another deal? Let's hammer it out now if we do."

"Babylonian god is worth more than sixty thousand. We're good, witch. Save Greek plates for next job."

"Oh, good... I really liked those plates. I dreaded getting rid of them," I said, letting my sarcasm flow.

Mulan turned to smile at Rasmus. "I put victim profit from previous jobs in escrow for you. We will set up bank account for you and transfer money to it soon so you will not be financial burden to witch and high demon."

"Why do I have a victim fund?" he asked, looking at me and not Mulan.

I smirked at him. "Mulan and I deemed ya to be a victim

after ya changed back to yer true self and flew off. I'll explain the details later. Just go with it for now. The Wu Shaman is very good with money. I'm sure ya're earning interest as we speak."

Did the real guardians understand or appreciate material wealth? Or were they above such things?

I took a long last drink of my coffee and watched Rasmus finish loading the dishwasher in silence. Watching him doing something so mundane and common was oddly soothing to me.

But I'd forgotten Fiona was still watching. She aimed her smirk at me. "Since Dad put me into a demon sleep, do I get a victim fund too?"

I opened my mouth to answer but never got the chance.

"No," Mulan said. "You get room and board only until you are trained. Untrained witch with no magick is worth little as team member. Maybe you ask your tough mother for child allowance."

"Allowance?" Fiona repeated while rolling her eyes. "Why can't parents tell when you're grown up? I don't take naps, and I for sure don't get an allowance. I have an online business that does well enough to support my college party habits. Thank you very much."

Laughing at people who got burned was one of my favorite things in the entire world, especially if I was doing the burning. Now I could add Mulan's humorous obsession with making money to that list, even when being her friend and partner came with insults about my womanhood.

I laughed out loud the moment Mulan pointed a finger at my smug daughter.

"You are spoiled child like my sister. You are a Daddy's

Girl. He gives you money, fancy car, and finds you great boyfriend to keep you on his side."

Fiona had already confessed all that to me, so she couldn't deny any of what Mulan said. And to her credit, she didn't even try.

I admit I was surprised when she let a smirking Mulan walk out of the kitchen without offering a single defense of her mature character. Instead, Fiona moved to sit across from me as everyone else filed out to get dressed for the day.

My daughter stared at me for a long while before eating her pride and saying what she wanted to say. "I want to help you find out what's going on."

I finished the dregs of my coffee before answering. "I can't take ya into an actual fight when ya have no skills, Fiona. Watching ya die would turn me into the criminal ya think I am already."

Her eyes widened at my confession, but she nodded.

"Okay then... I'll do your paperwork to help. I will drive you places and make sure everyone eats. I swear I can be useful, Mom. Dad's demon sleep made me miss most of my finals anyway. I'm going to have to get a doctor's excuse and take makeup exams later to finish those courses."

I looked around the kitchen. Rasmus had wiped all the crumbs from the counters. It sparkled under his care, but this was a rare morning. Once we got serious about finding Jack and the lab, we would need someone to do the mundane things that kept the rest of us going.

Mulan had absorbed the task of feeding us. Most of the time Conn helped her. If Fiona was helping too, maybe Conn could help me and Rasmus instead.

I crossed my arms and stared hard at her. "I have to stop yer father and I don't know what it will take. He may get hurt, Fiona. Are ya helping me because ya're thinking that might save him from my wrath? Or do ya think what he did to yer Daniel fellow is okay?"

Her gaze flicked away from mine. "I don't want to choose sides, Mom. Can't I be neutral and still help?"

Shaking my head, I watched hope die in her eyes. Maybe I was a terrible mother, but it was better she hurt now than end up betraying our efforts. "If ya want to be neutral in this fight, go back to the dorms and don't come home again until I tell ya it's okay. Watch yer back and don't go anywhere with strangers. Stay as close to yer room as ya can. They call it 'lying low' for a reason."

I watched my daughter shake her head. "That would be me turning my back on our family, which is what I've been doing since you went away. That's why I called Gigi instead of you. I knew not talking to you was wrong, but I didn't want to choose between you and Dad."

I uncrossed my arms, leaned forward, and picked up one of her hands. "Ya're twenty in a different way than I was. Da trained me to fight like a man does when I was fifteen. When I was only seventeen, Ma trained me to use my craft for self-defense, and protection, and to stop my enemies. No one trained ya at all, Fiona. And that's on me for letting ya grow up so out of touch with yer magick."

"Dad said I didn't have any magick, and that your magick was the kind that caused trouble. Since you got sent to prison for using it, I thought maybe Dad was right."

I sighed. "Well, my magick indeed disrupts things, but not the way Jack meant. I cause trouble for the troublemakers. Otherwise, I go about the business of living my life like everyone else. Before yer father betrayed me, I was planning to open a store and sell witching supplies."

Fiona's gaze dropped. "Dad never liked your magick."

I glared at her. "Because I never let your father tell me how to use it."

Fiona shrugged. "Well, I have no magick to control, so Dad was probably right about me."

"Girl, magick is yer inheritance the same as it is mine. Ya have a similar magick as yer grandfather had, which I'm learning is even more special than what ya inherited from yer great-grandmother, Murieann."

Sadness was in Fiona's voice when she finally spoke. "So Dad lied about my magick as well?"

"Yes. Without practice, though, yer magick will not come to help ya when ya call to it. It demands both sacrifice and respect from its wielder. And it often demands yer blood. I intend to see that ya get all the training ya need to prosper as whatever kind of witch ya choose to be, but ya have to stay alive long enough to learn these things."

Fiona squeezed my hand. "I'm conflicted, Mom, but I'm not completely stupid. I want to believe Dad's not a bad guy, so I rationalize everything he does. I get that I'm trying to make excuses for him, but I can't seem to stop myself. Have faith in me while I figure out what story about him I can live with. I know I'll get there."

I shrugged. "And I believe ya, but I will still hurt him if he hurts ya again. Even if he destroys me, there is a line of other magickals waiting for their turn. Only yer father can choose to be good. That's why they call it free will."

Fiona nodded. "Who inherits Conn if something happens to you?"

"I asked The Dagda that very question when I was training with him. Are ya sure ya want to hear his answer? If I recall right, I think ya were barely walking when I talked to him."

When Fiona nodded, I reached out and touched her flat stomach with my finger. "If I survive long enough, one child ya bear will become his next keeper. If I don't live that long, Conn will pass to some cousin of mine temporarily until the chosen one among yer offspring comes of age. Conn won't bond with anyone but the next chosen child of The Dagda. Our god ancestor didn't tell me what would happen if ya chose not to have children, though. And I chose not to worry about that possibility. "

Fiona smiled at me. "You've always been a positive thinker."

I smiled and patted her cheek. "Love makes me one, and that's the best I have to offer ya, child. However, I will do what has to be done to keep the balance between good and evil, just as I have before. Ya might not agree with what I have to do, but we'll just have to talk it out if that happens."

"Gigi said you used to work with a paranormal group in Ireland called the Shadow Breakers. She said you were famous among them."

It was strange to hear that my mother bragged to my daughter about me. I laughed at her words. "I'm many things, sweetie, but famous isn't one of them. Let's get dressed now. The Shadow Breakers is a story for another time. Can ya mind the house while the rest of us do a little in-person research today? I can't afford to keep buying scrying tools."

"Yes. What else can I do to help?"

"Change the settings on your phone so yer father can't track ya. Make yer social media private. Move yer money to an account yer father doesn't know about. The last thing I can think of is to see if ya can take yer college exams in a month or so. Tell them ya're contagious and can't be around anyone for six weeks."

"Doing all that will take most of the day."

"Ya have no time limit. I'm just glad ya're here with us and willing to stay safe. You staying safe will help me focus on the right things."

My daughter's eagerness to help made me hopeful that Fiona had finally joined Team Aran, but the young were brash and kept their own counsel.

Sadly, my daughter had become one more being I couldn't completely trust.

But for now, that was a fact of life I couldn't change.

Chapter Twelve

It's true what they say about plans. Ya can make them all day long, but that doesn't mean ya're going to get to carry them out like ya hope.

Mulan found something on Jack's computer that required several hours of online research.

Fiona got deeply involved in cleaning up her social media.

Conn left to investigate the latest threat to Lilith's caste.

That left Rasmus and me doing low-level surveillance from a coffee shop across the street from the sports gym. He said it hid a hospital-type lab on the other side of a hidden wall.

He also shared that I wasn't the first person to ever put him in a cage. I was not surprised to hear that, but I still didn't feel guilty. I felt no regrets for protecting myself and the people I cared about from betrayers like Jack. I felt no regret for caging someone like Rasmus who seemed too heavily influenced by them.

"They made up most of that military story about ya, though the colonel I spoke with knew ya existed. Do ya remember what happened during the time ya spent with them?"

Rasmus leaned on the table. "I remember up to a point. After that, I recall being totally confused and always asking people to explain things. General confusion was a perfect way to distract me from my purpose. What they gave me worked well on my human body. I'm still not sure how they kept me from assuming my true form."

I gave up staring at the gym to look at the man sitting across from me. It was easy to forget he was anything other than what I saw with my eyes. "What is a guardian, Rasmus? Are ya a type of angel?"

Rasmus grunted as he thought. "We felt no need to define ourselves, so terms changed but meant the same. I knew for certain that I was created to watch over the beings inhabiting this planet. I knew my job was to keep them in balance. I've gone by many names but the term 'guardian' describes my primary purpose best."

"That's not an answer to my question, though. Ya have the ability to transform into what ya consider yer 'true' form, and yet ya can take a human form like mine. In yer head, ya must be placing a higher value on having wings and being able to fly off whenever ya wish."

Rasmus answered as if I'd asked a question only a two-year-old would ask. "We were made immortal so the creators—beings humans often call gods—wouldn't have to repeat their work eon after eon."

"So ya said the gods created ya to watch over the caveman versions of us."

"No," Rasmus said, snorting a little at my summary. "Humans were two hundred thousand years away from existing when I was created."

"That's mind-boggling. What species were ya guarding way back then?"

Rasmus hesitated before he told me—a very human trait I found fascinating given his normal arrogance. It was beyond me to feel awe for the human he appeared to be, even though I'd seen his feathered form several times... and watched him fly.

I saw Rasmus a bit like I saw Mulan. I considered him to be a quirky friend and a fellow magickal. If I hadn't been lusting for Rasmus, I might not have been so aware of him as a male.

But I was lusting.

The memory of running my hands over those abs of his had never left my mind. I'd been checking for demon compulsions at the time I'd indulged, but it was impossible not to recall the tingle of my fingers brushing over his skin.

That also brought to mind the electric spark that his innocent kiss ignited against my lips. The sexy bastard had given me just enough carnal knowledge of him to make it impossible to think of anyone else.

Was I resentful of that fact?

Yes, I think I was.

"The first species my kind monitored on this planet were the Dragons," Rasmus said.

All lust and resentment were forgotten as my mouth dropped open in shock. *"Dragons? Like real ones?"* I asked.

His nod was solemn. "Yes, but not all of them were the flying versions of your mythology. Only military Dragons were altered and given wings, but they are the ones most remembered. The majority of dragonkind looked like your Komodo dragon lizard except for walking upright. They possessed humanoid bodies and limbs. I think you would describe them as reptilian. They lived here for a very long time."

"*Dragons?*" I repeated because my brain was still trying to take it in. Was he talking about dragons?

"Dragons were long-lived, which they found tiring. Eventually, most put themselves into stasis and woke at different points in their evolution. They got out of sync with each other, which created a division in their society that never healed."

"Dragons," I said again, but with less shock in my tone.

Rasmus nodded. "However, skipping ahead in time is not allowed for the same reasons as going back in time is forbidden. You will cease to exist if you go backward too far and rapidly age if you go forward too much. Most Dragons lived out their typical five thousand years each like humans live out their eighty or ninety now. Their numbers dwindled for reasons no one could explain then... or now. The creators devolved them into less sentient beings, which cleared the planet for the next species."

"Dragons," I said one more time, smiling at his story. I refused to think about the mysterious "creators" devolving them. "What species came after Dragons?"

"The Venusians were moved from their dying planet and put here on Earth. They looked a lot like humans but had very different views of their bodies. They only developed their minds to experiment on each other. They were brilliant, but too self-absorbed to care about their environment. They did things to the Earth that nearly destroyed it. The creators evolved them into beings of light to stop their physical body's evolution. Finally, they were sent to another dimension to live."

"And after the Venusians?"

"The creators developed a cross-species culture consisting of beings who relocated here from several dying planets in your galaxy. The primary group were the humanoid ancestors of all the advanced human civilizations you still have traces of today."

I grunted. "Despite what ya said about the Venusians, that culture sounds more like the first alien invasion. What kind of problems did they cause?"

Rasmus gave me a stink-eyed glare over my tone, but I ignored it.

"They worked out quite well and the creators made sure your entire planet had some faction of them dotted around the globe. They were the ones who built the megalithic stone monuments still existing today *and* who brought civilization to the entire Earth. Over time, they were redistributed to other planets in your galaxy where I believe their people still flourish. This is the story we were told."

Rasmus sipped his coffee as he talked. "The behemoths you call dinosaurs came next. They were a true experiment and the creators instantly regretted them. The behemoths used Earth's resources in amounts too large for the planet to sustain, even though the creators tweaked plant life and sized it in proportions that satiated the behemoths better."

I shook my head sadly. "And we all know how the dinosaurs ended, don't we?"

"Yes. It was unfortunate. The creators eradicated them and decided to promote your early human ancestors instead. Unfortunately, a meteor struck Earth before the matter could be handled. The long unnatural winter caused most of the behemoths to die natural deaths. It was a tragic time in your planet's history."

If I hadn't believed in my gods and actually met one, I might have been rolling on the floor laughing at the stories Rasmus was telling me. But as a child of The Dagda, I knew that a plethora of extraordinary beings *still* shared this world with modern humans. Magick existed everywhere in our world.

Legends said the *Tuatha de Danann* grew tired of all the wars and fights over land and people. They made bargains with the other tribes to take care of the land, and then they moved into another dimension to live.

Only a few living people knew what I knew, which was that my ancestors could come back and visit this world whenever they chose. They just chose not to most of the time.

"What about the flood? Did that really happen?"

Rasmus shifted in his chair. "Yes. The flood was natural, but my kind brought the source of it into the world. We had discovered our ability to shift into whatever form we chose. We shifted into early human ones and mated with human females. It was not forbidden to us at the time—not the way your mythology says. But..."

"Let me guess. There were *unexpected consequences*," I said, finishing for him.

Rasmus shrugged both shoulders. "The offspring of our pairings grew into giant humanoid creations, but with small brains like the dinosaurs. The giants were too large and demanding as well. As the ice from the long winter melted, it caused massive floods. We were forbidden from saving our offspring after some of them cannibalized humans to survive."

I blew out a breath. "I guess the number one rule during that time was 'thou shall not eat thy fellow Earth creature', right?"

My snark was my way to deal with the overwhelming things he was sharing with me. But I could see the memories upset him. My heart broke for him a little. "That must have been difficult for ya, Rasmus."

"It was devastating in ways I can't explain. We begged to be allowed to save the remaining humans and vowed never to take them for mates again. Our request was granted, but we were too late to save all of them. Natural forces are stronger than anyone's magick. Only a few survived the floods."

"I'm sorry ya've had to deal with so much pain and loss."

"After the flood waters receded, several advanced civilizations came into being, but with limited technology. We taught them to use the Earth's resources wisely. The hope was that they would become caretakers of each other and the planet."

"I think I get where ya're going with yer story. Even the advanced humans—the ones we call gods—like to make war," I said, interjecting my thoughts. "The Egyptians fell to their conquerors, as did the Babylonians, Assyrians, Sumerians, Mayans, and Asian dynasties. When I think about it, I suppose no great human culture ever survived more than a few thousand years."

"Correct," Rasmus said flatly.

I shook my head. "History tells us all this, but I guess we tell ourselves it's not something we can change. Peace—true peace—is a foreign concept. All of us live in fear of being conquered. The fear of losing our freedom drives all of humanity."

"Wars seem to be the only real catalyst for change that humans acknowledge." Rasmus spread both his hands. "Humankind is complicated. We watch over you knowing full well you will most likely destroy each other. The creators continue to allow you to be like this, even though thousands of years have passed since your beginning. We do not understand why they allow you to keep on surviving. Because your kind has become very dear to my kind, we still care enough to guide you to positive outcomes when you let us."

I watched his face but didn't understand what I saw in his expression. "Yer explanation about feeling compassion sounds like the exact description of a guardian angel."

Rasmus tilted his head as he considered it. "Some have called us fallen angels, but we differ from angelkind. The Sumerians referred to us as *watchers* in their language. Once we took human mates, that moniker no longer fit us. We started calling ourselves *guardians*. It seemed more appropriate. Then, like all powerful beings who help humanity, we decided it was best to hide our existence so as not to risk being used."

I leaned on the table. The *Tuatha de Danann* didn't hide from others like them, but they did eventually choose a home outside of normal human reach. His explanation fits perfectly with what I was taught about my ancestors, so I still couldn't imagine what kind of problem Da had with the guardians.

I needed time to think about all this.

"What's it like living forever?" I asked, trying to stave off my information overload.

"Lonely," Rasmus said quickly, staring at me.

Surprised by his answer, I leaned back to stare at him. Movement across the street caught my eye, and I saw Jack enter the building. "Did ya see Jack go in just now?"

"Yes," Rasmus said.

I turned at his wistful tone. "Are ya still feeling friendly toward him?"

"Jack took part in my capture, but he was also a kind caretaker. Rarely is a being all evil, Aran. This was the root of why I questioned your hasty acts against him, even before I realized my captive circumstances. You should have had a discussion with him about his motivations. Discussion and compromise could be the saving grace of your people."

When Rasmus visited me at the cottage, I'd had to explain

myself to the confused human version of him. Now here I was still trying to convince the more enlightened one that all I did by divorcing Jack was make sure he couldn't keep using me or Fiona as bargaining chips.

I took a calm, no-bullshit approach as I covered the same ground again. "Jack made promises to me when we married —when we *mated*. He betrayed those vows by trying to control my powers. When that didn't work, he had me locked away for seven years. Every word he spoke to me was a lie of some sort, but his malicious actions made things clear. I took the steps I felt were necessary to prevent the possibility of Jack continuing to hurt me or my daughter. I don't know if yer kind acknowledges *love*, but my kind values it greatly."

Rasmus lowered his gaze to the table. "I have felt love. I understand it well."

That was curious news, but I charged on. "Well, Jack's betrayal killed my love for him. He made himself my enemy and I'm still angry at him for it. Part of me still wants to hurt him for the harm he did to me and my child, even though I never will because Fiona is traumatized enough. But I swear to Goddess Danu that I'd rather bed a demon than be with Jack Derringer ever again. As devious as demons are, at least they respect me. Jack does not."

"You may not see it, but in his way, Jack truly loves you," Rasmus said.

I rolled my eyes at his one-track mind. "If ya think that, then I guess we're never going to agree about Jack."

Perhaps I was too quick to judge a person by their actions. It was a flaw The Dagda often pointed out to me while we were training. Maybe I was less judgmental now that I was older, but I felt no kindness or sympathy toward Jack. Compassion for my ex-husband and for those who captured Rasmus continued to elude me.

I stared at the soft-hearted guardian. There was only one matter we had left to discuss.

"If I tried to kill Jack in front of ya, what would ya do?"

His answer was immediate. "I would step aside and let you do what you felt was right, even though I think it would be a terrible mistake for you."

I smirked at his answer. "So ya wouldn't help me fight him?"

Rasmus shook his head. "No. Guardians work at staying neutral. Remaining neutral keeps us dedicated to our bigger purpose in aiding all of your kind."

Shaking my head, I dug in my purse for coffee money. I pulled that out and a couple of bigger bills for Rasmus, because I knew he carried no currency.

"Take this and use it. It won't last long, but it will pay for coffee and food."

He took the money from my fingers and studied it.

What good was having a powerful being like him fighting next to me if Rasmus wouldn't help me stop Jack and his buddies from making more fake guardians? It was his blood they were using for their wicked serum. Ya would have thought Rasmus and his kind would be completely invested in putting an end to them.

From my perspective, there was neutrality, and then there was stupidity. The inherent evil in Jack's man-made guardians was clear to me. Why wasn't it just as clear to Rasmus?

Maybe I better understood Da's skepticism of the guardians and their higher purpose after this frustrating conversation. Sure, my woman parts still longed for his attention—and I wanted his lips on mine again—but the witch in me mocked my wishes.

Didn't I once open my body and my heart to Jack only to get betrayed for following my feelings? Was I supposed to view my daughter as a consolation prize for losing the game Jack had been playing with me?

There was no choice except to see that what Jack was doing was wrong. I'd not stand by and watch worse happen simply because this version of Rasmus wanted me to reconcile with the traitorous man I divorced.

"When Conn comes, he and I are going into the gym to investigate. If ya can't or won't help me, ya should stay here drinking yer coffee. That's what the money is for."

Rasmus stared at me without blinking. I couldn't read the guardian's thoughts, which was just as well. If he could read mine—good. It would save me from having to explain that I'd written him off and now considered him to be of no use to me.

The world was full of men. I refused to share my bed with yet another male I couldn't count on, no matter how much I was drawn to him. I would resist temptation and make the most of my forty-ish maturity as I walked away from this one.

One of the first things I'd learned during my training with The Dagda, a being with powers even an immortal like Rasmus would have respected, was that ya couldn't change things merely by wishing they were different. The Dagda would never have stood by only watching when he possessed the power to stop evil from taking over.

I didn't have the luxury of being neutral in Jack's never-ending thirst for material gain. I couldn't stand by and watch my ex-husband destroy all the beings who came into contact with him. Jack wasn't my responsibility any longer, but the demons he paid *and* our daughter would always be mine to protect.

Help from a guardian would have been useful, but I didn't need him. Others would help me. I bent over my phone and sent out my request to prove it to myself.

Chapter Thirteen

Mulan met us on the street corner less than a block from the man-made guardian gym. The Wu Shaman had dressed for a yoga class, which meant her petite, muscular curves were highlighted in the latest sportswear.

She wore tight black leggings, a black sports bra, and a red sports tank as her outer layer. Even in tight-fitting clothes, I couldn't tell where the woman carried her shaman staff, but it had to be on her person. She never was without it.

I hadn't bothered to pull together a workout costume for myself. I planned to stay hidden until Conn and Mulan got done with their information gathering. We'd collectively decided that Mulan and Conn should check out the inside of the gym, while I checked out the outside.

Conn chose the brother form, made himself a little beefier in the arms, and smiled at Mulan when she chuckled and poked at one of his much larger biceps.

I activated Conn's mantle for protection as I left them, grateful for its ability to make me invisible. I drew a sword The

Dagda gave me and jogged around the side to check out the building from the back.

Rasmus must have accepted my plans no longer included him because he had disappeared from the restaurant while I was using the restroom.

Outside the annoying feeling of loss in my gut, I was fine without him. I don't know why I expected him to help me take down the man-made guardians anyway. He'd made me no promises before flying off.

Conn and I saving him didn't appear to be a good enough reason for him to join Team Aran in any meaningful way.

I pushed thoughts of Rasmus out of my mind to focus on what I came to do. After chanting to activate my invisibility spell, I watched both exits in the back and searched the windows above them for signs of activity.

Ten minutes soon went by with nothing happening and no danger in sight.

I chose one of the two back doors and pushed on the handle. It easily swung open with no resistance. Despite my original intention to remain on the exterior, I stepped inside.

The hallway was quiet even though I could hear noises coming from the gym. Still cloaked from sight, my feet landed in whispers of sound on the commercial tiles as I made my way down the corridor.

A large power surge in the hallway dimmed the electricity for a moment. I hoped it wasn't Conn's mantle failing me... or something dumb Mulan had felt it necessary to do to some jerk in the gym.

I stopped walking when I thought I heard a man screaming in pain somewhere in the distance. But when I pressed my ear against the blank wall to listen, there was nothing more to hear.

I tiptoed by a large, blank wall before I finally felt the

magick of a demon ward tugging at me. Fighting off its attempts to stop me wasn't hard, but its presence meant I likely would get company soon. Maybe I'd get lucky and the demon would recognize my energy and run away from me. I'd prompted that sort of reaction before.

When I was wearing Conn's mantle of power, I energetically read like him. Demons would recognize Conn's sovereignty, even if I was the less scary option of the two of us. I never met one that didn't.

Because of the spell I cast, normal non-magickals would see nothing when I was near, but the man-made guardians were no longer completely human. I had no idea about their new capabilities.

Would they see me? Or sense me? Maybe I would soon find out.

At the end of the hallway was a one-way mirror used to discreetly look into the gym. I peeked through it and saw Mulan sitting on an exercise bike. Across the room, Conn lifted weights while his gaze remained fixed on the Wu Shaman's hips and legs as she pedaled.

A muscled giant leaned against a wall and watched everyone. I wasn't close enough to read his energy, but he fit the same physical stereotype as the man-made guardian we captured.

An argument erupted in a room down another hallway. I gave up watching Conn and Mulan and moved closer to the shouting voices. Despite the wall separating me from those on the other side, it was easy to hear them through it.

An agitated man made a disapproving noise before speaking. *"What went wrong, Rick? You said Will would be okay—that he would turn out like us."*

"No. All I promised was that he wouldn't die, and he's still

alive, isn't he?" the mysterious and very sarcastic Rick answered.

"He grew spider legs and demon horns. What if he stays like that?" the other man asked.

"Your friend did not turn into a spider. Shifter transfusions consistently fail to produce changes in full humans. Your friend has become an otherworldly being, similar to those we pay to help us. Now we've learned mixing demon blood into the guardian serum produces unpredictable results. This is precisely why we had to test it on someone more expendable than the rest of us."

"Will is not expendable. He thought he was getting a new kind of steroid shot. How is he supposed to live like that? What about his girlfriend? He'd just bought her an engagement ring."

"Relax. Your friend won't be like that forever. Whenever we cease serum treatments, the DNA changes reverse themselves. That's why we used those demon hunters as test cases. Every one of them returned to normal."

"You mean they're normal except for needing near-constant sedation to keep from foaming at the mouth. This deal is getting worse all the time, Rick. What will happen to us when the serum runs out? Are we going to be like them?"

"We're already testing serums made from each other's blood. The results from using Dane's blood are very promising."

"Good. Test that version on the damn Marshal," the first man grumbled. *"He's demanding to become one of us or else he's going to talk. You know he will not shut up until someone does what he wants."*

One of them laughed and I felt fairly sure it was Ringleader Rick.

"Maybe we should try the demon version of the serum on the Marshal just to be sure we want to rule it out. I warned him the science behind this was not precise."

The second guy laughed then. *"If he turned into one of those beings he hunts, the Marshal would probably try to take me and you both out."*

"If that happened, we'd have a good reason to kill him. Then he'd be off our payroll for good," Rick said.

A door opened where they were and their conversation faded away. It didn't matter because I'd already learned far more than I ever thought I would.

Before we went busting into Goddess only knew what kind of situation, we needed another talk with Lilith. Some demon was offering blood to those creating the man-made guardians.

Had they captured one of her people? If so, why hadn't she told us? Or was she profiting from the deal?

Demons took a middle stance in most conflicts, but Lilith was going to have to pick our side if she wanted us in her corner fighting for her child.

The door connecting to the open gym area opened. The muscled guardian who'd been watching people work out walked through it. I knew my cloaking was still in place when he lifted his wrist and spoke into the sports watch he wore.

"Where are you? You were supposed to replace me ten minutes ago. I'm bored out of my skull."

"Dr. Darwin had a snafu. The new serum fubar-ed some guy. I'll be right out. Brace yourself before you come back here. This one is worse than the last."

"After the crap I've seen already, I'm fairly immune, bro," the sports watch guy said.

I stayed where I was and held my breath because sound was nearly impossible to hide.

A large area of the wall I'd eavesdropped through suddenly swung inward and out of the way. Another muscle guy wearing a similar watch on one wrist emerged. He smiled at the first sports watch guy... and then he frowned.

Turning his head my way, the new guy searched the hallway. "Do you feel that?"

"Feel what?" Sports Watch asked as he tried not to laugh.

The suspicious guy's gaze searched the blank walls and the allegedly empty hallway where I was stealthily holding my breath. I could take on one of them alone, but probably not without creating a ruckus guaranteed to give myself away.

Neither their deaths nor being discovered was on my agenda. I needed to regroup with the others and share what I learned.

Since Rasmus and I had seen Jack enter the facility, the Marshal they mentioned had to be him. If they went through with their plans, the father of my child would get what he deserved, but my child wouldn't. Fiona didn't deserve to know the depths Jack had sunk to in his quest for power. As much as I'd like to see Jack pay for many things, standing by and doing nothing would make my life harder—not easier.

The element of surprise was the only advantage I had against these people. I couldn't lose it simply because one of the man-made guardians had developed some heightened sense of awareness. I backed up as quietly as I could when Suspicious Guy walked in my direction.

The second exit door stopped my retreat. The door handle rattled behind me when I leaned against it and I nearly gasped in alarm.

Someone on the outside chose that moment to knock on the door, which startled me again, but in a good way this time. I clapped a hand over my mouth to keep from making noise, and then slowly moved it down to my thundering heart.

Luckily, the adrenalin rush ramped my native magick higher which gave Conn's mantle a boost.

Someone knocked on the outside door again.

"Use the other effing door, moron," Suspicious Guy bellowed.

Sports Watch snickered behind him. "Hey, that was amazing. You felt someone outside."

Suspicious Guy snorted before he stalked back to Sports Watch. "If I had wings, there wouldn't be anything that could stop me. That's my idea of Darwinian Evolution."

"That's because you got more from the serum than most of us," Sports Watch said, heading through the door.

"We've been experiments up to now. Once we get that ancient creature back, the serum they make from him will give us all the powers he has," Suspicious Guy said, busting powerfully through the door of the gym.

I waited for the invisible door in the wall to close behind Sports Watch before sighing in relief. When I felt it was safe, I headed back down the hallway, watched Mulan and Conn wiping their foreheads with towels, and then hustled back to the exit door I originally came through. No one had ventured in through it, so the person who knocked must have gone around to the front to enter after being yelled at.

I slipped out and immediately heard a whistle. My head whipped from side to side looking for who'd made the sound, but I saw no one.

I felt a presence nearby but couldn't tell who or what it was.

Feeling a renewed need to be careful, I decided a fast retreat was the right answer. I didn't reverse my invisibility spell until I was leaning against a brick building only steps from Mulan's car.

Pulling my phone out, I sent a quick text telling them to meet me at home. I returned to the restaurant and claimed the seat I'd been in earlier. I even ordered another coffee. While I drank it, I ran over both conversations in my head a few more times before concluding the same things.

The most important was that people were becoming part of experiments they hadn't volunteered for.

Second, Jack—aka the Marshal they referred to—wanted to become one of the man-made guardians no matter what gaining such power cost him. He certainly wasn't thinking of his daughter. Or me, though I'd never believed he was serious about wanting me back.

And I'd also accidentally discovered that the serum they made from Rasmus could both wear off and go horribly wrong.

Not that he would care. Or own his part for allowing them to capture him.

But I cared, which meant I would do whatever I had to do to make sure the experiments stopped.

Chapter Fourteen

"You certainly don't miss much when you set your mind to a task," a man's voice said before he slid into the chair across from me.

I blinked over my coffee in surprise. "Did ya hear me talking to myself just now?"

Rasmus attempted to smile. "No, you were thinking loudly."

My mouth quirked at the corners. "Were ya eavesdropping on my thoughts then?"

The small smile on his lips widened a fraction. "Let's just say I have to make a special effort not to listen to your thoughts."

I ignored the broader implication of him knowing that I often thought about him and focused instead on finding answers about what I'd learned. "Are ya the one who knocked on the door, and then whistled later?"

One of his shoulders rose and fell, which told me everything he didn't want to say. I grunted in disgust. "That wasn't very neutral of ya, Mr. Guardian."

Rasmus looked my way and caught my gaze with his intense one. "I couldn't let them capture you. Your scientists can make a serum from just about anyone with paranormal abilities. Your world isn't ready to deal with the supernaturals they could make from your DNA."

I leaned on the table and smirked at his extremely non-neutral reasoning. "Are ya sure about that? Technically, I already replicated myself when I gave birth to Fiona. Maybe it could have been different if I'd been around to train her, but she seems to have inherited none of my powers."

Rasmus stared out of the window as he talked. "Power is naturally resident in every being. However, its development—or lack thereof—is up to the individual. Your daughter will manifest whatever powers she believes she can wield."

"Are ya saying the choice to become a witch or not is part of the free will thing?"

Rasmus paused with his mouth open as if to deny it but seemed to change his mind.

"Yes. I guess you could say that."

I sighed and looked away from his stare. "So Fiona *could* become a witch if she were properly motivated, but maybe she never will."

Rasmus shrugged. "Your daughter could become a witch, but even if she did, she would never be like a witch like you. It's not her destiny."

I frowned at his words. "Why? Because she wasn't born a child of The Dagda?"

"Correct. She didn't inherit the power you did from your ancestors."

"Neither did Da."

"No, it was your father's *understanding* of power, yet lack of having it, that drew my brethren to him. The ring you wear approved of your father, even though he did not approve of my kind being its caretakers. Your father considered us to be the fallen angels talked about in many of your religions. He assigned the beliefs of your angel mythology to us."

"Hmm..." I said, not commenting further.

I had yet to decide if the real guardians were friend or foe to anyone, so I didn't blame Da for his conclusions. The being talking to me was even older than Conn but seemed removed from the emotional maturity that living so long should bring to a being.

While I found his neutrality stance personally frustrating, how could I begrudge Rasmus the beliefs he'd spent eons developing? How could Da? Rasmus seemed both ancient and yet equally naïve about real life.

Call me naïve as well, but I believed his guardian stories. Being angry at Rasmus was like being mad at Conn for occasionally displaying the demon temperament he'd worked over a millennium to tame. Of course, I'd always felt a little show of temper was better than being apathetic, so I hadn't minded his passion.

The way I saw things if a person didn't care one way or the other, then they couldn't feel true compassion. Without compassion for each other, what was the point of living?

I wouldn't want a life without caring about anyone's fate, yet the being across from me thought not caring was his number one goal.

What Rasmus considered neutrality, I considered a bunch of crap.

But that was just me.

I knew I could never be neutral about certain things. The man-made guardians were one of them. Jack's betrayal was another. Making this world a place where my family, my friends, and even the demons I monitored could live without fear was paramount on my 'get it done' list.

Our goals seemed radically different to me, which meant Rasmus needed to take his neutrality elsewhere to practice it.

At least I knew he wasn't planning to stop me any more than he was planning to stop Jack. I would let that be enough.

"Thanks for helping me today, Rasmus. Yer timely knock on the door kept me from giving myself away. Given how strong and smart those two man-made guardians were that I saw, I'm going to need the element of surprise to get into their lab. By the way, I heard they're making serums from each other now because the one they made from you is nearly gone."

"Human bodies cannot support the DNA changes they're attempting. Humans will either revert to their natural state or their bodies will die trying."

"They were talking about a failure they had today, so their process is not without flaws. Plus, they said the early converts are mentally ill from the serum, even after their bodies reverted."

Rasmus nodded. "Some of my kind also suffered from simply being one of us. It took centuries of seclusion for them to heal enough to be useful guardians again. A few never healed at all and had to be destroyed. We were fashioned to survive nearly everything imaginable. Do you know how difficult it is to kill a guardian?"

I hoped his question was rhetorical instead of literal because I had no idea and hoped to never have to test the theory. My sigh was loud before I spilled the rest. "The worst thing I heard is that they mixed demon blood into the serum they made from ya and got a shocking transmutation out of the guy they used it on. That was the crux of the failure they were discussing. This whole situation is like a terrible science fiction movie."

Rasmus spread his hands as he talked. "Some DNA changes go viral in the body. The Venusians ruined their biology with too much experimentation on themselves. What started as someone wanting to change the eye color of their unborn child evolved into forced organ renewal for sale and profit. Marginal members of society were exploited as incubation units. Failures happened to them as well, but worse was the decline in their morality. Any time you value one being's health and well-being over another's it affects the balance of the entire world."

My head nodded in understanding, but my gut grieved such a terrible truth. "I guess yer kind sees that happening with us right now. Well, I won't disagree with ya that our morals are slipping, but I'm hopeful mankind will learn to draw ethical lines and not cross them. There's a life lesson in all this mess."

"What would that be?" Rasmus asked.

I lifted a hand as I answered. "Just because ya can do something doesn't mean ya should do it. It's one thing to bend the rules of nature to save a life. It's a whole other to give it a middle finger salute simply because ya want a child with a certain color of eyes."

Rasmus didn't comment on my response. Instead, he went on with his lecture.

"The Venusians ran into the same thing that all humanoid species eventually run into, which is that there is a mysterious randomness at work in the physiology of every being. Changes outside those made by natural processes are temporary in most cases. Let's hope that's true for those who received demon-infused injections as well."

None of what Jack and his military scientists were doing

made sense to me, but I'd grown up being magickal. I didn't desire more power because I had painfully learned its limits with my early failures to control mine.

"I know ya could stop this if ya wanted to, Rasmus. Why is yer kind allowing this unholy experimentation to happen in the first place?"

Rasmus lifted his chin and stared at me. "Who are we to interfere in the steps your kind takes in pursuit of growth? Your eventual failure to find contentment in life will result in your removal. When you're gone, yet another species will be given the chance to do things better. I've seen that cycle happen many times across many millennia. Lusting for the power to control everything is a commonality across many beings. I don't judge it anymore."

I wanted to yell at the eejit and tell him bad guys never did the right things until someone like me made them make that choice. Why should I bother trying to get Rasmus to see that maintaining balance on this planet was an ongoing job?

No one lived a life that was all black or all white when it came to morals. As I told Fiona, life was full of gray areas. I was no stranger to my own darkness, but my motivation to do right was stronger.

That was how true balance worked.

"If ya truly feel like that, Rasmus, then why bother helping me at all? Why not let the man-made guardians discover me? Perhaps me dealing death to them was my destiny today before ya interceded."

Rasmus was quiet for so long that I thought he was mad at me.

"I have no reason other than I don't want anything to happen to you," he finally said.

I nearly laughed at his declaration, but I could see he was truly puzzled that he cared that much about me.

Was I supposed to be flattered? Because I didn't feel that way.

Rasmus crossed his arms. "There's no reason for you to feel responsible about my decisions. I alone hold responsibility for them."

My eyebrow arched. "Are ya saying it doesn't matter to ya whether or not I appreciate it? Or whether it moves my woman's soul and makes me want ya in my bed more than I already do? No, I guess me falling for ya dips too low into human feelings for a neutral being like yerself to appreciate. A relationship between us would be like a royal desiring a peasant. I bet ya simply hate yerself for caring about me at all."

"Your anger about this seems both unreasonable and illogical," Rasmus said.

I rolled my eyes. "Yes, and I'm sure someone will carve that on my gravestone. *Aran O'Malley was both an unreasonable and an illogical woman.*"

My phone buzzed in my pocket before I could get snarkier with him. I'd silenced it earlier and forgotten to turn the ringer back on. It turned out to be Fiona.

The text was one I was dreading to receive but also expecting.

> Dad wants to meet with me to apologize and explain. Should I go? Do you think he will try to take me with him?

My thumbs moved over the keyboard.

> Wait for me and I'll make sure that doesn't happen. I want to talk to him myself.

Okay.

I pocketed the phone, put the money on the table, and stood. "It looks like ya're going to finally get yer wish, Rasmus. I'm heading to have that talk with Jack ya keep wanting me to have."

When I got to the door, I glanced back and saw Rasmus staring at me. If he'd been human, I would have considered his expression to be one of sad regret.

But he wasn't human.

I figured he cared about me because he was grateful I'd released him from his human bondage. He'd been nothing but nice to me since his return. Nice, though, was a long way from the level of wishing and wanting he caused me to feel for him.

The next time I felt this much for a man, I prayed I would feel it for someone normal.

I shook my head and headed outside where I could make the phone calls I needed to make.

Chapter Fifteen

F iona drove us to their meeting place. I left my daughter in
her shiny vehicle researching on her phone while I went
inside.

I spotted Jack sitting at a table doing something on his
phone as well. It was obvious that she was his daughter.
Nothing I did was ever going to change that, and I hoped it
wouldn't become a problem one day.

The dining crowd in the restaurant was light because it was
mid-afternoon. No man-made guardians or members of the
demon hunter council seemed to float around him.

Dragging a deep breath into my lungs, I searched for some
of that infamous neutrality Rasmus cherished so much, but I
didn't find much for Jack Derringer. I would just have to keep
Fiona in mind. Thinking of her relationship with her father
might help me get through this.

I slid into the seat across from him seconds before Jack
glanced up and flinched in recognition. "Hello, Jack. Were ya
expecting our daughter instead of me?"

He pushed out of the seat to leave, but I held up a hand to

stop him. "Don't make me get fierce with ya. I'm just here to talk."

His continued silence was surprising. Normally, the man wouldn't stop talking.

"What kind of mess have ya gotten yerself into?" I asked. "It must be pretty terrible since ya put a demon spell on Fiona to keep her out of the picture."

Jack leaned on the table and sighed. "I did that to protect her, not to harm her or cover anything up. And this is not a mess. This is my life, Aran. I've been waiting years to tell you the truth about it."

"Well, here I am, Jack—out of the prison ya put me in and finally willing to hear why ya did that."

Jack looked away and sighed. "I put you in prison to protect you. I work with the military as part of a Special Operations Unit. We track, monitor, and study people with paranormal abilities."

"Fascinating, but all ya ever talked about was becoming a demon hunter. When did ya jump from that job to the military one?"

Jack snorted. "One of my biggest regrets is that the demon problem worsened with you out of the picture. Something needs to be done to constrain them. They're a real problem."

I threw up my hand. "How can ya be paying them for favors yet still accuse them of being in the wrong? That's very bigoted of ya, Jack."

Jack lifted an eyebrow and stared at me. "Have you seen demons in their natural forms? They're nothing but animals, and they're hideous."

Bigoted wasn't even the right word to describe my ex-husband's poor opinions of creatures made when we were.

Demons were merely another type of us—just like all the other paranormal creatures on this planet.

The English language didn't contain a word pithy enough to put Jack in his place. I would have to use too many to make my point, which I knew would lead to Jack shutting me out. But I had to try.

"Have ya looked in the mirror lately, Jack? Evil can appear handsome, even though it's ugly underneath the surface." I snorted when his eyes widened. "And demons are not animals. They're another form of humanity. Ya can't kill them, Jack. They come back over time, just as we do. The creators gave demons the ability to completely regenerate."

Jack laughed. "You have all that power in your body and no idea about the truth."

"Ya're the one who has it wrong, Jack. I've been trying to tell ya that since we married."

"I didn't listen because I knew it wasn't true. The group I work for recruited me right out of college. I've studied paranormal creatures far more than you have."

My argument about being right died at his startling revelation. "Are ya saying ya worked for them *before* we married?"

Jack hung his head as he nodded. "Yes. Technically, I was ordered to marry you, but I didn't mind. By that point, I'd fallen in love with you."

I blinked in confusion. "I don't understand. Why did the military care if ya married me or not?"

"You're still not listening, Aran. I'm part of a global group that monitors beings with paranormal abilities all over the world. They sent me to Ireland to investigate you. I was supposed to discover the source of your abilities and report back to them how dangerous you were. No one was happy to learn that you had inherited your powers instead of gaining them from some artifact. It was fortunate Fiona didn't inherit them or they would have taken her from me."

I felt an angry heat climb my face. "If anyone associated with ya touches my daughter again, it will be the last aggressive act they ever do on this Earth. I will kill ya and all yer kind to protect."

"No one will ever touch her. Are you crazy? Her safety was part of my bargain. I sent you to magickal prison and they left Fiona alone. Everything was fine until you got involved with Rasmus."

I rubbed my forehead and tried to focus. It was hard when I was this angry. I needed to learn everything I could from this talk, but sifting the truth out of all of Jack's lies was nearly impossible.

"Why were ya nice to Rasmus, Jack? Ya became his keeper. He told me that. The guardian remembers some of what happened to him."

"I was nice to Rasmus because he wasn't doing anything to harm anyone when we captured him. But I couldn't convince anyone I worked for that he had more power than even you did. If we'd made him into an ally, things wouldn't be so messed up right now. It was not my idea to constrain him and keep him captive. I did what I could to make it easier."

I lifted both hands in the air. "How can ya paint yerself as a hero of any sort? Ya let them use Rasmus to make a serum that turns normal men into fake guardians."

Jack groaned and face-palmed. "How in the world did you figure that out, Aran? It's top secret."

"Once Rasmus reverted to his normal form, he remembered everything ya did to him. All the guardians now know. And Rasmus is not the only one of his kind, Jack. I've seen several different ones."

Jack closed his eyes and shook his head. "I warned the people I worked with that there were a lot of them, but they wouldn't listen to me. Are Rasmus and his people coming back to kill us all?"

I could have told him about Rasmus and his neutrality goals, but Jack didn't deserve the truth. He deserved to live in fear.

"I couldn't begin to know what motivates him. Rasmus is an ancient being—one of many—who have seen whole civilizations come and go on this planet. I don't think he's overly impressed with our species. That should worry everyone walking around and breathing. He and his people have destroyed all life on the planet when their creators told them to do so."

Jack rubbed his forehead. "I did what I could to protect him. Maybe that might make a difference to him. I can't believe you single-handedly destroyed five years's worth of my efforts to befriend him by insisting on working with him."

"Ya were never his friend, Jack. That was a lie ya told everyone, including yerself."

Jack shook his head. "I knew once Rasmus witnessed your powers that his own might resurface. It took a lot of drugs to keep Rasmus in check and you removed him from my reach so I couldn't keep giving them to him."

"Wise up, Jack. He was never yer captive. His brethren could have removed him from yer reach any time they wanted. They intentionally left him with ya to see what ya planned to do with him. *It was a test of yer intentions and ya failed miserably.* Rasmus still has a small soft spot for ya, but his brethren would like to wipe ya and the people ya're working with from the planet."

Jack blew out a breath. "There's no one here but us, Aran. I deserve to know the truth. Do you still have a soft spot for me?"

It was so like him to ignore the real matter and change the subject to what served his interests. How had I not seen this in him before?

"Give up yer delusions about us, Jack. Ya betrayed me and put me in prison. I wouldn't spit in yer direction even if ya were on fire. I'd be more likely to pile wood at yer feet to make sure there was nothing left of yer miserable arse when the burning was done."

Jack blew out another breath. "I know you don't believe me, but I loved you when I met you... and I love you still. I love our daughter. You and Fiona were the only happiness I ever knew in my life. All I want is our old life back, Aran. All you have to do is share your secrets with me and it could happen."

I leaned on the table and stared at him. "That life ya dreamed about us getting back was based on lies and culminated in ya betraying me for yer work. That's not the path of love and happiness, Jack. That's a whole heap of selfishness on yer part and I'm done dealing with it."

Jack lifted a hand and swiped it through the air. "Who are you to say what love is for me? You always do this, Aran. You think your opinion counts more than mine."

I swiped one of mine in the air as well. "How are ya not hearing yerself? Ya just confessed to not even being the man I thought ya were. Ya lied to me about yer life from the moment we met. Did ya know that my family knew the truth all along? Ya're lucky they said nothing about yer wickedness until I'd seen it for myself. We'd have been over long ago if I would have seen that side of ya before ya sent me to prison."

"They wanted me to bring you in for testing. I put you in prison to save you from them. It took all I had to talk Hildy into doing that instead of turning you over to my bosses."

I shook my head. "No, Jack. Ya talked yer girlfriend into helping put me in that place to save the big plans ya had for yer life. And I stayed in that place to save my daughter from being mistreated by her lying, deceitful father. There's no one in my family ya haven't wronged in some manner. Not only do I not love ya anymore... I don't even like ya."

"Yeah, I'm sorry about what I said to your father. He intended to tell you what he suspected. Threats were the only way I could think to stop him. I thought when I talked you into moving to Salem with me that your parents would stay behind in Ireland. I never dreamed they'd move here to be close to you."

"It wasn't for my sake only that they moved here. They were protecting Fiona. Ma is close to putting a curse on ya, Jack. It's her witching specialty. I've been holding her back because Fiona has enough to deal with where her parents are concerned."

Jack grunted. "Let your mother do whatever she wants. I don't believe in curses—witch caused or otherwise. I've seen what witches can do and I'm not impressed."

My mouth twisted at his comment. "How could ya not believe in curses? Yer military scientists created one that robs men of their sanity. Insanity is the consequence of magick gone wrong."

"That's not a curse causing their insanity. That's the reality of being a test subject. And they're going to be fine."

"No, they're not going to be fine. Why are ya lying to

yerself? Rasmus told me humans can't handle having guardian powers. No matter what ya think, Jack, science and magick aren't very far apart. And there are *rules* governing both for good reasons. Yer people are breaking those rules and harming others. Rasmus and his kind are watching every move and counting every slight against us."

"That's what he told us too, but it doesn't have to happen. Help us fight them. Work with us and we can overcome them."

"The guardians are not our enemies, Jack. *We* act as our own enemy every time we take advantage of those who are weaker. Yer scientists are converting people against their wishes."

"Progress requires sacrifice."

"Jack... listen to yerself. It's the nature of evil people to not know they're being evil, but I'm telling ya true, that's what ya are in this case. If ya aren't freeing yer fellow demon hunters from that lab, ya're acting like a villain."

"If you'd only share the secrets of your power with us, you could change everything. We could create beings as powerful as the guardians. Those I work for would give you anything you wanted."

"Jack," I said sadly, shaking my head. "The guardians were created to stop us from destroying ourselves. Yer attitude is the perfect example of why they exist."

I could see he didn't get it—that he thought I was the one being naïve.

All the hatred and anger left me in a whoosh. Jack was a fearful child who needed reassurance that the boogie men weren't coming after him. It was ironic that Jack seemed incapable of believing that the boogie man he most feared was himself.

As much as I hated admitting it, Rasmus was right about

Jack. My ex-husband was not completely evil. He was worse than that. Jack was too fearful to see the real truth of his actions.

I stared at him as I spoke. "The magick I possess is both a burden and a blessing. The way I live my life is what makes it either. If I wasn't honoring the gifts I've been given, the gods I serve—gods who are still part of this world—would have no choice but to come take my powers away from me. I am a child of The Dagda and a hereditary witch. I honor everything that means. Ya can't steal it from me or trick me out of it or convince me to give it to others."

Jack snorted as he glared. "You're still as selfish with your powers as you ever were."

I shrugged deeply. "And ya're just as fearful of them as ya ever were. Ya never understood my magick nor wanted to. All ya wanted was to control it."

"So where does this leave us?" Jack asked.

I had no suitable answers, but I could see he needed to hear something in closure.

"I have nothing good left to say to ya, Jack. Both Rasmus and I are gunning for yer kind now. He won't be helping me and I won't be helping him, but ya need to be thinking hard about whose side ya plan to be on when things go down. I also suggest ya apologize to yer daughter and tell her to lie low until this is over. Death could find both of us before this is done."

"Aran, please don't side against me this time. You could choose me and things could be vastly different. Your attitude about my work is the main problem we have."

I stood and sighed. "I'm not siding against ya, Jack. I'm taking the side of the average person who hasn't been given a say in what ya're doing. And I'm including the demons ya keep blackmailing and paying to help ya. Thanks for telling me yer story. It leaves me feeling like the biggest of fools, but it also helps me not to hate ya so much. Let's just say we were young and gullible. That's going to be how I look at our past from now on. I'm sorry we didn't talk sooner."

"Think about it, Aran. Your decision could save our relationship."

"Goodbye, Jack."

"Wait... will you send Fiona to see me?" Jack asked.

I indicated the exit with my head. "She's outside in the fancy car ya bought her—waiting her turn to talk. I'll send her in to ya shortly. Think about what I said, Jack, and stop hiring the demons for yer dirty work. If I have to take off some demon heads, yers might get lopped off too."

"Is that a threat to my life?" he asked.

I shook my head. "No, it's a friendly warning to the father of my child that he's messing with the job I was born to do. I wouldn't want our daughter to have to grieve yer loss because ya disrespected me in the one way I could never tolerate."

Chapter Sixteen

"Diversification was key to handsome ex-husband's wealth," Mulan said, blinking her tired, red-rimmed eyes.

I slid a cup of her own rejuvenating tea blend in front of her before sitting in a chair near the desk. She muttered something to me in Chinese and I muttered she was welcome in English. Many of our conversations went like that.

As Mulan sipped her tea, I sipped from a bottle of cold water and pondered the day's events. Fiona had talked to Jack for barely ten minutes before she exited the restaurant in a huff. Whatever he'd told her hadn't sat well, but she wasn't talking to me about it. So far, I'd been afraid to ask what Jack had said to her because I was still stewing over my conversation with him.

Jack hadn't mentioned his missing computer or notes to me. Either he had a duplicate set of the data somewhere, or he didn't care about what was on the computer. Maybe he hadn't yet discovered my theft, which was also possible.

Fiona said Jack wasn't spending much time at home. He was either with the people he worked with or the woman he was involved with. Neither boded well for Jack heeding my words.

I sipped the cool liquid again and pushed Jack from my mind. "Pretend I have no idea what ya mean and explain diversification to me."

Mulan giggled at my confession. "So much power is within you, and yet you use none for yourself. You could be wealthy beyond your dreams."

I blew out a breath. "Ya've tagged along with me on my unpaid assignments enough to understand I'm a non-profit witch. I have a hereditary obligation to help keep demons and humans in balance. If my hours were stable, maybe I'd take a job like yers, but ya know they're not."

"I don't have job, witch. I have hair business. I do hair myself only to show stylists how to do it right."

I fought off rolling my eyes—barely. "Of course, ya do it for those reasons. I never doubted that. Now, explain diversification to me because I have no idea what that is."

Mulan's face crinkled in disapproval before she launched into her lecture. "Checks in ex-husband's account come from many sources. Conn says two are from his extortion of demon businesses. One is from military government. Another is from demon hunter council. Two more are from sources I have yet to identify. Your ex—or someone on his behalf—invests some of the money, saves some of it, and the rest goes into his checking account. All bills are paid automatically. His morals are bad, but I envy his financial talent."

My grunt of disgust was loud. "Do ya know what he told me? Jack said he only came to Ireland because meeting me was a military assignment. His bosses told him to marry me. It wasn't even his idea. I spent all those years with the man and just now discovered I was nothing more to him than a freaking job."

Her eyes darkened in anger. "Did you make him suffer for his dastardly deception?"

I glared at her question. "No. I warned him to leave the demons alone before he got his head chopped off."

"How can you be tough mother and brave fighter, yet wimpy woman with dastardly men in your life?"

I lifted a shoulder and let it fall. "Because talking to Jack is like talking to a tree, Mulan. He can't see beyond his own leaves."

"Weak analogy," Mulan said, turning back to shut down the computer.

I nodded. "It was the best one I could think of under pressure. The actual answer is that I don't know why I keep letting Jack off the hook. Every time I think of something awful to do to him, I think of Fiona and let him go."

Mulan lifted a shoulder and let it fall before going back to explaining what she'd found.

"There are no files with data on man-made guardians. Little notes are all we have. He accesses secret lab through internet portal or something. Everything juicy would be in cloud or on lab local server."

"So the rest of Jack's notes about the man-made guardians are not on his computer?"

"No," Mulan said firmly.

"Was there anything else interesting on it?" I asked.

"He has naked photos of many, many women—hundreds probably."

I laughed at the irony. Jack's declaration of love for me

didn't include physical faithfulness in any way, shape, or form. "Did ya look at all of them?"

"No. I had Conn do it. We would have deleted those of you, but we found none."

I chuckled and sighed in weak relief. "Yes, well, I don't think Jack ever found me sexy. It was my power that interested him, not me personally."

"That is surprising since men are visceral about sex."

"So are women," I said, rubbing my stomach as I stood. There was an ache of shame over Jack that refused to go away. I felt so stupid for ever trusting him. "I thought I'd done a good job in getting over him, Mulan. Today, I discovered another layer of pain and betrayal. Hopefully, this will be the last one I have to endure."

Mulan used her toes to twist herself back and forth in the desk chair as she watched me pace. Her feet didn't touch the floor even with it set on the lowest setting. She didn't fit normal furniture any better than I did.

"I loved like that once," Mulan said.

I stopped pacing to stare at her. "Was it with one of yer well-trained-in-bed boyfriends?"

"No. It was with another shaman. Most are women. Hung was special. He was also a lover of men but hid it well. Hung used me to fool others about his sexual preference, but I was also fooled. We were excellent lovers, but I never had his heart. Of all men I've known, he alone is unforgettable. This makes no sense to my head, but in my heart it is truth."

"It wasn't fair of him to deceive ya like that. I'm also sorry ya haven't gotten over him yet. That must be a tough thing to live with."

She spun some more in the chair. "Is Conn lover of men?

Most demons I meet don't care about gender. I have not found courage yet to ask."

I crossed my arms and grinned. "Conn said something once about Rasmus being good-looking in his human form. He teased me about not sleeping with him. I told Conn if he liked Rasmus so much to sleep with him himself. Conn said he'd kissed a man once but it had done nothing for him. He has known many women, though, Mulan. Conn indulges his carnal urges whenever they hit him. He doesn't care what kind of female—human, demon, witch, or anything else. He also doesn't care about age or looks. Conn is indiscriminate in a selective way. I tell ya this only because I care about ya. I love Conn like the brother he pretends to be to me, but I wouldn't sleep with someone like him."

She nodded. "This I know already. Sleeping with high demon is big risk."

I nodded in agreement. "It could be, but I also need to share that I've never known Conn to act with a woman the way he does with you. He respects you but is also very attracted to you. I think his feelings for you have surprised him."

"He is not only one surprised by our chemistry."

I walked over and patted her shoulder. "If ya want him, I say go for it. Despite what men write about women saving themselves for true love, celibacy is not some holy thing. It causes its own set of problems, especially as ya age. I'm suffering for my own."

"Use it or lose it," Mulan said.

"Yes, and doctors are not lying about that," I answered, thinking of the oils I used to keep myself in good shape down there. "As soon as this man-made guardian mess is sorted out, I intend to date for real."

"What about Rasmus?"

"He's got too low an opinion of our kind. I know he's capable in his human form because he mentioned somewhere in his history there were women in his life—early human women. But that turned out to be a mistake and one he's determined not to repeat. I would never seduce him for my own sake, Mulan. That wouldn't be fair to either of us."

"And no woman wants to be someone's mistake," Mulan said.

I chuckled. "I for sure don't. I'm tired of dealing with mistakes—mine and other people's."

"Keep protection in your empty purse," Mulan said as she sprang off the chair. "Just in case guardian seduces you."

"Are ya carrying protection in *yer* purse?" I asked.

"Demons and shamans are not compatible. I will not conceive with him. And they carry no disease. If I take Conn as lover, I have no fears other than that he will break my heart with his treacherous, womanizing ways."

I fisted both my hands on my hips. "Goddess, I hate men sometimes. Wouldn't ya rather kill one than fall in love with him?"

Mulan laughed at my outburst. "Demons can be obliterated, but I read guardians are impossible to kill."

"Well, I think I could find a way to take Rasmus out for the rest of *my* lifetime at least," I said, grinning when she giggled. "Thanks for your sleuthing work. Can I send the computer back to Jack by Fiona?"

"Unless you want me to sell it," Mulan said.

"No, let's stick to selling our appropriated antiquities. They're worth more."

The money-loving Wu Shaman walked away laughing.

I picked up Jack's computer and carried it to my room. I

didn't dare give it to Fiona until she calmed down enough to deliver it to her father in one piece.

AFTER TALKING TO MULAN, she left to go to her shop and I went to the backyard to sit.

Conn was off warning Lilith that she'd better turn down offers to do jobs for the man-made guardians. We didn't have a way to monitor her or her caste's compliance. So instead, we warned them that when the time came for us to take down the man-made guardian operation, all demons wanting to keep their body parts had best be absent.

I closed my eyes as the weight of what we planned to do settled on my shoulders. I kept them closed even when I felt someone sit in the chair beside me. His energy was so familiar to me now that I didn't have to open my eyes.

"Did ya come to lecture me again on the sad inevitability of our destruction and replacement as a species?"

"No, I just wanted to see how you were doing."

Snorting, I opened my eyes and glared at my unhelpful companion. "Today I learned that Jack worked for the military before we met and that they *ordered* him to marry me. They figured it would be the best way to make sure my powers were monitored for life. Ya could have told me this, Rasmus."

Rasmus shrugged. "It wasn't my revelation to share."

I turned my face away from him. "Everything about Jack's life is a bunch of lies, and yet he professes to love me."

"Jack does love you," Rasmus said, smiling at me.

I laughed dryly and shook my head at his empty words. "What Jack feels for me is a mixture of fear and respect at best. That may be as close to love as he's capable of feeling for anyone, but it's nothing I want or need. What Jack offers is not the kind of love I need from a man."

"How can you be so sure that loving Jack is not your true destiny?"

"Ya may be smart about human history, but ya're foolish about love, Rasmus. My parents are a perfect example of what love is really like. They had each other's backs for decades. They sided with each other even when they disagreed about me. And for damn sure, they never took other people into their beds."

Rasmus turned away as if avoiding my angry speech. I was so done with his half-ass sympathy. I leaned back in my chair and stared at the nicely trimmed yard. Conn had hired a neighborhood kid to care for it.

"Let's cut to the chase here. Have ya come to stop me?" I asked.

I felt his head whip toward me in surprise. "No. I would never interfere with your choices."

"Then ya're no good to me as a friend or companion. What I'm about to do is a fool's errand. Anyone with a lick of sense would leave it alone, but I can't. What Jack and his people are doing is wrong. Maybe yer Venusians didn't have people like me living among them. I refuse to let all of humanity suffer simply because I fear the fight."

"Heroes have existed among all the species who have walked the Earth."

I barked out a laugh. "Yes, well, I'm not Hercules or Perseus or even Greek. I'm just a witch, Rasmus, but I'm a smart one. Magick alone will not fix this. Conn and I will have to physically stop them before I can use my magick to change their view of things."

"That's a serious deception you're planning to place on Jack and his people."

"Yes, and one I learned from demons. They routinely wipe the minds of humans they interact with to keep themselves hidden. Do ya have a better idea about how to stop the military scientists? The way I see things, either I re-program their minds to stop their actions... or I kill them to do it. After deciding both paths were acceptable, I chose to try the less bloody option first."

Rasmus sighed softly before speaking. "It's not my place to talk you out of anything. But even if you succeed this once, others will rise and repeat what these military scientists are doing. It may not be tomorrow or the next day, but it will happen."

"Well, then, I suppose I'm just buying everyone a little more time before mankind destroys itself." I smirked at his crestfallen expression. "Letting this go on leads to more pain and suffering of innocents. I can't sit by and watch without trying to save the ones I can. And I can't let the demons keep being part of it. My job is to keep things balanced. I plan to do my job."

"Does Jack know what you're intending to do?"

"I don't know what he knows, and I can't care how he feels about it. Jack's planning to take the serum himself, Rasmus. He says it's so he can monitor what happens to people, but that's a lie. I know him better than that. Jack wants to experience the kind of power you have. That's his true motivation. He doesn't care what it will do to him. He doesn't care about what that means for me or Fiona. Jack cares only about Jack, except in rare circumstances."

Rasmus moved from his seat to kneel by mine. It forced me to stare down into his face. "The creators have given us a set of guidelines to follow. They have worked for eons. You're asking me to set them aside."

I shook my head in denial. "No, I'm not asking ya to do anything, Rasmus, except stay out of my way. Given yer devotion to neutrality, I figured it wouldn't be a problem for ya."

He reached into my lap and lifted the hand with Da's ring on it. The surface immediately changed from a solid gray granite into the Seal of Solomon. "With this ring, you could conquer the world and become its ruler."

I studied the raised symbols before shrugging. "And then I'd be responsible for everyone and everything that happens. I'm too old to be everyone's mother."

"Yet you possess the power to be a queen."

"Do I look like queen material to you?"

"Yes... you do," he said with his gaze holding mine.

It was hard to set aside such a comment from someone who'd seen royals rise and fall across multiple cultures.

I pulled my hand from his and the stone reverted to normal. "This ring wasn't meant for me. Just like your power wasn't meant for those like Jack. It would be wrong of me to use it for personal gain."

Rasmus shrugged. "I think you would also make a good guardian. Your soul is full of goodness."

I studied his bent head and the streaks of silver running through it. My fingers itched to pull the tie from his strands and let them cascade into my lap.

I closed my eyes to keep from acting on the urge.

"My soul is not as pure as ya might think, Rasmus. I selfishly want the same things in life that every other human woman on this planet wants. But wanting those things doesn't mean I'd take them by force or use my magick to get them. When I use my power, I do so for the greatest good I can see in a situation. The most selfish thing I've done lately was scry to find ya when ya flew away from me. Even then, all I wanted was to know ya were okay. Yer physical transformation was a scary, violent process that worried me."

"Your interest in my well-being humbles me, Aran."

I smiled at his admission and gave in to my urge to touch him. A woman didn't get to forty without learning the risks of revealing yer feelings to a man. But I wasn't counting the risks in that moment.

My fingers tingled as I pushed them across his scalp until the tie fell out.

I gathered his loose hair in my hands, divided it into two sections, and then brought them to the front so they could fall over his shoulders.

I kept my gaze focused on his hair as I spoke the truth of my feelings for him. "My interest in you is like any woman's interest in a man. I don't crave yer power, but I crave many other things from ya. But I also know the man I'm touching is not a human. Ya're some ancient being with a sacred calling I resent because it divides us. Wanting ya feels like lusting for a priest. I've never been one of those females and I don't want to become one."

Rasmus didn't answer me with words. Instead, he rose and covered my mouth with his. The reverence in his kiss seeped through the hot sweetness of his desire for me.

His kisses were highly distracting. I barely felt my body being lifted until he sat down in my chair with me in his lap.

His lips never left mine until he dragged them away to trail kisses down my neck. He'd been with a woman or two because he knew exactly how to make me feel every nuance.

When I heard myself moaning, I wondered if I should be grateful or appalled at my reaction.

One large hand slipped around my waist and pulled me harder against him. I couldn't remember ever feeling this cherished before. It was odd how safe I felt with the most dangerous man I'd ever known outside of Conn.

Rasmus used his hands to gently explore me lovingly. It had been so long since I'd had anything from a man that I didn't complain about what he gave me.

"Are ya allowed to fool around with me this way?" I asked, barely whispering the question.

"Sexuality is allowed, but there are consequences."

"And I bet there are consequences for yer consequences too. Nothing is ever easy or simple with men," I said with all the snark I could muster.

His body shook in quiet laughter in my arms. I could get used to this, but I didn't think Rasmus and I had much of a future.

"I enjoy holding you," he whispered against my temple.

I would have liked a lot more from him than just holding, but cuddling with him was nice too. The movement of his hand stroking my side sparked contentment in me that was foreign to my soul.

I tucked my face against his neck to breathe him in. Then I closed my eyes to enjoy the heat of all the places our bodies touched and let sleep claim me.

Saying I was merely disappointed when I woke up alone in bed several hours later didn't begin to describe my frustration about what had—and had not—passed between Rasmus and me.

It had been so long since I'd felt the comfort of a man's arms that I guess I passed out from sheer relief. Or maybe from exhaustion. Goddess only knew, I'd had nothing but worries and concerns since I left the cottage behind.

Ya'd think at forty I'd know better than to be longing for a man so far outside my reach, but the heart wanted what it wanted. It was just like Mulan said. What the heart felt was its own truth.

Disappointed in myself and Rasmus, I put on my shoes and went to find my daughter. Regardless of how sad my love life was, I had bigger problems to solve.

Chapter Seventeen

Fiona was putting two foil-wrapped pans in the oven to bake when I got to the kitchen. I got a bottle of water from the fridge and sat at the table while I waited for her to finish touching hot things, like the stove.

"Frozen lasagna was on sale. I got salad and bread too. That should feed everyone this evening, don't you think?"

My girl was hanging tough, but there were a ton of hurt feelings in her tone.

"Pasta always sounds good to me," I said, rasping out my support of the menu. My throat was rough from sleeping so soundly in the middle of the day, especially when I hadn't meant to sleep at all. I'd probably been snoring too. That would explain my parched throat and dry-as-dust mouth.

I ran a hand through one side of my hair, yanking out tangles. I repeated it with the other hand, declining a trip to the bathroom to find a comb or brush. If Mulan had been here, I'd have gotten a dirty look. The joke was on her, though, because I was now doing things on purpose that I knew would earn me her glares.

I hated, hated, hated having to pry the reason for Fiona's pain out of her. It involved Jack, which was explanation enough for me. I preferred to let her process her anger before hearing the gory details. Since I was planning to disrupt Jack's plan to turn himself into a mentally deranged version of Rasmus, I couldn't let anything involving him go unaddressed —not even fights with his daughter.

I cleared my throat while I worked up the courage to ask. "So... can we talk about what happened with yer father?"

"What is there to discuss, Mom? Dad apologized but insisted he did it for my own good. He ordered me to go back to school and hide out."

I sipped my water while the mother guilt rolled over me. Honesty won out. "If ya recall a similar argument we had about yer safety, I suggested ya do that as well."

Fiona stopped banging around the kitchen and plopped her slumping form into a chair across from me. "You told me to choose a side, take precautions, and figure things out for myself. You said to do that OR go back to college and hide. You gave me options because you're worried about my safety. Dad just gave me orders. He honestly thinks I'm supposed to follow them."

My grunt was barely audible. I didn't want to point out that between all the financial help he'd given her and her new car, Jack did sort of own her. But I couldn't say that without really setting her off. "At least yer father wants to look out for ya. That's a good thing. Right?"

"Dad threatened to put me in stasis again if I didn't go back to college. Who does he think he is making threats like that? No one died and made him king of the world. What he did to me was kidnapping and assault. I'm not moving back home until he learns better."

Her irritation made me chuckle. Sure, I'd called removing her from the house a 'rescue' but what I did was remove Fiona's unconscious body from her room. Some might call that kidnapping, but what Jack had the demon do to Fiona was a personal assault.

It wasn't funny—not really. Jack and I were both terrible parents in some ways.

What was funny was my spitfire daughter. When Fiona got into a temper, she sounded exactly like me.

"Fiona... sweetie... calm down before ya burst a blood vessel. I threatened yer father's life if anyone laid a hand on ya again—demon, fake guardian, or human. I've already proven I can take yer father in a fight. He won't mess with ya, either."

Fiona lifted her face and smirked. "Dad's completely willing to put me into stasis again to get his way. Who does that to their daughter? I know Dad thinks he's smarter than everyone else, but it's like he truly thinks I'm a small child still. Do you think of me that way?"

I snorted. "No, Fiona. Yer mother's a witch and a child of The Dagda. My only regret is that I didn't arrange for ya to be trained when I was away all those years. I want to protect ya as much as yer father does, but I also want ya to be able to protect yerself. As soon as we shut the man-made guardian program down, we'll look into yer training."

Fiona nodded, rose, and checked the food before returning to the table. "I want that too, Mom. I want to make sure no one can do anything to me. I never even put up a fight with Dad. I just stood there and listened to the demon chanting like I'd never heard a spell being spoken before."

"Had yer father ever given ya reason not to trust him before that day?"

Fiona sighed loudly. "No. Not that I can remember."

I spread my hands. "Then given what ya knew at the time, ya can't blame yerself for trusting him. Ya won't trust him blindly ever again, though, right? That's called a life lesson, and I think ya've learned it."

"Is adulting always this hard?"

I laughed at the question. Before I left the cottage, I would have lied to her. I couldn't do that now. My gaze met hers and held it.

"Before ya had yer awful ten minutes with yer father, my ex-husband informed me he had worked for the military before he and I ever met. He traveled to Ireland for the sole purpose of investigating me and my powers for his government. They ordered him to marry me so he made sure he did. If I had known any of that about him before today, Fiona, I would never have stayed in demon hunter prison. I still loved him when he betrayed me. It took me two years to stop crying over what he did."

Fiona frowned at the story. "You might never have married Dad or had me if you had known the truth."

I reached over and picked up her hand to hold it. "While that is probably true, it's too late to play the if-only-I'd-known-then game. Plus, I can't imagine my life without ya. Jack said he fell in love with me *despite* his mission to control my powers. Part of me wants to believe him because I fell hard for him when we met. Ya came from the love I once felt for yer father. We both have to let that be enough good."

Fiona nodded and ducked her head. "I'm sorry I never saw how unfair Dad was being to you. I thought he was mad because you saw your work as important as his. He likes to feel like he's the most important person in the world."

"Yes, I realize that now as well, but I didn't see it back then. And not all men think like yer father so don't be going down that path. It's my fault Jack had to hurt me badly enough for me to figure it out. And I have. But I can't undo the past. All I can do now is see ya get trained."

"Dad wouldn't even tell me what happened to Daniel. He told me to forget about him. That's why I left so soon. What was the point in staying if I wasn't going to hear the truth?"

I leaned forward. "While we were doing our research, I learned the serum they made from Rasmus wears off unless follow-up doses are given regularly. That means at least some of the things done to Daniel will be reversed if he doesn't get more treatments."

"Can I talk to Daniel about what happened?" Fiona asked.

I looked deep into her eyes. She needed personal confirmation that Daniel was lost to her the moment he listened to Jack. It was simple for me to see—but not so simple for her.

"Talking to the boy is yer call, Fiona, but ya need to take proper precautions when ya do. Ask yerself how much Daniel means to ya and whether or not he's likely to betray ya to yer father. The people who worked on Daniel are both mean and strong. Even if ya once trusted the boy himself, ya can't trust any of them. Take more precautions than ya ever think ya might need. And I'll be praying they'll be enough to protect ya."

Fiona frowned but nodded. "That sounds like good advice."

I sighed loudly. My daughter's true maturity was running parallel with mine. I wasn't sure how I felt about it, but there wasn't anything to be done.

"Maybe we can get Conn to bring Daniel here. Inside my wards, there's not much he can do to ya. How does that sound?"

"Or..." Fiona said with a tired laugh. "I could simply use the phone and call him. A chat on social media might do as well, but I'd prefer to hear his voice. I'm not completely stupid, Mom. Anyone could type for him."

"Goddess, I hope those are yer survival instincts kicking in and that ya're not that jaded about men yet."

Fiona shook her head and groaned softly. "Aren't you planning to kill those scientists, Mom?"

"No," I said, staring at her. "I don't randomly kill humans or demons. Conn is going to mind-wipe them of their findings and reprogram them to think differently about their biological tinkering. We're tweaking the truth to slow them down. Hopefully, that will be enough to change their opinions."

"Scientists all around the world are doing DNA experiments. Is stopping the rest of them going to be your new job after this? It sounds both dangerous and impossible."

I crossed my arms. "Ya just had to point out the short-sightedness of my plans, didn't ya?"

My daughter laughed. "I'm a practical person like Gigi."

My arms fell as I sighed. "Goddess bless, Fiona, that's the truth if I ever heard it uttered." I snapped my fingers and pointed a finger at her. "Okay, that's something I need to take into consideration, but first I have to disrupt the mess I'm attached to. The ones working with yer father intend to trap Rasmus again. He won't let that happen and neither will his brethren."

"Brethren? Is that what he calls the others like him?" Fiona asked.

"Yes. It sounded old-fashioned to me as well, but if ya saw the other two, ya'd see it fits them. They're ancient bird men, Fiona, with powers like the Gods. I suspect most would call them angels, but they don't call themselves that."

"Does he kiss like an angel, Mom? I saw you two making out in the chair earlier."

I scrubbed my eyes with my fists. "That's none of yer business. And I haven't kissed an angel before, so I couldn't say. Ya can ask me about the Faerie Folk if ya like. I've kissed quite a few of those."

"You're babbling, which means *yes*," my daughter said with a grin.

Mulan knocked sharply on the front door, then entered without waiting for an invitation. She burst into the kitchen with her usual gale-force energy.

"I brought brownies," she said, setting a large container of chocolate wonderfulness on the table. She studied my face and frowned. "Your face is red, Aran. Tomorrow I will make you lotion with chamomile and peppermint. It lessens redness."

Fiona burst out laughing at the makeup advice. "Mom's face is red because she's blushing. I saw her and Rasmus kissing today."

Mulan's expression betrayed her confusion as she looked at me. "The guardian chases you like lovesick puppy. Why does this make your face red? He has very nice package and could be good lover. Seduce the man and see."

"How do ya know what kind of package he has?" I demanded.

Mulan snorted. "I was there when he changed from human into giant flying creature."

I scrubbed my face and moaned in humiliation. "Oh. That's right. Everyone saw his package, didn't they?"

"Mom's jealous," Fiona said with a smirk.

"I'm not..." I began but stopped protesting to sigh in defeat.

I was jealous.

I hated the idea of anyone seeing Rasmus naked but me, especially after our make-out session earlier. My fingers itched to play with his hair again. I wanted to feel it falling over me. I wanted to feel every inch of him touching me, even though I knew it was foolish to want someone like him.

Mulan nodded in approval. "Look... the guardian gives her dreamy eyes."

Fiona giggled. "You should have seen them, Mulan. It was so romantic. Mom fell asleep in his lap and he carried her to bed before he left. She slept for *hours*."

Mulan let loose an enormous sigh. "You are so lucky, Aran. High demon is too busy with his old girlfriend to have time for needy Wu Shaman. And I have no time for his nonsense. I do not wait for men to have time for me. When I want man, I go get one."

I ignored her rant about Conn but made a mental note to warn him that he was losing her.

"Okay, yes. Rasmus kissed me. But it's not like anything significant happened."

They both giggled at my words. I knew I was protesting my innocence, but I was also trying to escape the conversation.

"The two of ya make it sound like Rasmus and I are a thing, but we're not a thing. Maybe he likes me—maybe he even wants me—but being with me is against his religion. Goddess, that's something I never thought I'd be saying about a man, but that's the truth of the situation."

Mulan opened the container of brownies and got one out for each of us. "Where does the guardian go when he leaves you?"

I frowned at her. "I don't know. Why would I ask him? I'm not his keeper."

Fiona bit into a brownie before speaking. "You should find

out, Mom. Rasmus could be plotting with Dad against you. You said yourself that Rasmus has a soft spot for Dad."

That unhappy observation settled on me like a cold, wet blanket. My smart child was too observant—too much like her grandmother. What could I do about that? Nothing. She'd been that way since she was born.

I glared at my daughter. "I'm going to have a long talk with Gigi for encouraging yer skepticism about everyone's motives."

"I'm being practical," Fiona declared.

And she was. Plus, she could be right. I certainly hoped that wasn't the case, but I hadn't questioned the guardian's loyalty to me lately. I was too busy thinking about the way he kissed me.

Nothing Rasmus said made me believe he favored Team Jack more than Team Aran at the moment. But I certainly didn't trust Jack's calm reaction to knowing Rasmus was running around loose. He seemed almost too unconcerned. Was Jack's lack of fear because he thought they'd already created beings equally powerful as the guardians? Surely, he wasn't that much of a fool.

I ate my brownie and a second one while thinking about it, but more thinking didn't change what my instincts were telling me needed to be done.

Short of tying Jack up and compelling him to explain things to us, I had no way to see what was going on inside that lab. I'd considered putting a compulsion on him to get him to talk, but I didn't want to deal with any other compulsions he had on him that might work against us.

Lilith had said she'd lied *for* Jack and *to* him. I didn't ask for details, but I did take her words for the warning I felt sure they were meant to be for me.

No, the experiments were getting worse. I had no choice

except to stop this madness. We would go in tonight after the gym closed for the evening. Conn and I would enter our way. He was right now gathering a demon team to watch the building and be there if we got into trouble.

The last thing I needed was for Fiona to be conflicted about me and her father again. It was best to take my chances by being surprised by what I found. Breaking up a troll thievery ring or disbanding a black witch coven wasn't easy either, and I'd survived both.

"After dinner, I'm going to do my preparation rituals," I announced.

"May I watch you do them?" Mulan asked.

"So long as ya don't ask me a bunch of questions. I can't afford to be distracted."

"Observation only. I will remain in my room and view from the window," Mulan promised.

"Do you need to do anything to get ready?" I asked.

Mulan blinked at me. "I am Wu Shaman. I am always ready."

Fiona laughed. "Did you hear that, Mom? No rituals and always ready—I want to be like Mulan after I'm trained."

Mulan tilted her head and studied my daughter. "Your energy is not like your mother's. Maybe you will make a good shaman. We will talk this out later."

"Did you hear that, Mom? Mulan might train me to be a shaman."

The girl had no idea what she was in for and I was not going to enlighten her.

Fiona cheekily grinned at me when I rolled my eyes and left the kitchen.

Chapter Eighteen

W e opted to eat early since it was going to be a long
evening. Rasmus didn't show up for dinner. Fiona
offered to make him a plate, but I declined on his behalf... and
mine.

He wasn't returning today and I would not allow myself to
hope he would.

Conn didn't join us for dinner either, but Fiona made him
a plate on autopilot.

Conn would return and the first thing he would want to
do was eat. He preferred food we'd prepared to eating out
because his instincts deemed it safer.

Goddess only knew how much fuel we were going to need
this evening. I wanted Conn to be at his best.

It felt strange to have kissed a man so thoroughly yet have
no idea if I'd ever see him again. Rasmus had tucked me into
bed and left without even saying goodbye.

Who knew what he was even thinking about our situation?
I sure didn't. Maybe our little make-out session was enough
closure on our not-quite-a-relationship for him.

Whatever the case, I refused to be starry-eyed about the attentions of a man who came and went as he pleased without explaining himself.

At forty, I wasn't sweetly naïve like my daughter. I didn't look at males as strange, wonderful beings with the capacity to make my insides sing. Maybe I sometimes *wished* I could feel like that again, but my maturity wouldn't let me get too hopeful.

I understood that Rasmus promising not to stop me differed vastly from him being willing to fight at my side.

It would have been doubly foolish for me to long for the guardian's presence tonight and to count on him having my back if things didn't go right. Given our discussions and the guardian's philosophy, I had no choice but to conclude Rasmus would stay as far away from the action tonight as he could get.

How else could he claim to remain neutral? His weakness for me might cause him to intervene even if doing so was against everything he believed.

No reasonable being would put himself through that sort of mental and spiritual agony if he could avoid it.

Pulling my thoughts away from what I couldn't have, I lit a fire in a metal fire pit I'd purchased for the yard. Purification herbs dropped from my fingers as I chanted a prayer to the Goddess I served and the ancestors who gifted me their powers.

The herbs crackled as the fire turned them into fragrant green smoke. I closed my eyes, breathed in the smoke, and let my heart fill with gratitude.

I prayed for calmness, for strength, and for the people helping me to be kept safe. I prayed for my daughter.

And even though I felt it was a waste of my spirituality, I prayed for Rasmus too.

I WAS FINISHING my magickal preparations when two small dogs rounded the yard in a full-out run as they raced toward me. I recognized one dog, so I waited for the yipping and yapping to settle before I greeted them both.

"Evening, Conn. I see ya picked up a friend while ya were out. Are ya planning to introduce us?"

Conn morphed from a small furry dog to a fully dressed human in a blink. He stooped and scooped up the other small dog in his arms. He gripped the dog—almost too tightly—and seemed to do his best to keep the animal from squirming out of his hold.

"I recruited a friend to guard Fiona and the house while we're out tonight. I granted him access through the wards in case they had to flee. I hope that was okay."

Nodding, I reached out to scratch behind the little dog's ears. The grateful whine I got for my efforts made me smile. "Ya're a beautiful doggie, aren't ya? Is it a he or she?"

The dog finally wiggled itself free of Conn's hold. Before its paws touched the ground, the dog smoothly shifted into a tall, attractive man with snow-white hair to his waist, a muscular chest, and two sharply pointed ears.

I stiffened in surprise but made myself nod to him. Some of his kind recognized my connection to them. Others did not. Since Conn brought him here, I hoped it was the former in this case.

Conn held out a hand. "Aran, this is Murray. He's a friend of mine."

"I believe calling us friends is a stretch," Murray said with a masculine chuckle as his sexy lips formed a knowing smile. "I, unfortunately, owed Connlander of the Fir Bolg a favor. But it is my greatest pleasure to pay my debt to a daughter of The Dagda."

Murray gently lifted my hand and kissed the back of my knuckles. Magick coursed through me at his touch—very familiar magick. It felt a lot like my own and I suspected I knew why.

"Conn did not warn me about yer beauty, Aran of The Dagda. I see us being life-long friends and perhaps even more."

My answer was instant, but I softened it with a small smile. "I thank ya for the compliments. Unfortunately, being friends is all I can offer ya at this time, Murray. My daughter is not available for romancing either. She is young and I'm a vengeful mother to those thinking to harm her."

I was relieved when he inclined his head in acceptance of both statements.

"Call me Aran, though, and tell me truly if ya're one of the Faerie Folk. I haven't seen one in quite a while."

He gave a courtly bow. "Labels mean little, but blood runs true. I am what I appear to be, which is a descendant of the *Tuatha de Danann* like yerself. But I can see yer power dwarfs mine by quite a bit. It may be even greater than Connlander claimed. Ya're both witch *and* warrior."

"Ya flatter me, Murray. "

"Oh, I doubt that's the case. Ya must know The Dagda's human descendants amaze the rest of us, especially when someone like yerself is born. I met the lovely Murieann who was Conn's previous caretaker. She was powerful too. I assume the two of ya are related somehow since yer sort of power only passes through families."

I inclined my head at his praise. The Faerie Folk thrived on formality and their ability to cite their heritage. I suppose I was no different. Maybe I wasn't a braggart like some, but I was very proud of my family.

I smiled at Murray. "I consider myself doubly blessed to claim The Dagda as my ancestor and Connlander of the Fir Bolg as my friend. However, my daughter was raised by her non-believing father and has not been educated in the ways of our people. I plan to rectify that oversight soon, but it will not happen today. I apologize in advance for whatever she might say to offend ya."

"Never fear, Aran of The Dagda. I promise not to take offense nor to bind your daughter to any recompense. Conn insists I stay in small beast form until the two of ya return from yer task this evening. I have agreed to the arrangement with no stipulations otherwise."

I smiled at his admission. "One thing I can promise ya, Murray. No dog will ever be more spoiled than ya will be at my daughter's hands tonight. Her father forbade her to have a pet. She's longed for one all her life."

Murray arched a white eyebrow. "How barbaric of him to deny his child such a small pleasure. What kept ya from overriding his wishes?"

"I was in magickal prison," I said, refusing to cower from the truth. "My ex-husband betrayed me. I just recently got released."

"And ya stayed there for the sake of yer child," Murray said, staring very hard at me.

I lifted my chin and nodded. "Yes, and I appreciate ya saw that so quickly. That alone has earned ya my friendship."

"Why else would someone as powerful as ya are tolerate such circumstances? Murieann did the same. She gave up seeing her only grandchild because..." Murray stopped talking and then pointed his finger. "Ya're the grandchild she rarely got to see, which means she likely never got the chance to train ya to take over for her. Ah, Aran... that breaks my heart for both of ya."

I shrugged. It was old news to me. My parents had good reasons for keeping us apart... or thought they did. But parents aren't always right and I had parented long enough to understand that. Seeing Jack's true nature for myself made forgiving them much easier.

"Who trained ya then? Did Conn do the honors?" Murray asked.

I smiled at Conn. "Conn began my training, but The Dagda himself incarnated to continue it. I don't tell that story to many, Murray, but I share it freely with ya. Goddess only knows, I have done my best to honor The Dagda's gift of entering this physical world again for my sake."

Murray dropped to one knee at my feet. "Ya're as special as Conn said ya were. I will protect yer child with my life, Aran of The Dagda."

"Thank ya, Murray. Ya honor The Dagda as much as me with yer promise."

He rose to face me again, towering over both me and Conn. Murray was about the same height as Rasmus. I studied his handsome face before my gaze ran over the rest of him. His clothes hid nothing and showed off his assets all too well. Looking as he did, Murray could be a problem for any woman without ever intending to be.

His smile at my perusal was wide. "Yer eyes speak quite loudly. Do ya like what ya see?"

"Yes. As much as I'm sure many other women have liked it as well. My daughter is young in age, but even younger in heart. I ask ya not to show yer true self to her unless it is necessary. She is easily swayed by male beauty, and I would hate to have to hurt ya for taking advantage. Especially since ya're doing me a great favor by guarding what is most precious to me."

Chuckling, Murray lifted my hand again and kissed it. "I prefer seasoned women. My offer to be yers and prove it will remain open until I pledge to a life mate. The magick we would create between us, Aran, would serve us both well. Please consider taking me as a lover."

Murray was right about the magick, and I was getting more desperate by the day. But I couldn't roll under this beautiful man while desiring another one as much as I did. That would betray my own heart.

All I could do was counter his tempting offer with honesty.

"The gods seem to be testing me, Murray. I'm currently obsessed with an ancient being who tempts me with his kisses. What can ya do, though, except suffer while the gods laugh at yer pain? I'm hopeful this longing I feel for what he withholds from me will eventually pass."

Murray laughed like I'd told him the funniest joke ever. It probably was funny to a being who slept with a different female every night.

"Not *every* night..." Murray declared, favoring me with a wicked wink and an even more wicked smile.

"Are ya reading my mind without permission?" I demanded as my face heated and turned red. Silver strands had replaced most of the burnished copper ones in my hair, but my flushed skin still shouted 'redhead' to the world.

Conn's wicked masculine laughter made my face flame even hotter. "You spoke your thoughts aloud, Aran. The guardian is not worth this humiliation. Take Murray up on his offer. I've heard he's quite good with women."

"Guardian?" Murray repeated, sounding surprised. "I

thought those were a myth. Aren't they tied to the Abrahamic traditions?"

I shook my head. "No, but that's a common misconception because of all the fallen angel hype. Guardians are much older than angels. They pre-date Dragons and dinosaurs. Guardians say they have seen multiple civilizations rise and fall on this planet. I find them fascinating, but one in particular. Conn and I rescued him."

"And I find that ya had to rescue him to be fascinating. That's probably quite the story for retelling. I don't believe I ever met a being that old, nor do I think I want to if he's immune to yer amazing charms. Good luck seducing him, though, Aran. Does he even have needs of that sort?"

I lifted both hands. "Outside of kissing, I honestly have no idea what he wants or needs. This is my dilemma."

"It would be my pleasure to make ya forget him... and yer pleasure as well. Do think about my offer."

I smiled at him. Murray's offer was one I once would have seriously considered and might have even accepted. Too bad I wasn't selfish enough to embrace that side of myself today. "How could I not think about it? Of course, I will keep yer offer in mind, Murray."

The male fairy looked at Conn. "Are we ready to charm the child?"

"The *child* is twenty human years old," I said to remind them both of Murray's promises.

"That's not even a blink of time," Murray said before spinning his male form back into that of a small dog again.

Yipping, Murray jumped from the ground into my arms. I could barely hold his squirming body. His unruly tongue swiping across my face made me squeal and push him away.

Conn laughed as he took Murray from me.

"Behave yerself," I said, ruffling the fur on Murray's doggie head. Neither his barks at me nor Conn's laughter were reassuring.

It was nice of Conn to call in a favor for Fiona's sake. Neither of us trusted Jack, the people he worked with, or the demons taking payment. Wards weren't perfect and could be broken, even ours.

I returned to my ritual fire and raised my face to the sky. "Thank ya for answering my prayers before I could think to ask someone to protect her, Danu."

The fire surged in reply and sent a flurry of bright green sparks into the air. I stared into the embers that remained and counted my blessings that I served a goddess who'd also been a mother.

I chanted a spell to help me see what was concealed and another to sharpen my senses. When I'd done all I could, I spoke another gratitude prayer and poured purified water over the embers.

When I turned, I saw my daughter sitting in a lawn chair petting the dog in her lap. It was a beautiful scene and one I tried to commit to memory. Then she reminded me she was no longer a child.

"Mom, this creature I'm holding is not a real dog. I'm not sure how I know. I just do."

Since I had no reason to lie to Fiona, I didn't.

"Ya're right, Fiona. He's not a dog. Murray is one of the Faerie Folk—a distant cousin of yours. After all the centuries that have passed since the *Tuatha de Danann* left Ireland, the bloodlines of our family are too mixed to sort out relatives easily. Whatever the true case, Murray is doing us all a favor by being here."

Fiona nodded as she continued to stroke the dog. "Conn

said the dog is going to guard me and the house while you're gone tonight."

I nodded in reply. My throat was tight with regret which made speaking hard. Why? Because I hated having to admit she was in danger, but it would be foolish of me to keep it from her.

As bad as I hated admitting it, I was having as big a problem as Jack was in accepting our daughter was now an adult. Thank the Goddess that Fiona dealt with my protection of her better.

If I'd been her, I might have been mad about the dog and ranted more about not being so easily fooled.

She sighed as she looked at me. "Do you seriously think the people Dad's working for might come after me?"

"Yes, and they would do that to use ya as leverage. Getting ya a bodyguard was Conn's idea but I agree ya need one. Ya're in good hands with Murray."

Fiona ducked her head. "Is there anything I can do to help while you're gone?"

I stopped by her chair and lifted her chin until her gaze met mine. "Ya can pray we're not too late to save those people trapped in that lab, Fiona. Pray for our success and send us good energy. We need all the prayers and good energy we can get."

"What gods should I pray to?" Fiona asked.

I studied my daughter's clear gaze and smiled. "Pray to whichever ones ya think will listen." Then I leaned forward and kissed her forehead. "Next week, we'll begin yer magick lessons. Everyone starts with learning to conjure fire. This is the last time I want ya to feel unprepared to deal with our enemies."

I moved beyond her, but her hand on my arm stopped me.

The girl had a strong grip. "Will you try to save Dad? I know you don't love him anymore, but I still do."

I blew out a breath. Given what I knew of Jack's goals that would be a hard promise to keep, but I nodded. "I swear I will do what I can for yer father, Fiona, but Jack hasn't been listening to me. What drives him speaks a louder language than his love for ya, which is immense. I wish he could see reason in this for all our sakes. I can't tell ya how much I wish it."

My daughter nodded and dropped her hand. "So what's he look like?"

"Who?" I asked.

I felt my face crinkle in confusion until she put her hand on the dog who barked in reply.

I narrowed my eyes as I glared down at Murray. "Don't be forgetting our agreement, Murray."

He grumbled in his doggie throat and laid down across Fiona's legs to pout.

Fiona chuckled. "He's a good-looking guy, isn't he? That's why Conn made him promise to be a dog."

"No, he's hideous," I whispered, winking at her to ruin the lie. "Murray didn't want to scare ya with his multiple deformities. That's why he vowed to stay in dog form unless attackers get through the wards. Brace yerself before ya have to look at him, Fiona. Ya won't be able to look away."

Fiona grinned when the dog set loose two fierce barks while staring hatefully at me. "Thanks for the warning, Mom. Would you think I was a wuss if I confessed to wishing I was just an oblivious kid again?"

"Goddess, no. Adults wish that for themselves all the time. Then they go out and do what has to be done anyway. There are benefits to adulting, not that ya've had a chance to appreciate them yet. Remind me when this is all over to tell ya about them. We'll have ourselves a pleasant chat about the good things about growing up."

Her giggle was music to my ears. "Thanks, Mom. I'm going to hold you to that."

"Hold me to what? Being too honest? Having a job that puts ya in danger? Making promises to ya about yer father that I might not be able to keep?"

Fiona smiled and shook her head. "Thanks for being you, I guess. I've known all my life that we were not a normal family. It feels important for me to be involved this time. I love you for trusting me not to do anything stupid to mess things up."

"Ya're the light of my life, Fiona. I love ya the way flowers love the sun. I can't even imagine my life without ya."

Her answering smile held love and soothed my soul.

"Good luck with the bad guys tonight, Mom."

I smiled back at her. "My luck is coming with me in demon form. I'll be fine."

I hustled into the house and away from my still-chuckling child before I knelt at her feet and cried in happiness that we weren't at odds anymore.

What happened later tonight could change our ease with each other, but I chose to believe it wouldn't. I wanted to think that Jack would get a clue and step up to do the right thing.

It wasn't all that hard to remain positive about the situation.

When it came to Jack, denial and I were the best of friends.

Chapter Nineteen

T he ride took longer than we thought it would because of all the traffic downtown. A big event of some sort had congested the streets so our driver took an alternative route to where we were going.

I should have been thinking about what we were planning to do and how we could rescue the people who'd become science experiments, but I wasn't thinking about any of that yet.

No, I was pondering why weird thoughts get stuck in yer brain no matter how many other thoughts have passed through yer gray matter since ya heard them.

The driver Mulan and I hired to take us downtown was not much of a talker. He agreed to drop us off at a restaurant and hadn't said anything else. He also hadn't given our matching black outfits more than a cursory glance. There was no reason at all that I should be remembering the last time the three of us went out dressed in all black. Or that our driver then accused us of doing cosplay for *Charlie's Angels*.

I glanced at Mulan. She looked very Asian with her sleek,

black hair pulled into a high ponytail. The Wu Shaman always looked beautiful and sleek, but there was an ethereal quality to her tonight that increased her allure.

Maybe Mulan's beauty was the reason I was thinking about stupid stuff instead of the mess we were about to get ourselves into.

The Wu Shaman looked like she was going clubbing. I looked like a lazy housewife who didn't feel like dressing up but had to throw on real clothes anyway. My silver curls were haphazardly pinned to the back of my head and the stragglers were barely restrained behind a wide black headband.

The walk to the gym from the restaurant where we got dropped off was blessedly short. We found Conn on the street in front. Dressed all in black as well, he looked like a young Sean Connery and wore a smile just as sexy. It didn't do anything for me, but I saw Mulan trying hard not to stare at him.

Conn and Mulan were perfectly matched and both looked like they came to the gym every day. My layered shirts and too-tight black leggings emphasized my much softer figure in unflattering ways. My stomach bulged a bit and rolled over my waistband. My more than ample butt pushed the stretchy fabric to its breaking point.

I sighed and admitted to myself that my leggings were too tight. No more mediums for me. Next time, I was going to buy large regardless of how depressed the size on the label made me. What did I care if I looked like the older woman I was?

I could easily blame my weight on Mulan's brownies. They were heavenly in the pan but looked like hell on my hips. When ya were five feet tall, every pound ya gained looked like five in yer clothes. It wasn't fair that happened to those of us who were shorter, but life was seldom fair.

Sighing, I set aside my vanity and did the spell to cover myself in Conn's mantle of power. What was one more layer going to matter to my roundness?

At least the mantle served a good purpose, unlike those extra pounds I'd gained from consoling myself with all those yummy brownies.

Eating all those brownies was not my substitute for sex, though.

I'm sure every shrink in the world would have called me a liar for denying it, but whatever. I'd analyze my weight gain later.

Rasmus would have to factor into that analysis too, but thinking about the purposely absent guardian was more unacceptable than my too-tight clothing. Thinking about the guardian's opinion of my actions could easily send me spiraling. I pulled myself back from it but it took more effort than usual.

Conn and Mulan were staring at me when I finally surfaced from my pity party.

"Sorry," I said to both of them. "I'm ready. Let's do this."

Conn glanced around. "Lilith's people have surrounded the gym. I told them not to join the fight unless I called to them."

"Good," I said before I turned my attention to Mulan. "I still think ya should wait out here. I don't know what we're going to find inside."

"The man-made guardians are strong. I prefer to watch the lab from a place where you can more easily reach me," she said.

I nodded in agreement. "Okay. Then we're as ready as we can ever be."

The three of us trekked around to the back of the building. Conn opened the door I showed him and disarmed their security in under a minute. James Bond had nothing on my familiar.

We left the lights off as we entered, but I conjured a little blue fire in my palm for us to see by. When we got to the wall that opened, I let the fire die out.

Conn felt along the wall and found the outline but could not discover how to enter. Mulan pulled her staff from a holster strapped to her thigh and extended it to full size. Ten seconds of chanting later, a large expanse of wall slid backward and out of the way.

We entered an empty dark room with no windows or light. I conjured the blue fire again but kept it to a glow instead of a flame. The outline of a faint gray door was barely visible. It had a small badge reader on one side of it.

All three of us froze at the sight. I looked around. Three white lab coats were hanging behind us on the wall. "Search for a badge," I said, holding my lit palm higher.

Mulan scrambled across the floor and went through the lab coats. "None," she said.

I swung around in the room. "I hate to break in, but I don't think we have any choice."

"Wait... give me time," Mulan said, heading back into the hallway.

I heard her opening the gym entrance and the door clicking shut behind her. A couple of minutes passed while I pondered how to infiltrate the lab without alerting the wrong people.

Mulan came back into the room with two badges in her hands. "I got them from desk out front."

"It can't be this easy," I said.

"Of course, it can. Why must everything be hard?" she asked.

The first badge slid through the reader and did nothing. The second lit the panel up with a green light.

Mulan attached the badge that worked to her shirt before starting her chant. She tapped her staff against the floor to charge it.

I looked at Conn who hovered by the door. "I'm ready anytime ya are."

Mulan nodded and then badged the door open. Conn ran inside before Mulan and I had a chance to go. As I came through, I heard a loud zap and a grunt. Lights came on and the first thing I saw was Conn on the floor in front of me. He was rolling over and struggling to push himself upright.

As I looked around, I saw a row of cages on each side of the room. A man's voice came at me from the side.

"He hit the barrier. They probably know you're here now, but maybe not because the night guard tends to fall asleep."

I turned to stare into a cage. "Colonel Benson? Are ya stuck in there?"

"Unfortunately," he said. He lifted his head and inclined his chin to the cages in the room. "We're tomorrow's guinea pigs."

There were two men in each of the cages, except for the one holding Colonel Benson.

"Are these yer people?" I asked as I took a step toward him.

"No, stop!" he commanded. "The cages are electrified. The floor in front of them is pressure-sensitive. You won't be fast enough to escape the charge." He paced the center of his cage. "I took your advice and decided to get involved. These men were assigned to help me."

"How did they take ya down?"

"With stun weapons and muscle," he reported.

Conn finally made it to his feet and carefully backed up to where I stood. "Why did you let me run in here?"

I snorted at him. "Don't blame me for yer impatience."

Conn chuckled at my remark while Mulan sighed in irritation.

I ignored them both. "How do we release ya, Colonel?"

"Take out the control panel. But I don't know where it is. Down below probably."

"Below?" I asked.

He pointed down. "There's another level under our feet. That's the lab. It's where they keep the abominations."

"I really wish ya would come up with a different term. In my line of work, *otherness* is quite normal."

"There's a man down there with spider legs growing out of him, Ms. O'Malley. They sedate him every few hours because he screeches at them when he wakes up. *That* is not normal and *this* is not TV. That shit down there in the lab is happening for real."

I nodded. "Yes, it is... and so are we." I swung to Mulan. "Got any shaman tricks to take out their security measures?"

Her gaze glanced around. "I can, but it means everyone gets wet."

"Do it," I said with a grin before turning back to the cage. "Colonel, tell yer people to stand in the middle of their cages. Things might get a bit tingly if this works."

While Colonel Benson barked out orders and woke up those sleeping, I looked around the room. At the end of it, I noticed the elevator. The lights on it were lit. Someone was coming up here.

"Do it now, Mulan!" I shouted.

Conn and I huddled together while she chanted at the ceiling. Sprinklers across the room burst one by one. The lights flickered and the floor sizzled. The cages sparked as the water cascaded down the bars and into the locks before running to the floor.

Mulan stood in the middle of it looking like a rain goddess with her arms spread wide.

I looked at the cage again. "Now, don't panic, Colonel, but I brought my 'otherness' with me tonight."

Conn shifted into his demon form. There were a few quiet gasps but mostly the Colonel and his men kept their cool.

"Elevator is coming," I said and drew an energy sword from my mantle.

Conn ran through the water to the elevator. The floor didn't stop him this time. I took that as a good sign and ran to Colonel Benson's cage.

"Move back and watch yerself," I ordered, slicing between the bars until the cage door flew open. I ran to the next one and did the same thing.

At the elevator, Conn doubled his size and grabbed the two man-made guardians as they exited.

"Don't kill them unless ya have to," I yelled to Conn, working on my fourth cage.

"I can help you open cages," Mulan said.

I watched her run across the water and tiles without ever touching the floor. How in the world did she do that?

I pulled my gaze from her and went back to opening cages. When I got to the end of the row, I stopped long enough to see Mulan glaring up at Conn.

"Lower them, demon. I cannot reach them."

Conn looked down at her. He held the man-made guardians by their necks and shook his head. He seemed fearful of letting her help.

Mulan used her staff to bop Conn on the knee. "I said, lower them!"

He rolled his demon eyes and lowered his arms until the two struggling men in his grip dangled a foot in front of the Wu Shaman.

Mulan chanted and struck each one of them on the head with her staff. All struggles ceased.

"Twenty minutes," she said as she looked at me.

I nodded and started up the other side of the cages.

Conn tossed his now unconscious attackers aside. The elevator doors opened again. A gun took aim at Mulan and fired. She barely deflected it with her staff.

The next thing I knew, she was running again.

Conn roared his displeasure and snatched up the gunman. Unfortunately, that left one more still in the elevator.

"Go," I heard someone yell near me.

I turned and saw Mulan was using her staff to melt the panels on the cages. When the man inside kicked it open, she ran to the next.

Fine. I guess my job was to be elsewhere.

I ran toward the second man who was creeping out of the elevator. "Hey! Put yer weapon down!"

He fired a large stun gun at me. When the first electric surge bounced off, he fired a second time. Then he seemed out of juice.

I watched as the man ran back into the elevator and started pushing buttons. The doors began to close.

Conn stuck a giant demon foot inside the door to stop it.

I vaulted over his foot and had my sword pointed at the guy's throat. His hands flew up as he pressed himself against one of the elevator's metal walls.

"How many more of ya are down there? If ya lie to me, I'm going to run ya through."

"Six more," he stammered.

"And what else?"

"No..othing... else," he stuttered.

I could tell it was a lie. I lowered the blade and pushed it into his chest. "If ya're just going to lie to me, ya're not worth my time or trouble. Now what else are we going to find down there."

"Guardians with powers."

"What kind of powers?"

"I don't know," he screamed as the blood started to trickle. "I swear I don't know."

I removed my sword and grabbed him. Then I tossed him over Conn's foot and he skidded along the floor. "Colonel Benson..."

"Got him," a male voice said. Then I saw the colonel bending over the guy with one of the stun weapons in his grip.

It seemed that we'd survived the first round. But the men with weapons were not man-made guardians.

That told me that our real fight hadn't even started yet.

Chapter Twenty

I exited the elevator by climbing over Conn's enormous foot and saw Mulan knocking out the gunman Conn had stopped.

Colonel Benson's men dragged our prisoners inside the cages and used their belts to keep them there. The resourcefulness of military men was not a myth.

After Mulan did her thing on the last conscious guy, Conn dropped him and shifted back down into human form. He stood in the elevator door to keep it open and to prevent people from coming up.

I frowned as I looked at them both. "There are six more guards and several man-made guardians with unknown powers down there. I vote Mulan stays up here."

"No. I go where you go. You need my help," Mulan said stubbornly.

"We need an army of Wu Shamans and Imperial Demons, but we don't have them," I said, lifting my hand. "Someone up here needs to be able to get help to retrieve us if we lose."

Mulan chewed her lip as she thought about my words.

Colonel Benson jogged over to us. He nodded to Conn once before giving me his full attention. Maybe he considered Conn a friendly abomination. There was no time to ask.

"I sent two men outside to call this in. Help will come within the hour, but that help may think stopping you is what is needed. Even with my military record, I couldn't find a truly sympathetic ear. No one believed this whole project had gone south. They gave me men and sent me here to check it out. You saw what happened to us."

I frowned and nodded. I looked at both Conn and Mulan. "My instincts are flashing a warning across my brain. Neither brute force nor magick will be enough to go up against a bunch of guardians with powers. It took all of us to defeat the one we came across at Lilith's. But if we wait for military help, it will probably go down exactly as Colonel Benson says. They'll go on making the fake guardians any way they can."

Colonel Benson hoisted his weapon up. "We all saw what they're doing down there. If you go down to the lab, I'm going with you. These weapons are charged up again and I'm a pretty good shot. I should be able to stop one or two of the armed guards. If we take two more men with us, the three of us might take out four or five of the armed guards using their weapons."

My brain hurt trying to decide what to do. I wasn't a military leader. Conn and I were used to working alone. Though I'd promised myself I wouldn't, I thought of Rasmus and wished he was here helping. I had no idea what a real guardian could do in human form, but even being a distraction would have given us an edge.

But it was just as well that he wasn't around since those running the program wanted Rasmus back. They wanted more of his blood. Jack was proof they would never give up trying to re-capture him. There were too few of us to get done what needed to be done... and I knew it.

I reached into my pocket and stroked the feather I'd tucked inside it before I left the house. I spoke to what there was of Team Aran.

"They weren't expecting us this time. Next time, they'll be prepared. Next time, they'll know how to take out Conn in a way he won't recover from so easily. We have surprise on our side tonight, but that's about all we have. The odds seem more against us than usual."

"I recruited a little more muscle for our side," Conn said, pointing to the door. A beautiful woman strolled through it.

"Lilith," I said, smiling at her.

"Conn said you needed my help."

"Is yer baby okay? Is he guarded well?"

"He is being guarded by the best I have," she said. "When they demanded demon blood, I gave them a young one to use for their test. Now they're demanding mine. You and Conn were right. They aren't intending to stop until they have an army capable of defeating every creature on Earth."

Behind Lilith, two more people rushed into the room.

"Fiona," I said, opening my arms as she ran to me. Her face was wet with tears, but she was in one piece. Her hug was fierce.

A handsome man with cuts on his face strode by her side. "Where are the rest of the people with a vendetta against ya, Aran? I left two of them tied up and tranced at the house. They came right after ya left. Yer daughter's cool head let us overcome them."

"Jack must have had people watching us. He must have seen Mulan and I leaving," I said, closing my eyes in dismay that the worst had come to pass. What if Murray hadn't been there?

My daughter pulled away and scrubbed her eyes. "They came to take me away. Murray didn't let them."

"Never on my watch, beautiful," Murray said, his blue eyes blazing. "She's only here because I didn't know where else to take her. I think they may be tracking her somehow."

I looked at Fiona who turned her back to all of us and walked to stare into one of the broken cages. This was my worst nightmare come to life. My child's illusions were dying while I watched and there wasn't a single thing I could do to stop it from happening.

But since she had to be here, maybe I could put her to work. "Fiona, a bunch of military men are going to show up soon. Can ya talk to them for us?"

My daughter swung back and nodded. "Are they friends or foes?"

"I don't know," I said.

"Is Dad part of this?"

My sigh was loud. "I don't know that either."

Fiona threw up her hands. "I guess it doesn't matter anyway. They almost broke my arm and I think kicked out someone's teeth. Murray bashed both their heads together until they stopped fighting. But I can't hide out from Dad's people forever. I want this to stop."

The mother in me longed to offer comfort, but I would have to soothe later. I couldn't do it now. The number of fighters on my side was greater than it was moments ago. This was the best that was going to happen.

Mulan took the badge off and clipped it to Fiona's shirt. "This is for door to this room. Keep people out or slow them down. Hide it when you're done. We need half hour at least."

Fiona patted the badge and lifted her chin. "Go, Mom. I got this."

I nodded and looked at those comprising the new and improved Team Aran. Adding a royal demon and a vicious fairy might be the edge we needed to survive this.

I lifted my chin just like my daughter had. "There are six guards with stun weapons and some number of man-made guardians with unknown powers waiting for ya all at the bottom of the elevator. The fake guardians are strong and have absconded with the powers of an ancient being who could destroy the whole planet if he chose. The fake guardians are the most serious threat, which is why we're going to stop these people from making more of them."

I glanced at my daughter who waved as we crammed into the elevator.

Seeing how snug we were, Conn morphed into a dog to save space. Mulan gave Lilith a dirty look and then picked doggie Conn up to cuddle him. She didn't even complain when doggie Conn gave her face a few licks.

Colonel Benson, along with two of his men, crowded in to block the front of us. Benson carried two weapons and the other men carried one each. The weapons took up as much room as they did. I knew they expected to be met with weapons. But I didn't. I expected to be met with something beyond my imagination.

We'd soon see who was right.

When the elevator door popped open, we were confronted with a nightmarish monster that stood twenty feet tall in the underground space. He sported black demon horns on his head, had gray wings growing from his back, and was covered with feathers everywhere else.

But the scariest thing about the creature was that I recognized him.

For a stunned moment, none of us moved. I pushed through Colonel Benson and his men. "Jack Derringer, what in the world have ya done to yerself?"

He spread his wings out and smiled. "This form wasn't exactly what I planned to shift into, but I'm finally more powerful than you."

Was it terrible of me to be grateful beyond words that Fiona hadn't come down to see her father like this? My energy sword hummed in my hand.

"Jack, the power ya have is not yers to keep. It belongs to Rasmus and his kind. At some point, they'll destroy everyone on Earth to stop those like ya. Yer ambitions to gain unnatural power are jeopardizing all humanity."

"Don't be a fool, Aran. They can't hurt us. We're just like them now. I tried to tell you that."

Behind Jack, six guards with stun weapons aimed them at all of us.

"Don't do this, Jack. Fiona is upstairs waiting on the military. The people ya work for are coming to help us stop this madness. Ya took yer experiments too far."

Or at least I hoped my daughter's story might persuade the ones coming that Jack and his people were the bad guys.

"Please don't make me fight ya, Jack."

His eyes glowed blue and reminded me of Rasmus. "You have used your powers against me for the last time, Aran. Now I'm the one in control. I'm the one making the rules."

One of the armed guards chose that moment to get antsy. He shot his weapon at us but luckily missed. Colonel Benson didn't, though, when he fired back.

Suddenly, all weapons were discharging as fighting erupted around me.

It was hard but I kept my gaze on Jack as monsters streamed on either side of us.

I feared for my team as I glared at him for what had become.

Jack laughed in a voice deeper than his normal one. He looked like a cross between a giant bat and a large bird of some sort. Had his scientists mixed bat DNA with guardian blood to make him?

"I kept samples from Rasmus and watched every experiment. My transformation is unlike any other. What I've become has made me unstoppable. Once I master shifting back to normal, I will have everything I ever wanted. I am the future of all men, Aran. You and your inherited powers will one day be useless against my kind."

Jack used his strange new arms to clap his webbed hands together. It caused powerful sound waves that knocked both my team and the other monsters down. I barely remained standing throughout it all. When I glanced behind me, I saw Conn's demon form shielded Lilith and Mulan.

I looked back and tried once more to reason with my former husband. "Jack, no one is unstoppable. Even Rasmus was able to be captured. And ya should know that leaving him was a choice his people made for their own reasons. If they'd wanted him back, ya couldn't have stopped them. One day the real guardians will return to fix this planet again. When that happens, they'll replace humankind with a different species. That's how this planet works. The guardians were created to stop the current species from destroying it."

"We took his memories and his powers. We will do it again if we need to. The guardians are no longer to be feared. We have made ourselves in their image. From now on, those like me will decide what happens on this planet."

"I can't let ya do that, Jack. I can't let yer kind be the ones in charge."

"*Don't. Get. In my. Way,*" Jack said, bellowing each word.

I stabbed forward with my sword and pierced Jack's thigh. He let loose a screech that assaulted my ears. I reached up with my free hand to see if they were bleeding.

Had Jack truly done this? Had his people replicated guardians in every way possible?

I pulled out the feather and held out my hand to show it to Jack. "This is from a real guardian." I blew it toward Jack who was glaring at me. His blood still dripped from my sword.

Jack caught the feather and crushed it in his hand. "Do you think I fear its owner?"

"No, but ya should," I said.

Jack's bloody hand morphed into a claw that he used to swipe at me. I sliced off his fingers and shuddered at what I'd done. He screeched in pain again.

"Please, Jack. For our daughter's sake, please stop this madness. I don't want to kill ya, but I will."

He straightened and let the blood drip from what was left of his hand. "Fiona is mine to control. You will have no say in how she uses her paltry powers. *I* will make those decisions. *I* will be the one who decides her fate."

"Jack," I whispered, shaking my head. "Ya know I can't let ya do that to her."

Conn in demon form chose that moment to rush Jack. Laughing, Jack used the hand I hadn't damaged to scoop him up. He even enlarged his demon form but Jack still kept hold of him. It took no effort at all. Jack's strength was beyond anything I'd ever seen.

"Aran tells me your kind can recover from anything. How long will it take you to heal a broken back?" Jack demanded, squeezing Conn harder.

A sickle adorned with jingling turtle shells sliced Jack's gripping hand off at the wrist. Conn fell to the ground as Jack's claw fingers released him. The liberated demon scooped up the angry Wu Shaman and pushed her behind him as he inched backward.

I stooped to the floor and picked up the feather from Rasmus that Jack had dropped. I looked around the room. "Either ya stop him, guardian, or I'm going to do it the only way I can."

I stuffed the feather back into my pocket and lifted my sword.

The room suddenly lost air as hundreds of feathers fell from the ceiling. They covered all of us... and all of the monsters.

Jack stood still, frozen in place. His severed limbs no longer dripped blood onto the floor. As I looked around, I noticed most everyone in the room was still and unmoving. Conn, Mulan, and I seemed to be the only ones not affected.

Before I had a chance to wonder what was happening, Rasmus appeared in front of me in his human form.

"I knew what choice you would make when Jack pushed you too far. I came to spare you from having to make it," he said.

I sighed into the silence. "I would have killed Jack to stop him and I would have killed the others too. Killing is not what I want for these people, but what else can I do when they won't listen to reason?"

The guardian bent and picked up a random feather from the hundreds littering the floor. "As usual, you did the only thing you could see to do, Aran. I'm glad you at least talked to Jack before acting this time."

I held out my hand toward the being Jack had become. "Does this creature look like someone ya can reason with? Rasmus, he took blood from ya and kept it for himself. This monster form is the result of what he did. Never let yerself be taken prisoner again. Tell yer brethren as well."

"The other guardians already know your feelings," Rasmus said as he looked around. "The royal demons can extract the effluvium from those who received it. Changes to their blood will be undone in approximately three days. I will undo what was done to those made from my blood. Those changes will be reversed instantaneously."

I frowned at his words. "All that sounds great, but I'm still going to mind-wipe the scientists and compel them to say this was a mistake."

Rasmus stared at me as he shook his head. "That's not how free will works."

My jaw tightened. "Would ya rather I made everyone involved believe they were crazy? There is no good answer about how to stop this. I'm trying to leave them functional."

"What will you gain from your manipulation of their memories?

This I could talk about all day. I'd thought of nothing else for a week now. "The scientists will think they failed. The military will think they wasted money. Everyone else goes home and forgets it ever happened. I call that a win-win."

"Would you be willing to let my brethren and I fix this?"

"Will the military scientists be making more of ya?"

"No, but they likely will be making stronger soldiers. Not guardian strong—but stronger than normal from what they learned."

I sighed. "Fine. I can live with that... with one exception."

"Jack," Rasmus said.

"Yes, *Jack*," I said back, as sarcastically as I could. "All he ever wanted was to have more power than I have. Jack is a loathsome, power-hungry man. I'll not have him causing me and Fiona problems for the rest of our lives. He wants to control her as well."

"So I heard," Rasmus said, looking off. "Put a feather in the pocket of anyone you want to wake up. You have one hour to do what you feel you must. I'll help you heal people. I will not help with the rest of what you intend to do."

"Fine. Start yer help with those that reverted back to human but lost their minds. Heal them first."

Rasmus shook his head. "No, I'll start with Jack. Once he's back to normal—or as normal as I can make him—you can do what you intend."

I nodded. "Am I in trouble with yer kind?"

His mouth twisted. "No. Quite the contrary. They're encouraging me to spend more time with you."

My grunt of disgust amused him because Rasmus grinned and chuckled. I could count on one hand the number of times I managed to get any sound of amusement out of him.

"Don't do me any favors, guardian. There's a fairy back there on the floor who's offered to make me forget yer kisses. I was tempted to take him up on it."

"It wouldn't make any difference, Aran. We're trapped in each other's realm of influence. You and I are like two planets caught in the same trajectory around the sun of our mutual interest in each other."

My lips pressed into an even firmer line. "Yer poetic speech does not impress me, nor do yer philosophical leanings. I'm not going to trade being heart bound to one controlling arse only to get tangled up with another. If I decide to forget I want ya, Rasmus, I will. And if I decide to invite dozens of men to share my bed to accomplish that feat, I will do that as well. I'm not Fiona. There are no stars in my eyes for love everlasting."

Rasmus grinned at me again in that rare manner he had. "Yes, I'm sure you would do your best to forget me, but I would never let you succeed. I'm not done with you, Aran of The Dagda."

I narrowed my eyes. "If ya're thinking I'll be some kind of human pet ya can study for yer own purposes, *that* will not be happening either. I know who I am, Rasmus. I know *what* I am. Yer brethren and ya will not be making me into yer fool. This is *my* world and *my* planet. If ya believe in free will as much as ya say, then ya must know that my will is like iron."

Rasmus smiled. "I do. It's one of my favorite things about you."

Glaring at him, I gathered up a handful of feathers. I should be more grateful he'd interceded after all. It was what I'd hoped he would do all along.

Yes, I fully intended to kill Jack... and I still wanted to. I'd hesitated only because of Fiona. Since I couldn't change the fact that her father was a bastard, I had no choice except to take the drastic measures I planned.

The guardian could work his magick on the others. I would work mine on the worst man I'd ever met.

With my thoughts churning like the wind of a storm, I walked over to Conn and Mulan. They instantly snapped out of their shock and blinked back at me.

"Everything's fine now. I'll explain later," I said, frowning at them.

I took Conn's hand and pushed some feathers into it. "Put

one of these in the pockets of all Team Aran people, including Colonel Benson, but skip his men for now. I want to get the monster undoing done before we wake up the rest of the full humans. The fewer people who witness these atrocities, the better off we'll be. *Do not wake up Fiona* until we get done with Jack."

Conn stared at me. "You were going to kill him, Aran. I felt it building in you. You were one sword swipe away from completing the deed."

I huffed at hearing the facts, but I wasn't afraid to own them.

"And I still might kill him, Conn. This vile situation is not all Jack's fault, but a lot of it is. Rasmus insists on healing him, and I'm sure he's going to make me leave Jack's military job in place."

Conn's gaze locked onto Rasmus who knelt by Jack. "The guardian came to help us after all. Do you know why he intervened after saying he wouldn't?"

I shook my head. "No, I honestly have no clue. They don't think like the rest of us, Conn. Ya can't figure guardians out the way ya can a human."

"Huh..." Conn said, his gaze fixed across the room where Rasmus was studying a still-frozen Jack.

Now for the hard part. "Look... I know putting demon compulsions on people is against yer beliefs, Conn. Will ya see if Lilith will do one for me? I plan to lose my ex-husband for good this time. Rasmus is allowing me a concession for Jack, and by the Gods, I plan to maximize what I do to him."

"Did the guardian save us?" Conn asked.

I glared at him for reminding me. "Yes... and don't make me say it again. Let's just get this mess cleared up and go home. I'm so tired of dealing with Jack and his messes. I have to make sure he doesn't come after Fiona again. That's what I'm focused on at the moment."

"Okay," Conn said. "Let's get things done before you spin any higher. You're still too bloodthirsty to be reasonable. Did the guardian make you mad?"

"Mind yer own business, Connlander. And ya need to thank Mulan for what she did. She's the real hero tonight," I said, turning my back on him. Thinking about the fight, I turned to look at the Wu Shaman. "Can ya turn yer staff into anything ya want?"

"It takes much practice, but yes," Mulan said.

"Fascinating. Thank you for helping tonight."

"I am good partner," Mulan said.

A small smile found its way to my mouth as I walked back to where Rasmus was kneeling over a human Jack. He appeared nearly normal as he moaned on the floor.

Rasmus had reattached Jack's hand and was now reattaching his fingers. The wounds were still there, but I had no doubt Jack would be using all those body parts again. I tried not to resent that, but it was impossible.

It also hadn't missed my notice that the guardian was doing all his healing while in his human form. I wasn't up to mentioning it to everyone else yet or discussing it. My mind was still working on accepting what I was seeing.

When a now-conscious Lilith came over to see me, she glanced at the guardian as she stepped to my side. "Conn said you needed my help."

My head moved up and down. "I never thought I'd be asking for this, but I need ya to do me a demon favor—very similar to what ya did for Jack. I need a compulsion put on him."

Lilith held up a hand. "My caste and I are at your disposal.

And I mean that literally. You are a powerful being with even more powerful friends. What can I do for you?"

"This hasn't got anything to do with my work. Right now, I'm just a frustrated woman who's dead set on removing her ex-husband from her life. Can ya help me with that?"

Lilith grinned. "Anything you wish can be done. Will the guardian allow it?"

"Yes. It's part of a bargain I made with him," I said and left it at that. "When Jack comes around, I'll help you place the stipulations. If we need to remove other compulsions, let's do that first. I want one thing only from this, but the one thing is complex and will have lots of layers. I want to make sure Jack can't find a way around following it."

Lilith put her hand on my shoulder until I looked at her. "Conn said trust can only occur when you turn loose of fear. I want you to know that I trust you, Aran. His name is Zaren."

My irritation melted and I smiled at her. "Zaren is a big name for a child to grow into."

"No, my son's name is Bartholomew. Zaren is his father's name. He was not a human, but neither was he a demon. He is like that one," Lilith said as she pointed to Murray. "Zaren helped me in the last stages of my regeneration. We became lovers after I healed. After I came here, I discovered I carried a child. It must be his because I took no other man into my bed after him."

I stopped fidgeting over Jack to really listen. "Does the babe's father know about the child?"

She shook her head. "No, and I was afraid to tell him. We both assumed we were not compatible. Zaren probably wouldn't believe me. But if he did believe me, would he take the child away from me? His kind sees any with their blood as being theirs. There are too many questions without answers for me to approach him yet. I am waiting for clarity."

I smiled at her and nodded. "Well, yer secret is safe with me. I believe babies belong with their mothers. I let Jack come between me and Fiona when she was still young and I should never have allowed it."

Lilith smiled a genuine smile at me. "It will be my privilege to keep your secrets as well. Conn's help has been invaluable to me. I hope you both will come back and visit after you move away."

"Always," I said, thinking about what Conn must have told her. "But we have the rental house for a year. We're not leaving until I train my daughter in magick."

"Is she a witch?"

I shrugged but offered her a small smile. "We don't know yet, but there's magick in her. Mostly I want to make sure she can take care of herself. Her father wants to control her. I will never let that happen."

"Then we will not allow him to keep wanting it," Lilith said.

And with that 'we' statement, I knew I had gained a woman friend for life.

"When this is all over, let's do lunch, Lilith. I want to hear what ya think about the caste from New Jersey."

Lilith chuckled. "I am glad I did not choose to support your ex-husband more than you. The demoness of that caste will probably wish the same when you're done chastising her."

"Let's hope so because I'm still mad about not getting to chop off a few more of Jack's limbs."

"Does the guardian know about your lethalness?"

I grunted as I stood. "Yes, but despite that, Rasmus incites my wrath whenever possible. I doubt he fears me or anyone. I've never met anyone so... calm."

"See to the others for now," Lilith said. "I'll call you when I'm ready to set the commands."

I rose and walked over to Colonel Benson. "Are ya doing okay, Colonel?"

"No," he said, shaking his head as his gaze roamed the room. "No one could be okay with this."

I patted his muscular arm. The colonel looked pretty youthful for someone who was allegedly retired. "See if ya can get names from them. It will be helpful to know what kind of person they were and how they looked when they were normal. And if ya have a couple of people free later, there are two more man-made guardians at my house. Murray put them in some sort of stasis. He also comes from gods so I doubt they'd be able to escape his hold."

"When are we waking everyone else up?"

I studied the cages. Rasmus was walking through the ones holding man-made guardians who had reverted. Like the heavenly creature many thought he was, Rasmus was curing their mental illness with a touch. Some might have called his actions a miracle, but I suspected the guardian was winding their biological clock backward to reset them. I doubt they would remember ever being converted at all.

"If ya need yer men to help ya, tell Conn which ones to wake up. I showed him how to do it. Honestly, I think it would be best to wait until we finish our damage control here before we wake them. Rasmus has given me an hour, but he's nearly done with his part."

"Are you going to make me forget this happened?"

I lifted an eyebrow. "I guess ya deserve to ask that question. My answer is no. I'm not planning to erase yer memories because it would serve no purpose to make ya forget. And I don't want ya to. Ya're human and part of this. Genetic manipulation put our whole human civilization at risk with those charged by the creators to look out for us."

"You seem to be in touch with a part of my world I never knew existed, Aran O'Malley. I'm sorry I didn't pay more attention when you visited me."

I chuckled. "And I'm sort of sorry ya did. If ya had left things alone, Colonel, ya could have spared yerself all that time ya spent in a cage. I never meant for that to happen to ya."

"So..." Colonel Benson said as he took in the whole scene. "What are you planning to do to Jack Derringer?"

I looked at where Jack lay on the floor. "It's best ya don't know the details. Jack won't be permanently harmed, but I can't have him causing problems for me or our child any longer. He flat-out told me he planned to control her."

"Oh, right. He's your ex-husband. I forgot about that."

I wish I could have forgotten, but that was never going to be the case. "Jack's been quite resistant to the idea that we're divorced. I've learned the hard way that Jack has problems with boundaries so I'm going to help him correct that in his character."

Colonel Benson grinned. "What's next for you and your team after this is all over? I heard a rumor about a werewolf pack staking a claim to the woods outside of Salem."

I shrugged. "Lycans do tend to be territorial. They also band together in packs. They're more annoying than harmful."

"People say they're abducting women and converting them into werewolves."

I shook my head. "It's not happening. Such conversions are an urban myth. Lycans are a separate species from humans but were made when we were. They replicate like the rest of us.

They don't howl at the moon or change into hybrid creatures. All they do is shift to wolf and back again. Running with the pack is important to them and so is keeping to themselves."

"Will you be checking them out?"

"No. Why would I?"

He gestured to the room with a hand. "You got involved in this."

"Not willingly," I said, pointing at Jack. "My ex-husband is the reason for my involvement. I planned to open a magick store and plant a big garden when I got away from the demon hunters."

"You're too young to retire."

I eyed him. "So are ya, but ya did it anyway."

He chuckled. "I did, but I received an interesting job offer recently. If I take it, I could use a witch slash child of a god slash bad-ass on my team."

"Ya're making fun of me."

"No, I would never do that, especially since I've seen what you can do. Want to have coffee and discuss us working together?"

Rasmus appeared at my shoulder. "Aran is unavailable. Her coffee dates are all taken."

Colonel Benson raised his hands. "I'm not trying to step on toes here, dude. I'm married. It wasn't that kind of a coffee date."

I shoved Rasmus and made him stagger. "Not that it concerns ya, but it was a job offer."

Rasmus righted himself and seemed to grow three inches in the process. He blinked at Colonel Benson's grin but didn't seem to realize he was acting jealous. His eyes were a clear green and full of innocence.

I rolled my own eyes before turning back to Colonel

Benson. "I have a lot on my plate at the moment. My original plans included a move back to Ireland."

"That would be a loss for our country."

I bowed my head. "I won't be going anywhere for a year, but my plans aren't fixed after that."

"My offer of coffee still stands. You know where to find me."

I nodded and Colonel Benson walked off. Reluctantly, I turned to the guardian. "Are ya done?"

"Not completely."

"Well, hurry because I haven't even started yet. All I've done is talk to people."

"Are you interested in the military man?"

I knew what he was hinting at but I wasn't in the mood to share anything with him. What if Jack had broken Conn's back or what if he'd done something to me? Conn was right. I was mad at the guardian because he hadn't helped me until he was ready to help me. He considered his judgment superior to mine.

"What I feel or don't feel about Colonel Benson is none of yer freaking business."

Rasmus caught my arm in his hand before I could leave. "Yes, but you know I wish to make it my business."

When I sighed and glared at him, Rasmus finally turned me loose.

"Why would someone as *superior* as yerself care about my *inferior* feelings? Ya always think ya know better than I do about everything."

"This is not an appropriate time for this discussion. Let's discuss it later."

"Well, I wasn't the one who started the debate. Ya butted

into my conversation with someone else about things that didn't concern ya," I said, and then I walked away.

When Lilith motioned me over to her, Jack was sitting up and staring at me. I couldn't prevent my glare, but I managed to keep my voice soft when she told me to state my demands. Having rehearsed them in my head dozens of times as appeals to his better nature, phrasing them as orders fell effortlessly off my tongue.

Five minutes later, I was done. Lilith sealed the compulsion. Jack blinked at both of us, confusion marring his handsome face. Thank the Goddess Jack wasn't the father of Lilith's child. That would have made my friendship with her very sticky and I genuinely liked the woman.

I didn't want to deal with Jack—the old or new version— so I used my magick to knock him out again. Lilith only smiled at my actions. We left him on the floor to be dealt with along with the others he'd worked with.

I wasn't perfect or a saint by any stretch, and where Jack was concerned, I was never going to feel any kinder towards him. Rasmus had regressed most of his memories about the experiments. But while Jack might not remember what he'd done, I was never going to forget how deep his manipulative, power-hungry nature ran.

I picked up a feather from the floor and headed to wake up my daughter.

She'd asked me not to kill her father and I hadn't.

Yay for both of us that it hadn't come to that.

Chapter Twenty-One

Ironically, it was the compulsion I placed on Jack that turned a hot mess into less of one. I woke Jack in the middle of people changing back. He saw them reverting to normal and had a shocked reaction that surprised even me.

Now he was talking to Colonel Benson, who'd helpfully lied and informed Jack that he'd been drugged. Which I guess wasn't a lie—not technically. Jack had consumed some kind of monster cocktail to become that thing he became.

The lies about what happened were becoming so thick that I could barely spot the truth among them.

When the extra white coats and military people showed up to take over for us, Colonel Benson cleared me and my daughter from the suspect list. In the eyes of those who were not so informed, Jack's presence there justified ours.

Let's say I wasn't surprised to see the head of the demon hunter council show up and rush to Jack's side. Fiona sneered at her for both of us. Honestly? I was too tired and too jaded to care about the woman who'd been cheating with my former husband.

As tired of this as I was, though, I also couldn't shake the fear that I'd traded surgical justice to let Rasmus slap a band-aid on what I'd uncovered. The guardian left as suddenly as he'd arrived, and he'd oddly taken all his remaining feathers with him. The only feathers left on the floor were the ones from Jack's conversion back into a human.

Maybe Rasmus left those for my sake, so I would know I hadn't imagined his intervention.

I was still angry with the guardian. Maybe it was unfair of me.

He had helped us in the end, but not because of anything I thought, said, or did. And Rasmus didn't help me specifically. No, what Rasmus did, he did for some sense of greater good—a greater good that extended to Jack.

But to me, all I saw was some big-picture thinking that kicked individual justice completely to the curb.

As usual, Conn found his own way to hide from our alleged rescuers. He wisely took Murray and Lilith with him when he disappeared, and I was grateful for that. They didn't need to be involved any further, but I would never forget they'd come to help. I owed them both.

The absence of most of my team left me and Fiona looking like family-related victims. I let Benson's story stand about our involvement because of Jack and didn't have to prompt my daughter to go along with it.

Fiona hugged me and then her father. But clearly, I was the parent she intended to go home with that day. Jack had burnt a bridge with our child that might never get rebuilt.

We got a military escort home thanks to Colonel Benson. I don't know how he smoothed our exit path so quickly, but he did. I also learned that he'd sent Mulan home before I woke Fiona. Or maybe she left on her own. I'd learned not to underestimate the Wu Shaman's ability to take care of herself. It was one of my favorite things about her.

Dinner had been eaten and my child was sufficiently soothed enough to rest.

Conn stopped in long enough to say that Murray and Lilith were back to their respective homes. He'd gone to check on Mulan discreetly. I told him I wouldn't wait up for him if he wanted to return to her. They had a lot of talking to do, while I needed to do a lot of thinking.

It was well after midnight when I built a fire in the fire pit to soothe myself. I sent a prayer of thanks to Goddess Danu and another to The Dagda for all they'd done that helped me to survive a day like today. It never occurred to me until after it was over that I easily might have died fighting Jack. As I faced him, my only worries were about having to kill him and what Fiona would think about it.

How had I gone from being madly in love with the man to thinking of him as the worst of my enemies? Every time I saw him, all I wanted to do was punish him. If it were not for the child we made, his being in my life at all would have seemed like nothing more than a bad dream.

Was my judgement about men the problem?

Goddess knew, lusting after Rasmus was as dumb as lusting after Jack had been. The guardian was no prize and his loyalty would never be wholly mine.

As I'd feared in the beginning, Rasmus was another form of Jack.

Perhaps Rasmus didn't think he wanted to control me, but the net effect of his bargain had stopped me from avenging myself and all those others who'd suffered for nothing more than the greed of selfish men lusting for more power.

My brain hurt thinking about how much I'd had to cave on

my own beliefs. If he saw something with more clarity than I did, he should have explained it better. Because all I saw was people who committed horrendous acts and mostly got away with them. Some of the people in their experiments had died. Where was the justice for those dead people?

I closed my eyes to shut it all out, but moments later, the other chair was pulled close to mine by the fire.

"Well, it's finally over," I said to Rasmus who quietly gazed at the fire. "We both kept our parts of the bargain. But we also both know the scientists will continue experimenting on unsuspecting people. Thanks to yer healing Jack gets to live out his selfish life. Nobody pays for their sins except me."

"What punishment did I inflict on you?"

"Ya made sure I still have to be involved with a man I nearly made dead. Just because a woman was foolish enough to marry the wrong male, she shouldn't have to keep seeing him her whole life. There has to be a way for ya to see that I need to permanently lose him."

"Do you not think Jack can be redeemed of his wickedness?"

I turned to the fire and snorted. "No, but it's very *angelic* of ya to think he's redeemable. I've read most angels are all about helping humans repent of their sins so they can be forgiven. Redemption is a wonderful idea, Rasmus, but never sinning goes against human nature. Some people take evil into themselves and it becomes their religion. Ya speaking so optimistically about Jack makes me think ya might be an angel after all."

"But you know I am not one, Aran. I am part of all belief systems and yet part of none. Of all beings roaming this planet, you know most about what I truly am."

I swung to glare at him. "Do I? Because I don't think I

know much about ya at all. And what I do know makes me uncomfortable most of the time. If I was Fiona's age, yer lips on mine might make me forget how much ya annoy me. The truth, although it sickens me, is that my hormones caused me to forgive Jack too much over the years. Thankfully, I'm forty now and know better than to listen to them. May Goddess Danu save me from my terrible taste in men."

Rasmus chuckling was the last thing I figured would happen, but there he was, chuckling with a smile as bright as the moon. I glared harder at him for being amused. His humor was so rare that I always hated to stop him from laughing, but in this instance, his amusement hurt my pride.

"My rant wasn't meant to be funny."

"Yes, I'm aware your intentions are as serious as mine," Rasmus said.

"Go away, guardian. Ya're an extremist. Either ya want to save everyone in the world, or ya want to wipe everyone off the face of it. What I do is hold the evil doers responsible for how they exercise their freaking free will in hopes others like them will get a clue about the consequences. I've found no other way to make sure people don't keep doing wrong things over and over again. Jack is the perfect example. He's focused on being more powerful than me. That's his intention. That's all Jack cares about. This is not the mindset of someone who can be redeemed."

Rasmus stared at me. "Yet you spared Lilith, a wicked demoness, for the sake of her child. The demoness got paid to fool you, which she willingly did for the sake of her people. Jack paid many people to fool you because he thought that was better than the alternative of you finding out the truth too soon. You've forgiven everyone except Jack. Are you completely incapable of forgiving him?"

"Ya know what? I don't feel the need to justify my thinking or my actions to ya. We both know the compulsion I put on Jack is the only consequence he's going to suffer for all the pain he caused all those people, including his fellow demon hunters who were turned into demon zombies. Lilith did wrong things, but she's fighting for the survival of her child and her people. She's working toward that greater good ya keep throwing in my face. Jack is doing bad things only to gain power for himself. His motivations are selfish. Ya might not see a difference between those intentions, but I do."

"Jack is full of good intentions. It's his execution that needs work. Jack sees gaining power as the only way to accomplish the things he thinks are important in life. If he were convinced there was another way, he might use his talents for the greater good, instead of for himself."

I glared at Rasmus in the firelight. "What greater good can there be in changing yerself into a guardian-level monster? He was stronger than Conn. My sword and Mulan's sickle were all that stopped him. If ya hadn't come along, I would have chopped him up in pieces to make sure he stopped hurting people."

Rasmus sighed at my tone, but what did he expect? That I'd flutter my eyelashes and invite him to my bed out of gratitude that he showed up at the last minute? That wasn't happening. Goddess, I hated his arrogance and his air of superiority. Maybe I needed counseling. Why did I always end up attracted to the worst males?

"My brethren and I have made some decisions. Some of them concern you. Would you like to hear about them?"

I snorted over his nerve. "If the guardians are bent on destroying the world and all of us in it, I'd appreciate it if ya would do it while I'm asleep. I haven't gotten a full eight hours in weeks and I'd rather not be meeting my Goddess with bags under my eyes. I don't have a lot of vanity, but I do have a little."

"I'm afraid Danu is going to have to wait for your soul, Aran of The Dagda. You're not done using it yet. Your calling is barely upon you."

I grunted in disgust. "How about ya translate yer hints into pagan speak? Maybe then I'll be able to understand ya because I don't speak guardian."

Rasmus grinned at me but didn't outright laugh again. I hated the urge I felt to change the topic and stop bickering with him. All I wanted was to sit in his lap and feel safe for five minutes. The illogical desire for the worst of men seemed to be my curse in life. Even Ma couldn't have put a spell this effective on me.

My nemesis cleared his throat before speaking again. "I'm sorry it seemed like I didn't support your actions. It wasn't like that. I just didn't understand your decision-making. Guardians can see the entirety of a person's intentions in a way humans can't seem to see in each other. Many of us believe humans choose not to see the greater good in each other."

I shrugged in the dark. There was some truth in what he said, but I didn't have to like it. "Sorry that I can't change how being human works. If I could, I'd be spending my days brewing potions to heal people instead of scrying for the wicked and wielding a demon sword to get them to mend their ways."

"I would like to spend time with you and learn how you think."

I grunted. "Well, it's not like I can stop ya."

"I could also observe you from a distance, but that wouldn't be the same."

My arms crossed in irritation. "All I wanted when we met was to divorce Jack so my lusting for ya could be done legally. I'm a simple witch and a simple woman. I refuse to keep fighting with ya over Jack. If that's our destiny, then keep yer distance."

Rasmus shrugged. "What if I could show you why I keep defending him?"

"Will ya shut up about him afterward?"

He chuckled before he answered. "Yes, I think that would be helpful to both of us. Come sit in my lap."

"No."

"Are you protesting on principle? Because I know you want to."

I glared back at him. "Maybe I do want to, but ya're bastard for saying so."

He glared at me for daring to question him. "I have to touch you for this to work. Having you sit with me was an expedient offer."

I took a deep breath and pushed out of my chair. I was glad Conn wasn't here to see me cave into pressure. Rasmus made room for me on one leg, then boosted me closer once I was settled.

I wasn't as comfortable as I'd been the first time I sat on his lap, but that was mostly because I didn't trust him as much as I did the other day.

"Relax. This will be an inward journey. Nothing physical will happen to you." Rasmus picked up my hand and held it to his chest while he closed his eyes. I kept mine open and studied his face in the dark.

His lids cracked. "Would it help you concentrate if I kissed you? I can tell you're thinking about it non-stop."

I smirked at him. "No. Kissing you would make me hate myself more than I already do."

His sigh spoke volumes about his tolerance. It also made me feel as contrary as Fiona could be at times. I wished I could be different with him today. I wished we could reach some sort of understanding with each other.

"Fine," I said and squeezed my eyelids shut.

And just like that, I was sucked backward in time and through the stars.

Chapter Twenty-Two

When the stars going by me slowed to stop, I felt myself drop down somewhere. It was a strange feeling because I couldn't see any part of myself. It was like I knew I was there, yet I was invisible, even to my own eyes.

However, I saw someone in the distance—my younger self —walking through the fields surrounding the house I'd been born in, while I gathered herbs for Ma. My young thoughts were light and full of hope. I'd met someone.

My parents didn't like the man, but I longed for him something fierce. He was smart and accepting of my power. I reassured my heart that whatever misgivings my parents had would resolve themselves over time. I'd seen my parents survive many struggles in their married life. I felt sure Jack and I would do the same and prove to them our love was true.

Stars rolled by the edges of my vision as the scene sped forward. My younger self roamed the inside of the house this time when we stopped. Da—Goddess bless him—was in the kitchen fixing Ma's rocker for the hundredth time. Pieces of it were scattered on the table. The boards across the back kept breaking because Ma was such a fierce rocker. The rocker had a failing in basic craftsmanship but she wouldn't let him buy her a new one.

I smiled as I saw him. Goddess, I missed the man who helped make me. I missed his counsel and his company. I hadn't been trying to replace him with Jack. No, I was trying to find his twin so I'd have a good man of my own.

I was just living my life like Ma and Da was living theirs. We couldn't keep all the people in our lives forever. I think I always knew that.

Soon the stars zipped by once again but only for a few moments. This time when they stopped, I moved like a ghost through a closed door and into a room we called Da's study. The average person might have considered it a parlor for entertaining guests. It was the only formal room in the house and the one where Da talked to the guardian who visited and where he met with the being who brought the second King Solomon's Seal to him.

The only landline phone for four miles lived in that room, which I think was the point because Jack was in there—a very young Jack—and he was talking on the phone to someone who was arguing with him.

"Aran's no danger to anyone unless you make her mad. Even then, she's not going to harm a person. She doesn't have that kind of power or that kind of inclination. Her witch power is significant when it comes to brewing potions. Whatever inheritance she got from her alleged god ancestors is either dormant or non-existent. She's young and I got to her before she developed it. Whatever the case, I can see to it that it never manifests at all. I just need time."

Jack went silent and listened to what the person was saying

to him. Then he pulled the phone away and glared at it before holding it back to his ear.

"*Stop worrying about how. I already told you I would marry her. Aran loves me and I love her back now. Everything will be fine because she trusts me. I won't let her use her powers for the wrong things. That's my solution and you're going to have to live with it.*"

Stars flew by again before I could process what I'd heard. When things stopped this time, I saw myself as a young mother scooping up a two-year-old Fiona into my arms and dancing her around.

"*The job is in Salem, Massachusetts.*"

"*Good Goddess, Jack. That's the place where they killed the witches.*"

Jack's laughter was light. "*Nobody is going to kill you, Aran, and I already told them I'd take the position. You know being a demon hunter is all I ever wanted. Please don't fight me on this. For once, can't you just say yes without arguing?*"

I bounced a giggling Fiona in my arms. "*Ya should have talked to me first, Jack. I have a job here in Ireland that I'm happy doing. I have a purpose and that's to learn to use my magick. I have Ma and Da who watch the baby when both of us have to be away. There's a demon hunter branch in Dublin. Maybe ya can work there instead of us going all the way across the ocean.*"

"*Aran, we're going to the States. I've taken the job. We're leaving Ireland in two weeks.*"

"*Fine. But I'll not be this easy on ya again, Jack. When ya love someone, ya consider their needs and not just yer own. Ya should have talked to me before making yer plans. I don't know if I can close down my entire life in two weeks.*"

"I've spent years away from my country, Aran. It's my turn to have my way."

Everything suddenly fast-forwarded again and the stars zipped by my shoulders. When they stopped, I saw a bored, teenage version of Fiona reading a book in the backseat. She'd been complaining the whole time we'd had to wait for Jack to do whatever it was he was doing.

I never knew what he did when he was with the demon hunters. He never spoke to me much about the details of his work. It was just as well because I knew his job was in vain. I tried to tell him he was wasting his time with that group because ya couldn't kill a demon, but he wasn't able to hear it.

An adult version of me—one who seemed only slightly older than the version with the two-year-old—marched into the demon hunter building and rapped on one of two fancy wooden doors that opened into their main chamber.

"Hello. Is anyone in there? I'm Aran Derringer and I'm looking for my husband. Jack's been in there for over an hour. My daughter and I have been sitting in the car waiting for him. Can ya tell him I'm going home without him? Fiona has school tomorrow and she needs her supper."

One moment I was the one knocking on the giant door. The next, I was on the other side of it. The real me—the one looking at these memories—suddenly realized where I was. This was the judgment room of the demon hunter council where Jack had taken me when he betrayed me.

Jack and the head councilwoman were in the front of the room talking.

"How many times are you going to surprise me, Jack? I'm still shocked that you married the witch just to watch over her. Now I find out she once belonged to a rogue group of magickals in her homeland. And there's a rumor floating

around that she controls a demon. I'm telling you that she's just like that cousin of hers who got away from us. Our demon hunter reputation is at stake here. Something has to be done."

"I can't act against her without cause, Hildy. I have to think of my child," Jack said. *"And I have to do this in a way that Aran won't suspect will render her power inactive."*

"We should have done this years ago. You're the one who has us dealing with government officials and mad scientists. Nothing's been simple since they captured that creature they were stalking. I can't believe the idiot flew right down into their facility and tried to reason with them. That ancient being must be dumber than a bag of rocks."

"His name is Rasmus and he's not dumb at all. They're making me his keeper."

"His keeper? Why on Earth would you do that? Isn't keeping tabs on your wife enough of a job?"

Jack shrugged and grinned at her. *"Once Aran is out of the picture I'll be a single parent. I'm going to need all the money they're willing to pay me to do this. I'll agree to Aran's imprisonment but only if you promise me she will not be harmed in any way. Harming her will bring the wrath of her family down on our heads. You have to let me handle this."*

"I don't know, Jack. If that witch can control a demon, we can't have her running loose in Salem. We only recently got the demons under control. No one would blame you for taking her out permanently."

"You're talking crazy. She's the mother of my child and I love her, Hildy. It's not the way I love you, but I care enough to make sure she doesn't have to die. Think of what an asset Aran could be if she would agree to help us. There won't be any need to drug her, either. She'll stay where we put her if we let Fiona visit. Family is

everything to Aran. Trust me, after thirteen years together, I know my wife."

"She's knocking on the door and asking for you, Jack. She's growing tired of you already. One day you may wish you'd killed her when you had the chance."

"No, I will never wish that. Now kiss me goodbye, Hildy. I have to go."

The moment they locked lips the scene faded like a bad dream. I could feel myself aging as the stars went by this time. I could feel I was getting closer to the present.

The next stop startled me with its abruptness. Jack was in the master bedroom of his house and weeping. All the bedclothes I picked out were still there. My personal things were scattered about the room on dressers and nightstands. Abandoned clothes had been dropped in a pile on the floor.

A half-empty bottle of liquor sat on the nightstand. A picture of Jack and me perched next to it. Jack scrubbed his face and cried out his frustration.

"If you'd shared your secrets, I'd have killed your demon, and none of this would be necessary. Now you're in prison and I'm practically a widower. You brought this on yourself, Aran. You brought this on both of us. I did my best to protect you. Why couldn't you have taken my side for once?"

Before I could process what I was seeing and hearing, time sped forward in a rush again.

Suddenly, I was staring at a familiar man in a hospital bed. But wait... this wasn't my memory. I'd been locked up in the cottage when this happened.

Doctors came and went, checking on the first human version of Rasmus. Military men stopped by to see him. They murmured to each other and then left quickly.

Rasmus tried to sit up in the bed, but he seemed lethargic

and not himself. When no one was with him, he touched the IV lines and examined his own body. He seemed to be taking stock of where he was and what was happening.

This was the version of him who first came to see me. It was so bizarre to see him like that again.

A nurse dressed in military garb quietly came into his room and replaced his IV drip without telling him what she was doing. He stared at her but never uttered a single question about his care.

A normal hospital nurse dressed in light blue scrubs came in right behind her, saw the new drip, and put a hand over her mouth.

"That's too much to give him," the nurse in blue protested. *"We don't know what that might do to him. His memory is already gone. Isn't that enough? Are you trying to kill him too?"*

"Hush, woman. No one is killing anyone or being killed. We don't do that to people. We're the heroes here," Jack said as he strode into the room. He smiled down at Rasmus. *"How are you doing, big guy?"*

Rasmus blinked up at Jack. *"I'm not sure. What happened to me?"*

"You had a bad accident," Jack said, patting Rasmus on the arm. *"You lost a lot of blood, but you're going to be just fine. Your ex-wife doesn't want to see you but don't feel bad about that, though. Mine doesn't want to see me either. Women are nothing but trouble, am I right?"*

I tried to talk—to tell Jack our estrangement was all his fault—but no words escaped my throat. I couldn't speak or interact.

Jack studied Rasmus. *"My name's Jack Derringer, Special Agent of the Army and Marshal Demon Hunter. Once they get you fixed up, I'll help you get settled. I know what it's like to not know where you belong."*

Rasmus looked up at him. *"I feel like I'm in danger. Am I suffering from PTSD?"*

Jack chuckled. *"Yes, but only from that woman you married, dude. Come on, laugh with me. That was funny. Seriously, though, we're taking good care of you here. Some military guy with the first name of Colonel stopped by and said your pension will kick in by the time you're released. We have temporary housing at the place where I work. I know you don't remember anything, but I figured I could put you to work hunting demons with me until your memories return."*

"Anything is better than this nothingness. I hope I remember things soon," Rasmus said.

And then suddenly I found myself back in the present.

Chapter Twenty-Three

I opened my eyes and looked straight into a gaze that claimed to know all my secrets. The fire in the pit had burned down to nothing and the cooling embers crackled as they fell apart.

I slid from the guardian's lap and stood on my own. "Everything ya showed me validated that Jack lied to me, to his child, and everyone else with shocking regularity. I'm not sure Jack is capable of being an honest, upright person with a moral center. What I saw makes me more ashamed than ever that I let myself be fooled for so long."

"You loved Jack."

I snorted and shook my head. "I thought I did, but I see it differently now. My relationship with Jack was just a series of manipulations, deceits, and me caving to his blind ambition. The only thing I feel marginally better about is that he cried the day he sent me to the cottage. But he also had another woman in his life to replace me. Jack only grieved my loss for one day while I cried for two years about what he did. My feeling of betrayal is even larger now that I have a solid confirmation of his ongoing affair. I only suspected it before ya showed it to me."

Rasmus stood up too. "The point I was trying to make by letting you see the past is that Jack isn't completely bad. He has many flaws, but among the flaws are some good things that make him valuable to the world. He stopped his government from neutralizing you the way they did me. He made sure I was cared for and treated humanely, even though I was technically their prisoner. There are far worse people in the human world than Jack Derringer."

I stared at him. What did he expect from me? Did he want me to say I would forgive Jack? Or that I regretted defending my child from her wicked father?

The guardian seemed to be fishing for something, but I couldn't tell what.

"I never said there weren't worse people in the world than Jack. That would be hypocritical of me since I've had to deal with plenty of them in my life." I looked at him and spread my hands. "Some of what ya showed me were things I didn't know about Jack or had different memories about."

"I thought it would help you to see both sides of your experiences. I thought it might ignite your compassion for the challenges of his life."

I chuckled without a drop of humor. "I see. Did ya think that trip down memory lane would make me regret putting the demon compulsion on him? Jack's value to me is relative to his treatment of me, which means I hardly value him at all. His value to you is relative to you, Rasmus. Feel free to think well of him if ya want, but I would be thrilled to lose him out of my life forever."

His sigh was loud in the dark.

"If it helps any, I miss ya far more when ya're gone from me than I ever missed Jack Derringer being away."

Rasmus walked closer. "And that's the bigger thing I've been trying to tell you. I don't have to go back and I want to stay. If you'll let me, I'd like to learn more about how you see things. My brethren and I all agree you are not an average human. The mercy you show some and not others intrigue as much as it worries us."

I walked away from him, chuckling and shaking my head. "Oh, no... I'll not be part of that trap. Ya won't be judging all of humanity by what I say and do."

I swiped a hand in front of him.

"I joke about religion, but I'm serious about my ethics. Generally, I tell the truth and only hurt the bad guys. The compulsion I put on Jack gave me a good reason I have not to kill him. See? I know my flaws and work around them. That's what sets me apart from other humans."

"What's clear is that you're a dangerous woman when provoked."

I snorted at the admission. "So says the man who controls time like he's a *god*."

"I promise I'm not a god—not even close."

"Me neither... but I work for one."

I blew out a breath and rubbed my forehead. I was tired and my snark level was through the roof.

"I guess if ya want to visit me, ya can sleep in the garage when ya come. Conn moved into his old room, though he may not be coming home this evening. He and the Wu Shaman were overdue for a talk, which I believe they're having as we speak."

"I can't stay all night, but I can stay for some of it. Are you sharing your bed with Fiona still?"

"Yes, but I thought I'd sleep on the couch tonight and let her get some true rest. The couch is not comfortable, but at least I won't wake her up with my restlessness."

"Maybe I can help you not be so restless. May I sit with you until you fall asleep?"

I grunted. "Ya're a guardian. It's not like I can stop ya."

I retrieved a pillow from beside a sleeping Fiona and carried it to the couch. I was short enough that a large throw served as a cover. I curled up on one end and did my level best not to let any part of me touch any part of Rasmus. He'd parked his large body on one end of the couch and turned to stare at me.

"I will not let anyone disturb your sleep tonight, Aran."

"Too late for that," I said, tucking the cover under my chin. "The most disturbing person I ever met is sitting at my feet. I'm highly disturbed that he won't leave me alone."

I knew the moment I'd pushed him too far. Maybe I meant to snap his leash. I couldn't be certain.

Before I could laugh at my own joke about how much he disturbed me, Rasmus dragged me down the couch and into his lap.

He put a finger over my lips when I started to fuss at him for doing so. "Stop talking and go to sleep," he ordered.

"Ya can't order someone to sleep... or to stop talking."

"No, but I can put that person to sleep if I want."

I used a finger to poke him in the chest. "If ya use yer guardian powers to put me to sleep, I will chop ya to pieces when I wake up. I read a guardian couldn't be killed, but I know how to make it hard for a being to regenerate. Ya might say it's my specialty."

He pulled me closer and held me tightly. "You have no right to call anyone else contrary. You're the epitome of a contrary person."

I thought about that for a moment, and his use of big words, before I gave up and shrugged in his arms. "Ya're right. Being mulish is a failing of mine. My feelings are too strong at times, but threatening to put someone to sleep to shut them up is not right, Rasmus. It takes me a while to get peaceful when I can't tell right from wrong."

"Then that's something we have in common."

"Yeah, I've noticed. Are ya planning to neutralize me if ya don't like what ya learn about me?"

"Never," Rasmus said, his voice a husky promise.

"Fine. Then I guess ya can stick around. Just don't get in my way. I have things to do. Colonel Benson offered me a job, but I don't think I'd like working for him. He believes in science but doesn't believe in magick. That could be a big problem."

Rasmus stared at me like he hadn't heard a word of what I just said. He was staring so hard that his jaw muscle flexed and jumped. I reached my fingers out to rub and soothe it.

His words were soft when he spoke again. "Perhaps if I stay, you and I can share a bed."

I raised my head and stared at him. "Are ya suggesting we sleep together? Or that we have sex?"

Rasmus stared without blinking. "I'm suggesting the kind of intimacy where you let me satisfy your physical needs when we can find the time and opportunity."

Every cell in my body screamed *yes*, except for those two or three rational brain cells shouting loud enough to be heard above the rest. They warned me that I was being stupid for listening to him—that being with him might bring me more negative consequences than being married to Jack brought me.

I sighed in defeat. "I don't think that's a good idea. We have too many conflicting viewpoints. I punish bad guys but ya want to let them go. I hate Jack Derringer but ya like the deceitful bastard. I'm pagan but ya're unaffiliated. Or so ya keep saying."

Rasmus grunted as he nodded. "Yes, I agree. The two of us trying to be a couple is a terrible concept—perhaps the worst idea I've had in centuries. I spoke to my brethren at great length about it. After our combined past bad luck with human females, we've become extremely cautious about taking human lovers. It's not forbidden to us, but it's not encouraged. The other guardians have fewer reservations about you than I do. They felt you were worth the risk."

I chuckled in surprise. "That makes absolutely no sense to me. How can your brethren be my champions? They don't even know me. Did ya tell them what I did to Jack?"

"They know more about you than you realize, but they do not know more than I know. I am the expert on Aran of The Dagda."

I settled back against him and looked away. "Well, I wouldn't say *expert*. I can think of quite a few things ya don't yet know about me." When he didn't immediately jump on my innuendo, I giggled and buried my face in his shoulder.

Rasmus turned his face to mine and kissed my temple. "Sleep now. I'll try to be here when you wake up. We can argue again tomorrow."

"It's not like I'm living simply to argue with ya, guardian. It wasn't like I even intended to save ya from Jack and his scientist people. I didn't plan any of what passed between us. Life just happened."

He stroked a hand along my jaw the way I'd done for him. "That's how free will works, Aran. It's a whole bunch of little decisions after unexpected things happen."

I guess his declaration sent me into a panic. My brain

started doing that leapfrogging thing where it jumped from one unresolved task to the next. "I need to find my cousin Liam. In our walk down memory lane, the demon hunter council woman boinking Jack said Liam went underground to avoid them."

Rasmus shook his head. "No need to look for him. Your cousin is fine. Your demoness friend, Lilith, hid him. He and his demon princess are spending some quality time together."

"Good. My family will be relieved to hear he's okay. Next to me, he's the biggest troublemaker. Next on my list is finding out why the Seal of Solomon keeps hiding from everyone but me. Will ya tell me the secrets of Da's ring tomorrow?"

"It would be best if you spoke to the being who's responsible for the ring you wear."

"Would that 'being' happen to be an angel? Because that would be the best surprise ever. First I meet a guardian, and then I meet a real angel. Maybe the three of us can take a selfie together."

"You joke, but one ring's caretaker is an angel. The other is a djinn. Two rings have two caretakers looking out for them. I'm not sure which is the protector of the ring you wear."

"Goddess, next time I talk to Father Landerman, I'm going to blow his mind with all this. He'll be buying me the whiskeys and beer just for the privilege of hearing my stories. I bet angels are a hoot to talk to. I bet they're more serious about their work than ya are."

Rasmus bent his head and kissed me until I stopped talking. Things were just getting interesting when he pulled away. There was no place in the house where I could be alone with him. Maybe I should give Rasmus my room and move Fiona and me to the garage.

I sighed heavily. Something about my living arrangement was going to have to change soon.

I cuddled closer to him and sighed against his throat. The two of us as a couple was a terrible idea. Every cell in me knew Rasmus could break me in a way Jack hadn't been capable of doing. I realized that the first time he kissed me and magick sparked between our lips.

Even though I had indeed loved my ex-husband once, I never shared magick with Jack. What kind of magick would Rasmus and I make if I let our relationship progress?

And how would we ever co-exist peacefully? The man would fly off any time I made him unhappy, which I suspected would be daily. I had no idea where he went when he disappeared... or what he did while he was away from me.

Calling guardians a mystery was an understatement. Yet his very real, very human-like heart was currently beating under my hand, which rested on his equally real chest.

Living only in the moment suddenly held great appeal.

An amazing man had asked to sleep with me. No, it wasn't the wild night I needed to supercharge my powers, but I'd take the promise of it for now. Being held by a man and feeling genuinely wanted for myself was a lot better than the nothing I'd had this morning.

I just had to be careful not to get too attached to him. Rasmus wasn't the type to stick around. Like the 'guardian angel' I joked about him being, he seemed to have many responsibilities other than me. I might never know how much he valued me above all others or even if he did.

It seemed a selfish thing to ask, but it was a human one. I found it strange that a being I knew for sure *wasn't* human managed to remind me of how human I was.

Witch? Yes. Descended from gods? Yes.

But was I human? Yes, I was, and more than I wished, especially when it came to lusting and loving.

"Ya're as fascinating as magick, but the strangest man I've ever tried to figure out," I whispered.

"And you're the most wonderful woman I've ever known, even when you're babbling about nonsense," he whispered back.

As declarations of our affection for each other went, what each of us said could have used some finessing. Maybe pillow talk was something we would have to work on to keep from getting mad every day.

Conn would have laughed and told me not to get so hung up on semantics. I wasn't going to complain about a few challenges.

My Wu Shaman BFF would say that no man was perfect. I would say no woman was either.

What was happening in the rest of my life was perfect, though. For the first time in years, I didn't dread waking up tomorrow.

Or at least, not as much as usual.

All I really had to do to be happy was ignore that little voice inside me whispering that the chaos was just beginning.

— THE END —

Ready for more? CLICK HERE to get Book 3 or visit my website at donnamcdonaldauthor.com.

Note From the Author

Hi. I hope you enjoyed reading *40 Ways to Lose a Guy!*

If you enjoyed this book, please consider leaving a positive review or rating on the retailer site where you purchased it. Reader reviews help my books continue to be valued by resellers and help new readers make decisions about reading them.

You are the reason I write these stories and I sincerely appreciate each of you.

May thanks for your support!
~ Donna McDonald

40 Ways to Tell a Lie

TALES OF A MIDLIFE WITCH, BOOK 3

Click to pre-order Book 3 today!

Book Description

Am I just angry or having a true midlife crisis?

Life is easier when you're younger. My new bestie that I never wanted is in crisis. Rasmus left weeks ago and hasn't returned, so I'm in crisis. I put a demon compulsion on my ex to make him forget he was evil, so my daughter is in crisis.

All Conn seems capable of doing is laughing at me and my pain. We'll see who gets the last laugh, though. Mulan thinks dating him violates everything in her life and negates the reason she was given her powers.

Not that I would laugh at Conn's pain—I wouldn't. Okay, well, I would, but I'd feel bad about it. Maybe. Men in general aren't high up on my "things that make me happy" list at the moment, and I confess my attitude is quite fair to my normally very helpful familiar.

It's not helping my attitude that the one guy whose memory I didn't erase when we took down my ex and his military scientists is now offering my a job I can't refuse. The victim-funded paranormal organization I worked for in Ireland is now opening a branch here in Salem. I need the money, but do I need that much drama right now? I really don't think so.

But I need a change, that's for sure. Maybe I'll get Mulan to dye my hair red like it was when I was my daughter's age. Well, I will get her to do that IF she ever stops hiding out and returns to her hair shop. I tried to talk her into coming back, but it was hard because I envied her escape.

40 Ways to Tell a Lie is an exciting paranormal women's fiction tale from USA Today Bestselling Author Donna McDonald.

Chapter One

People talked about optimists as if they had glittering winged pixies circling their heads whispering the secrets of positivity to them. That wasn't the truth at all. A true optimist was someone like me—someone willing to repeat an action a gazillion times no matter what the outcome.

Or perhaps we all possessed a stubborn belief that we were right.

These are the deep thoughts I had as I pushed Fiona to try conjuring fire for the hundredth time even though the first ninety-nine attempts failed to produce even a tiny spark, much less a flame.

Now, that was what I called true optimism. But what else could I do except keep pushing her to learn the lesson I was trying to teach? I was her mother. My daughter possessed a lithe body and an elegance I never would, but beauty wouldn't protect ya. Well, she had a knack for talking her way out of things, but that wouldn't always save her.

Fiona plopped down in the nearest lawn chair to whine... again.

She did it every five tries and by now, I was mostly immune to her complaints and theatrics. Mostly immune, but not totally. The whining was wearing something fierce on my nerves, and I was working hard not to show how much it bothered me.

I gave up standing with my hands on my hips and sat in the second chair. It was hard not to sigh over how tired Fiona's "I can't do it attitude" made me.

While my daughter whined, I made another mental list of all the things I wanted to do. For one, I'd been meaning to ask Conn to get the other two chairs down from the garage storage so we could circle the fire pit with them. I only thought about asking when I was sitting out here, which was usually by myself —a situation that didn't show any promise of changing soon.

Or I kept falling asleep in the guardian's lap and waking up alone. My would-be lover kept saying all the right things to get my motor running, but he refused to drive me anywhere. His mixed messages were frustrating in all ways and not just the obvious.

No, I take that back. *He* was frustrating. I'm sure Rasmus had thousands of other more important things to deal with than me, but I had only one life to live. Was I supposed to live it without him? It would be easier to decide if I could have him by my side for longer than two hours.

Fiona's sigh was a heavy one and the kind only someone her age could bemoan. "Maybe Dad was right. Maybe I'm not magickal."

"No, yer father's not right, Fiona. I can feel the power in ya, even when we're just sitting here. So can Conn. But I am wondering if he blocked yer power somehow. We may have to look into that."

To ask Jack what he'd done to our daughter during those

seven years I was locked up, I would have to remove the demon compulsion I put on him. Why would I do that? I'd gone to great trouble to make Jack forget he was a cheating, manipulative scoundrel.

The current, demon-compelled version of my ex-husband treated me far more respectfully than the original one. That respect rolled naturally onto my daughter.

Sure, Jack was in danger of losing both his jobs because he wasn't his old self, but was that my problem? I was going with a definite no answer for now.

Fiona was nearly done with college and would soon make her own way in the world. Wasn't it time for Jack to finally let go of both of us? Even though ya could say I forced that inevitability along, I would argue that was probably the only way I could have ever made it happen. The old Jack refused to accept our divorce. I couldn't allow that to continue no matter what it cost to correct it.

"It's so odd that Dad had to take a leave of absence to recover from his ordeal. Maybe he needs to see a doctor. Do you think I should talk to him?"

Calling it an *ordeal* was the catch-all word Fiona chose to describe Jack turning himself into a half-guardian, half-bat monster. I regretted not getting a picture of Jack in his monster condition just so I could show it to her when she started feeling sorry for him. Unfortunately, he'd kept me too worried about whether or not I was going to have to kill him to think about memorializing his worst walk on the dark side with a photo.

A small, furry beast burst out of the back door of the house and ran toward us barking. He jumped up into Fiona's lap to look me in the eye while continuing his irritating yapping. I glared at him and barked back to annoy him.

I wouldn't have done that to an actual animal, but the dog

barking in Fiona's lap was not a dog. The dog was Connlander of the Fir Bolg. Gifted with powers no other demon possessed, Conn was an imp—an imperial demon and my familiar. Once the mightiest king of all demonkind, Conn sold himself into eternal service to my ancestor, The Dagda. The Dagda was the son of the Goddess Danu and the first and mightiest king of the Tuatha de Danann.

Conn saved his species from annihilation with his sacrifice but was now consigned to spend eternity at the mercy of his keepers. Not all of them had been witches, but I was one. I'd inherited responsibility for Conn and his demon powers when I was just over twenty.

Before that time, he'd belonged to my grandmother— Grandma O'Malley. No one had told me the history of my inheritance until I'd divorced the wicked man I'd married, not even Conn.

My family had a love of secrets that served no one, but they kept holding them close anyway.

The imp was officially my witch's familiar, but mostly Conn was my friend. Conn and I had been a team for many years, except for the last seven I spent in demon hunters prison. That was water under the bridge now and something never to be repeated, but my anger over Jack putting me there still lingered. I didn't trust my real ex-husband not to imprison me again, which was the reason I had no plan to ever remove the demon compulsion a demoness friend helped me put on him.

I sighed and stared at a barking Conn. "If I swear not to ask about what happened between Mulan and ya, will ya shift back to human and talk to me? Yer constant yapping is getting on my nerves."

A series of irritated barks was my answer.

Goddess only knew what I'd done to make Conn go canine

on me. It was his favorite brooding form whenever I'd inadvertently offended him. Maybe I should thank the stars he hadn't chosen to be a goat or something worse this time. He'd done the goat thing only once before, but once had been quite enough. Ya can't imagine what it's like to make up a story to tell the homeowner's association about why ya have a goat in yer backyard chewing on neighboring fences.

"Do not make me order ya, Conn. My patience has nearly reached its limit."

When he ducked his tiny, furry head, showed his tiny teeth, and growled fiercely, Fiona laughed and scooped him up to snuggle him close. He licked her face while she giggled and ignored me completely.

"Is it normal for you to let a dog answer your door?"

I swung in my chair and found Colonel Benson standing behind me.

Before greeting him, I glanced back at Conn, narrowed my gaze, and whispered. "Ya could have gotten me instead of just letting him in... *traitor*."

Conn barked twice before growling at me again.

I rolled my eyes and turned back to speak to my visitor. Whatever had brought Colonel Benson here couldn't be good, and I didn't want any part of it.

"That dog is not a real dog. He's a brooding shirker," I explained.

Colonel Benjamin Benson ignored my rant as his gaze cut to Conn. "Is the dog your partner?"

My mouth quirked at the corners. The man knew what Conn was. He'd seen him in full red demon form, black curled horns included. He'd also watched Conn fighting the monstrous creature Jack had planned to turn the Colonel and all the members of his team into.

"I come in peace today. I just want to talk," he said, pulling his hands from the pockets of his pressed jeans and holding them up.

Not only were the jeans and sneakers a surprise, but he was also wearing a Rolling Stones t-shirt with a motorcycle jacket thrown on over it. The colonel was quite good-looking in casual clothes. Maybe they were his retirement uniform. Ya could tell he was military because who else would bother pressing their jeans?

The last time I saw the man, though, he'd been in full military mode wearing camouflage gear and a matching hat pulled low on his head. He and his men had been prisoners held inside electrified cages by the wicked branch of the military both my ex-husband and the colonel worked for.

Technically, my ex-husband still worked for them, though perhaps not for much longer. Should I be so pleased about that fact? Probably not, but I was. Our daughter felt a bit differently about her father's career slide, but she hadn't wasted time pleading his case to me yet.

If I'd been the colonel, I would have been resentful, but Benson had taken Jack's betrayal in stride. Jack had told me he was in Army Special Forces. Benson had indicated he had the same special background.

I knew Benson worked with Jack in some regard on the DNA manipulation stuff because he'd confessed to it. The two men seemed to share little else, though. To me, they seemed more like enemies than comrades-in-arms.

Colonel Benson had handled Jack's betrayal of him and his people much better than I had handled him betraying me, but I was an Irish witch with a terrible temper.

Not being a soldier, I didn't live life expecting people I cared about to betray me. Jack had been sleeping with me.

Well, me and at least one other woman I'd learned, but I didn't know that back then.

As my husband, I had assumed all of Jack's loyalty belonged to me. But I'd been completely wrong. Maybe my mistrust had spread to people like Benson.

Today I wasn't so sure that aspect of my character was a bad thing.

Ready for more? CLICK HERE to get Book 3 or visit my website at donnamcdonaldauthor.com.

Also by Donna McDonald

NANO WOLVES SERIES (PARANORMAL)

Ariel: Nano Wolves 1

Brandi: Nano Wolves 2

Heidi: Nano Wolves 3

Reed: Nano Wolves 4

CYBORGS: MANKIND REDEFINED (SCIFI)

Peyton 313

Kingston 691

Marcus 582

Eric 754

William 874X

Nero 1000

FORCED TO SERVE (SPACE OPERA/SF)

The Daemon of Synar

The Daemon Master's Wife

The Siren's Call

The Healer's Kiss

The Daemon's Change

The Tracker's Quest

The Siren's Surrender

BABA YAGA SAGA (LITE PARANORMAL)

How To Train A Witch

How To Date A Dragon

To Yaga Or Not To Yaga

Baba Yaga Saga Collection

BABA YAGA ADVENTURES (LITE PARANORMAL)

Whole Lot of Shifting Going On

Witch's Guide to a Magical Life

Party Like A Witch

Baba Yaga Adventures Collection

ALIEN GUARDIANS OF EARTH (PARANORMAL/SF)

Bad Panther

Mad Panther

Dad Panther

MY CRAZY ALIEN ROMANCE (HUMOR/SCIFI)

Tangling With Topper

Touching Topper

Timeless Topper

Topper's Magical Christmas

The Topper Collection

ALIENS IN KILTS (HUMOR/SCIFI)

Matchmaker Abduction

Nate's Fated Mate

Shades Of Darcone

Non-Series

The Shaman's Mate

Want to hear about new releases and planned books?

Join my mailing list!

About the Author

USA Today Bestselling Author Donna McDonald published her first novel in March of 2011. Many multi-genre novels later, she admits to living her own happily ever after as a full-time author. Addicted to making readers laugh, she includes a good dose of comedy in every book.

Here are some easy ways to learn more about me...
www.donnamcdonaldauthor.com
email@donnamcdonaldauthor.com